Reckless Lover
Carly Bishop

Harlequin Books

TORONTO • NEW YORK • LONDON
AMSTERDAM • PARIS • SYDNEY • HAMBURG
STOCKHOLM • ATHENS • TOKYO • MILAN
MADRID • WARSAW • BUDAPEST • AUCKLAND

To Anita, Colleen and Carol
For terrific support and endless good times
over Sizzling Rice and Hot & Sour Soup....
Thanks.

ISBN 0-373-22357-9

RECKLESS LOVER

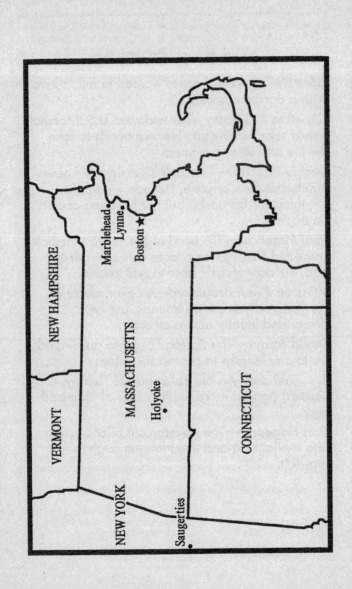

Marblehead
Lynne
★ Boston

NEW HAMPSHIRE

VERMONT

MASSACHUSETTS

Holyoke

NEW YORK

Saugerties

CONNECTICUT

CAST OF CHARACTERS

Eden Kelley—She'd never wanted to fall in love with a dangerous man.

Christian X. Tierney—The widowed U.S. Marshal would take the law into his own hands to save the life of a daring woman.

Margo Bancroft—Tierney's sister-in-law knew him better than anyone. Her son would do anything for his uncle, but her husband couldn't be trusted.

Paul Maroncek—The head of Boston US Marshals suspected Tierney was a loose cannon—not all bad, but dangerously close to real trouble.

Winston Elijah Broussard—A Cajun charmer, his generosity knew no bounds, but he demanded loyalty above all else.

David Tafoya—The Boston FBI go-to guy would go to any lengths to protect his witness.

J. J. Gelham—An old colleague of Tierney, he warned against more futile games of hide-and-seek.

Dan Haggerty—The government pilot bought into a hijacking and lived long enough to regret it.

Chapter One

Eden Kelley bade her last patron of that day goodbye with a bouquet of false hopes. The exquisite handmade camisole and tap pants, the trademark garments of her boutique, *Eden's!,* would not be delivered by the end of the week. Her reassurances were not worth the price of a cheap spool of thread.

The lie broke her heart, but no one must guess that when Eden left tonight, she would never be back.

Her life, as she knew it, was over. The hopes. The dreams. The wedding . . . her wedding.

She had been planning the design of her gown for as long as she could remember, from the romantic sweetheart neckline to the elegant train, kissed with hand-stitched pearls, each applied with the same loving care she gave every handmade confection in her lingerie boutique.

Instead of her wedding gown, Eden found herself busily stitching up the government's case against her financier and fiancé, Winston Elijah Broussard III.

Web, daaalin'. You mus' call me Web. I can see now I'm going to be heartbroken if things don't work out between us. . . . Web was New Orleans laid-back, Cajun and more sensual than the Big Easy itself. Add to that, Eden thought bitterly, a Louisiana-born Boston gangster. She'd fallen for it all—his financial backing, his long, sultry looks, the clouds of hothouse orchids he bestowed on her... his marriage proposal.

Eden swallowed hard and threw the dead bolt on the front door of the boutique. She'd learned an easy lesson the hard way. She would never again sit back and allow any man to take care of her. When had she grown so foolish?

She hurried now, anxious to make the break and leave behind the remnants of her dreams. In keeping with her routine, she locked the display case tastefully strewn with dreamy hand-sewn lingerie, plucked her antique needle-point satchel from the coat closet, then headed for the back staircase.

Web's handsomely appointed office occupied the entire third story of the Cambridge brownstone. She had to make this good, make this seem an ordinary farewell. Web already suspected a leak, a defector, a *traitor* in his organization. If she screwed up now and gave him any inkling that she had already gone to the Feds and would never be back, he would... stop her. Drop her into the Charles River, or whatever mobsters did these days.

In a lifetime of command performances, always bending herself to what she thought someone else wanted her to be just to survive, this one had to be Eden's most convincing.

The mahogany-paneled stairwell was dark. The stair runner muted the sound of her steps as she ascended to Web's inner sanctum, but the pounding of her heart echoed in her ears. The skirt of her peach wraparound dress whispered against her long, silk-stockinged thighs. She reached the third-story landing and took a deep breath to boost her nerve.

His door stood ajar. Eden sighed with relief. If the door had been closed, she would have been forced to wait on the deacon's bench outside. This understanding, which was carved in stone, should have been a clue to her months ago of something very much amiss.

She straightened her shoulders and slipped through the door of the outer office, calling softly, making herself into the besotted creature he supposed her to be.

"Web darling?"

No answer came. She crossed the thick burgundy pile carpeting. She could hear the low murmur of men's voices, Web's and one not very much like his except that they were speaking half in English, half in the Cajun-French patois.

She called out again as she pushed open the heavy door to his private domain and slipped inside. "Web? I'm leaving now. I just wanted to see you—" She broke off. He sat at his desk, his dark good looks appearing sinister to her now. He was, as ever, impeccably attired, his suit and shirt adorned by a scarf rather than tie.

But he wasn't alone.

Another man, pockmarked and dark and slightly built, stood by the windows overlooking the street. He stared at her a moment from unusual fiery, amber-hued eyes that chilled her. By the cut and skilled tailoring of his jacket, she knew he wore a gun.

The man flicked ashes at an old-fashioned brass spittoon and turned deliberately away. Eden smiled guilelessly, as if she hadn't a clue what kind of man this was. Only a few months ago, that would have been true.

Sitting at his ornate desk, Web stubbed out his cigarette and turned toward her. His dark eyes narrowed against the smoke into dangerous slits. "Eden. What are you doin' here, darlin'?"

"I..." She swallowed hard, remembering that the outer door *had* been left ajar. Her heart knocked painfully. Why would he leave the door open unless he meant her to get the message—his guest was a hit man. An assassin. A shooter. Whatever. She had gotten away with betraying his illicit operations to the Feds because he thought her essentially harmless and...decorative. Had he finally realized she must be the one?

Fear began to unravel her nerve.

Stop it! she commanded herself. If he knew anything, she would already be fish food. *Just say goodbye and walk out of here.* There would never be a better time than this. Web had arranged for her trip to the couture design show in Dallas himself. She had merely meant to make one last, convincing demonstration of her devotion, but instead she'd interrupted him and he was angry.

She gave a tiny, artless shrug. Her eyes flicked to the man at the window. She dragged her gaze back to Web and put longing into it. "I...I only wanted to see you once more before I left."

"Ahh see." He stood and approached her, blocking her view of his guest. "Poor darlin'. You'll miss me, won't you?" He smiled in the same slow, drawling way that he spoke.

Her skin began to crawl. "I will, yes." Her throat seemed to lock, but it didn't matter. Web would simply think her tongue-tied with her fascination for him.

How could she ever have been taken in by him, ever thought she wanted to marry him? It took everything she had to stand her ground and behave as if she couldn't bear to part with him without one last goodbye.

His small black irises shone. He reached out and stroked her cheek and let his fingers trail down to caress her obscenely through the peach silk. Eden shivered hard in a revulsion she hoped he would mistake for unrequited desire.

"Soon, my sweet, hungry virgin," he promised her, but his sultry tone lacked any real passion. She understood in a blinding moment of clarity that he hoped to so shock her or besot her that she would forget what, or whom, she had seen here tonight.

A soft moan escaped her lips. He laughed softly, deep in his throat, but Eden knew it was her horror in reaction to his caress that made him believe his goal had been accomplished.

"You go on along now, Eden, my little garden of secret delights. Miss me." She shivered. How she hated him and the lewd joke he made of her name. He laughed. "Ahh *know* you will."

She managed to produce a shy, demure little smile. He was going to burn in hell. And because he wished her to forget, she would remember till hell froze over the man with the skilled tailor and the cold amber eyes.

ON THE SEVENTH of February, five months later, Eden began her testimony in the prosecution of Winston Elijah Broussard III for the extensive, illicit use he had made of her *Eden's!* overseas connections. He sat there at the defense table day in and day out, never in all the unnerving hours of her testimony taking his eyes from her.

And each day, the defense table was adorned by a lavish display of fresh, dewy, hothouse orchids. A reminder, Eden thought, of everything she had sacrificed to testify against him. Wealth, privilege—a pampered life.

The boutique.

And Sheila Jacques. Eden's closest friend, an inner-city junior high school teacher, was tough as nails but more stupid than Eden about smooth-talking men. Eden had been allowed to write Sheila a note to be hand-delivered by the FBI so that she wouldn't worry Eden had come to any harm—but only that.

Sheila might have guessed Eden had become a protected government witness against Web—and was now the only key prosecution witness remaining in this front-page fiasco. Eden would never see Sheila again. Or share late-night confessions or ever again feel part of a real family.

Winston Elijah Broussard was a munitions broker, a monster making millions smuggling bullets and bombs that killed real people. Her testimony was supposed to have brought together the threads of a complicated but certain prosecution case, establishing the link between the manufacturers of death and destruction to Web's buyers.

Nothing came together as expected.

Three weeks ago, the Feds had come to the Maine safe house where she'd remained in isolated protective custody to tell her that the case against Web had all but collapsed.

"The long and short of it, Ms. Kelley, is that you're free to walk away from this. Under Witness Protection, of course."

Walk away from this? Eden couldn't believe it. "Why? You're going to nail Web, aren't you? You're going to put him away!"

The lead prosecutor, a woman, shook her head. "We had four key witnesses. The other three have bailed out."

Eden paled. "How does a key witness bail out? Can't you subpoena them? Make them testify? Threaten them?"

The prosecutor bowed her head, then met Eden's angry, confused gaze. "This is the way it works. We cut deals, Eden. It's done all the time. Immunity or reduced charges in exchange for testimony. Sometimes the slugs decide it's healthier in the long term to keep their mouths shut."

The prosecutor exchanged glances with David Tafoya, the FBI agent whose painstaking, bulletproof, highly

publicized case had now disintegrated. His features tight-
ened to a stony mask, but Eden had spent hundreds of
hours with him and knew he must feel deeply angered, even
humiliated about the outcome.

"*The best we can do with only your testimony,*" *the*
prosecutor concluded, "*is to go for wire fraud. Broussard*
will go away to prison, but he'll be out in two years—three
years tops....

Was it so foolish to believe that a few innocent lives
would be spared somewhere in the world because Web
wasn't brokering bullets for a few years? Eden felt she had
no other responsible choice than to go ahead with it.

In for a penny, in for a pound....

She had committed the unpardonable act of betraying
Winston Elijah Broussard III and so she would have to
disappear.

Become someone else. Again.

The courtroom echoed with the hammering gavel of the
judge, who was not only fed up with the defense antics, but
still irate at the prosecution's inability to produce its witnesses.

"Counsel, get on with it," the judge snapped at the
prosecutor.

Eden took a deep breath and cleared her throat.

"Ms. Kelley, help me to wrap this up," the prosecutor
said now, her hands flat on the table before her. The defense counsel had already cross-examined Eden. The
prosecution had one last chance on redirect to make its
most damning point. "You uncovered final proof among
your records of the defendant's illicit—"

"Objection, prejudicial, already asked and answered,"
Web's attorney interrupted in a bored tone.

"Rephrase."

The prosecutor thanked the judge, then went on. "You found evidence of the defendant's use of your overseas banking connections, your records and your accounts last July 21."

"Yes," Eden answered.

"Remind the court one last time what it was that led you to believe you were being used."

"A series of phone records and bank transfers on my books and in my business records."

"And what, in particular, snagged your admittedly belated attention?"

Feeling the forbidding waves of tension from Web, Eden lifted her chin. "I have no accounts in Banja Luka." The answer she'd been coached in framing focused her testimony for the jury to a single damning, startlingly graphic image. "I make undergarments. I don't make or sell AK-47s."

The courtroom erupted. Eden forced herself to take a deep breath in the presence of well over fifty of Broussard's extended family members seated that day in the courtroom.

Defense counsel roared to his feet, capping off half a dozen grievances with, "Your Honor, really. My client doesn't manufacture these heinous weapons, either, and I object to the implication that he does!"

The judge was forced to bang his gavel to silence the defense counsel and, in lieu of clearing his courtroom, excused Eden from the stand.

Eden stood. She couldn't avoid one last look at Broussard. He gave a slow, mesmerizing smile. Meeting her gaze, he plucked an orchid petal, rolled it between his thumb and third finger, then drew back his finger and flicked the crushed blossom over his shoulder.

Eden flinched. She was going to die. Web would see to it. A wild trembling began deep inside her.

Around her, everything seemed to unravel at once. The prosecutors burst into angry protests at Web's gesture. The bailiff came forward to escort her off the witness stand and out of the courtroom. The gavel pounded and the judge ordered the entire defense table thrown into jail for its client's barefaced contempt of the proceedings.

The swinging doors closed on the donnybrook behind her but Eden felt no sense of relief.

"Ms. Kelley, this way, please."

She turned and fell into step with a team of six deputy marshals outside the federal district courtroom, Boston, Massachusetts. Two to each side of her, one in the lead, one behind.

Funny, the way her mind was working, the way "this way, please" rattled around in her consciousness like an echo of too many times in too many government buildings at the mercy of well-meaning, overwhelmed child welfare workers. Sixteen foster homes in fourteen years. *This way, little girl. What is your name again?*

Standing at the elevator surrounded by deputies of the United States Marshal Service, exhausted by the weeks of waiting, the endless protection, the lack of any real privacy, the hopelessness of it all, Eden almost gave in to hysteria and laughed.

Wire fraud.

Two years at most.

That's all her sacrifice was worth. The brutal irony choked her. Her chest tightened with a fear she hadn't felt so fiercely since she was five years old and had been taken in by Social Services for the first time.

The verse was different, but the refrain was the same. Eden Kelley had no home.

The elevator came to a stop on a restricted-access floor of the Federal Building. Flanked by the deputies, she walked at her own pace, trying perversely to gain the tiniest sense that she was in control of her life. A maze of hallways led to the garage, where a car with darkened, bulletproof windows waited to transport her to Logan International Airport. Eden began to smell the automobile exhaust wafting in from the garage.

A small cluster of four men and one woman entered the unadorned hallway slightly ahead of Eden's protective entourage. The woman was taller than Eden's five-five height, with short dark hair and a three-quarter-length navy suede coat that nearly matched her own forest green one.

Eden thought the group composed a decoy team until the woman gazed adoringly up at the knockout, drop-dead gorgeous guy dressed in torn jeans and a black leather trench coat. "We're pregnant! Can you believe it, Chris? Baby *finally* makes three."

"Little loaf in the oven, eh, Tierney?" teased one of the other suit-clad men.

"Lead in the pencil after all!" gibed another.

"You're gonna name the kid after me, right?" a third one demanded.

"Right, Dilts," the gorgeous expectant dad returned, his deep voice vibrant with a Boston accent. "I been waiting since second grade to grow up and name my firstborn after you."

The five of them laughed as if this joke were the natural evolution of lifelong friends. Eden felt a wave of jealousy, a pang of longing, of not *belonging* so intense it stole her breath. She blinked and forced her gaze off them, and focused straight ahead.

The first man, Dilts, shoved through the heavy metal door with his shoulder, and the laughing fivesome poured into the garage. The deputy leading Eden's protective detail caught and held open the door after them, and in that instant, the deadly cocking sounds of a shotgun splintered the laughter.

One of the deputies roared, "It's a damned ambush!" and in the next second, a man swung wildly around from behind a concrete pillar, his head covered in a ski mask, the deadly shotgun aimed from his side. He looked no farther away than the woman ahead of Eden, and he brought the shotgun to bear on her chest.

His eyes seemed on fire.

Raw panic rose in Eden and she screamed, "You! No! No! God, no!" but the weapon erupted. Blinding bursts of light spewed out. The deafening blasts echoed and magnified and obliterated her scream.

Time seemed to warp, to stop. The woman who *belonged* crumpled silently back into the arms of her husband. The men surrounding her and the men surrounding Eden had already drawn sidearms and sprang into action. Someone shoved her to the ground. The men fanned out, shouting orders, covering one another, all of them firing. Eden saw the hit man duck and feint and run. He never made it to cover. He fell hard and facedown to the concrete floor in a terrible hail of gunfire.

One of the deputies held Eden down by the collar of her coat. She tried to scramble up, to shrug out of her coat, to go to the other woman. To stop her awful bleeding.

A part of Eden's mind urged her to break and run instead. The gunman was playing a dirty trick. The instinct nearly overwhelmed her. She knew he must only be pretending to be dead. Any second, he would curl up and around and take aim and this time not kill an innocent bystander, but her.

She didn't care. She couldn't face a lifetime of this kind of evil lurking behind every closed door. She almost hoped he'd come back to life and riddle her body with bullets. Amid the terrible chaos, she heard the woman's husband desperately commanding someone, anyone, to get an ambulance.

Eden began to hyperventilate as she writhed in the deputy's grasp. "Let me go," she begged, crying. "If I don't help her, she'll die! Let me go!"

He snatched her back.

"Stay down, damn it!" the deputy snarled. "It's already too late. Now breathe! There's nothing you can do. Breathe!"

She would never breathe easily again. The horror of that crushed orchid blossom filled her mind, gnawed at her awareness. The other woman had been blown away, and every instinct fired at Eden to run. She recognized the gunman from Web's office, but what could she tell these lawmen that they wouldn't already know? That the shooter was a crony of his?

The narrow hallway filled with more men armed with more guns. The shouting intensified. Eden felt unutterably cold and sick at heart and numbed and *guilty*. Another woman was shot dead with bullets meant for her.

The crushed orchid blossom . . . Oh, God.

The deputies finally dragged her up and poked her into the bulletproof car. The last thing she saw was the dropdead gorgeous expectant dad, holding the dead woman tight to his chest, his head bowed low.

"I'm sorry," she whispered. Such a brutal loss would forever deaden a man's heart. "So sorry." Emotion scalded her. Tears spilled down her cheeks, but they had dried by the time the deputies put her on the west-bound jet.

"Flying into the sunset," she murmured. "And she lived happily ever after." The deputies just looked at her, not knowing whether to smile or look tactfully away. Not knowing how to respond at all to the black humor that kept her from going quietly insane.

She couldn't get warm. After a while, two of the men accompanying her began to question her about the attack. She told them everything she could. She told them she knew the shooter was an associate of Winston Broussard's. That she'd seen both of them together, naming the time and place that she remembered exactly. She described the shooter's eyes. She agreed, numbly, fearfully, to be recalled when the case came to trial.

She dozed off and on. Each time she jerked awake, the image of the murderer's eyes, like flaming amber, filled her mind. The jet finally landed. The deputies and local FBI agents scouted the area and convinced themselves the destination was secure, and then, still numb, still cold, Eden disembarked.

It was colder here in Wyoming than in Boston. Her breath froze in the thin air. The jagged, snow-covered Tetons ruled the landscape. The deputies helped her into yet another car, but the drive was short, ending at the ice-crusted wooden steps of a mountain cabin veranda.

Seven hours after the gunman had murdered another woman in her stead, Eden Kelley became Lisa Hollister. She was helped to undress by a hardy, wrinkled old woman named Judith. The ritual felt familiar—kindly strangers taking an abandoned child into their homes. The old woman crooned softly and brushed Lisa Hollister's short, out-of-a-bottle sable brown hair one hundred brisk strokes.

Judith put her to bed beneath a well-worn handmade quilt, blew out the tallow candle and sat with Lisa Hollister through the night in a softly creaking rocking chair.

But by touch, to keep the shame and horror at bay, Eden counted stitches and squares in the dark and multiplied stitches by squares in her head until she knew there were 26,800 separate stitches in the quilt, give or take fifty.

WINSTON ELIJAH BROUSSARD didn't spend even two years in the country-club federal penitentiary where he'd been consigned. He served seventeen months and four days. His release was the straw that broke the camel's back, the cause of Deputy Marshal Christian X. Tierney's sacrificing whatever thin veneer of civilization he had managed to retain. His fellow deputies used to joke with him, changing Tierney into Tyranny. He didn't think they'd see the humor much longer.

Catherine lay dead and buried in a windy cemetery on Chestnut Hill with her unborn child still in her body. Chris thought sometimes, when he indulged a black rage and had to get totally drunk on Jack Daniel's to kill the pain in his heart, that he should have just lain down beside her in the frozen earth and been done with it.

No one in any law enforcement agency ever kidded themselves for long that justice prevailed more often than it was perverted, but Chris had a personal stake in dealing real justice now.

God's own justice. An eye for an eye, a tooth for a tooth.

Catherine was dead.

The day was overcast and windy, typical of Boston in May. The cold wind blowing off the Atlantic sliced through even his battle-scarred leather trench coat. Chris shoved through the doors of the Federal Building, flashed his badge and ID at the guards standing by to sweep their hand-held electronic metal detectors over anyone who set off the alarm system.

He looked like hell, but he was clean. He was always clean, though he hadn't shaved in days and didn't intend to. He didn't much resemble the clean-cut, Irish-Slavic eager-beaver deputy in the photo ID. His eyes were still hazel, his hair black, height six-one, weight one eighty-five. But his hair was way out of regs. His eyes were bloodshot all the time. And the unshaven whiskers made the angles of his face a little savage. Still, the guards recognized him and let him pass.

He got on the elevator, off on the restricted floor that housed the United States Marshal Service, Boston, and glanced up at the surveillance cameras. He pushed through another set of doors on an electronic lock, then passed rows of cubicles, finally letting himself unannounced into Chief Deputy Paul Maroncek's office. He stood, waiting.

Maroncek looked up from a bulky report. He leaned back in his blue leather chair, tossing his ballpoint atop the file folder. He nodded at the chair opposite him.

Chris sat.

"A job well done, Tierney," Maroncek said at last, gesturing to the report. "The attorney general is ecstatic. Seven captures in what? A year and a half?"

"Seventeen months."

It was true. Chris had reinvented himself. He'd become a merciless, dangerous son of a bitch. He needed some outlet for the rage, some way to burn off the violence in his soul. Even after he took to a mean vintage Harley, tracked down and captured seven of the most dangerous fugitives on the Eastern Seaboard, even after he traced Winston Broussard's activities and haunted his former bases of operation and consumed everything there was to know about the man whose assassin had killed the wrong woman, even then, Chris was left constantly spoiling for a fight.

He'd found more than one. The last brawl had left him laid up in a hospital in Whitewater, New Hampshire, where he suffered through five days and nights quaking like a man with malaria, only his shaking came from withdrawal.

When his mind cleared, the nightmares returned. The same disorienting, wildly disjointed images of Catherine's murder, like holographic images projected at an agonizingly slow pace of one per second.

Three weeks ago, Chris had cornered a domestic terrorist in one of the most bloody, bullet-ridden captures he'd ever executed. That night, his nightmares finally broke through to his consciousness and he knew. Eden Kelley, the intended victim of the bullets that killed Catherine, had been screaming beneath the echoing blast of the shotgun. *You! No! No! God, no!*

Eden had recognized the shooter.

He planned, then, to pervert the witness protection system he still believed in. He would dig out Eden Kelley's new identity and location so he could bring her back. She was the key. The only person on the face of God's green earth who could link Broussard to Catherine's assassin.

In the past few days, after poring over official investigation notes, Chris knew the FBI had already pursued that avenue. Eden Kelley had recognized the shooter and could even cite the day and time she had seen him together with Broussard because it was the night David Tafoya had taken her into protective custody. But guilt by association hadn't translated into a viable prosecution tactic since the Salem witch trials. Lacking any other link to Broussard, the FBI couldn't even bring him before a grand jury for indictment.

Eden Kelley's testimony would only further endanger her life. No charges were brought. No grand jury was ever called. Broussard was off scot-free.

He had not even served a full two years on the wire-fraud charges, but Catherine was dead for all time and Eden Kelley would live a fugitive's existence, in fear for her life, forever. Chris could no longer stand by and let it be. He wanted real justice. And for that, Broussard must die.

Maroncek wasn't stupid. He knew the seventeen months in which Chris had turned in those captures was also the length of sentence Broussard had served.

"Suppose you heard," Maroncek said, shoving his half glasses up onto his head. Narrow-faced, he had a full head of silver hair and penetrating, squinty blue eyes.

"Yeah. Broussard was released." Chris slumped. "Too frigging bad I had to hear it on the Channel 5 news."

Maroncek shrugged. "You weren't in yesterday. Or the day before yesterday, or the day before that."

Chris sighed sharply and shook his head. Maroncek knew Chris hadn't been in because he'd been on a round-the-clock stakeout trying to nab a heavily armed, cocaine-freaked fugitive. "This office knew, Paul. Everyone on that stakeout knew a week ago." Word had gotten around to everyone but him.

Maroncek pinched the bridge of his nose. "This office has a few higher mandates than keeping you informed. And frankly, it's of some concern to me that you refuse to let this thing with Broussard go."

Chris could no longer keep his anger leashed. "Frankly, I don't give a rat's ass that you're *concerned*. Frankly, I resent the hell out of your concern. It's insulting. I don't need a keeper."

Wearily, Maroncek let his chair spring upright. "What possible difference does it make that Broussard was released? Are you planning to take him out? Avenge Catherine's death? You think you're going to feel better then, like a real man? It doesn't work that way, my friend."

Chris met Maroncek's hard stare straight on and kept quiet. The silence lasted for over a minute.

Maroncek finally gave a heavy sigh. Chris knew his superior might worry about it all day long, but he wouldn't for a minute *believe* Chris capable of tracking Broussard down to blow him away.

Maroncek was wrong.

"Look," the chief deputy said at last, trying to make up for having insulted Chris's integrity, "the Feebs have got their shorts in a knot over this thing. Tafoya thinks Broussard has a fix on the Kelley woman's location."

Chris straightened. "Why?"

Maroncek shook his head. "Beats the hell out of me."

"We're supposed to take it on faith that her cover has been blown?" Chris demanded. He didn't believe in taking things at face value, and faith required a kind of spiritual conviction he no longer indulged in at all. "Is Tafoya suggesting Witness Protection leaked her location?"

"In a manner of speaking." Maroncek grimaced. The U.S. Marshal Service was inevitably going to be blamed when a relocated witness's cover was blown. He began toying with a pen. "The Feebs aren't talking," he went on. "Tafoya is playing this hand close to the chest. The most obvious conclusion is that Eden Kelley saw someone she knew, panicked over the chance that she'd been spotted and called Tafoya. Sheila Jacques's name came up, but Tafoya refuses to confirm or deny."

Chris shook his head.

"Do you know who the Jacques woman is?" Maroncek asked.

"I've heard the name." Chris knew Paul's question was carefully phrased. Bait in a fishing expedition. He wanted to know exactly how well-informed Chris was. How obsessed. But he also knew it would be deadly to deny knowing anything about the woman. "An old friend of Eden Kelley's."

Maroncek nodded. "Apparently, her closest friend. The closest thing she had to any family."

Chris knew that, as well, and more, but he didn't think Paul expected a comment. "I don't buy it, Paul. Even if Eden Kelley knew she'd been seen, she has to know better than to call Tafoya. She has an assigned contact in Witness Protection—"

"I agree. She was instructed in procedure, Chris," Maroncek interrupted. "But—again, neither confirming nor denying that she called him—Tafoya maintains that if Eden Kelley's witness protection identity has been compromised, then someone inside this office has either screwed up and leaked the information, or—"

"Deliberately sold her down the river."

Maroncek sighed heavily and tossed the pen down. "Exactly."

"So Tafoya can make the case that he's the only one she can trust."

"Again, exactly."

Chris didn't think Paul was done. "What's the bottom line?"

"Tafoya wants her relocated and he wants it done by his people."

"Bypassing Witness Protection altogether?" Chris asked incredulously.

"Yes."

"He'll never get the A.G. to approve that."

Maroncek gave a bitter smile. "The attorney general, bless her little pointed head, has already given Tafoya the nod. She's convinced that the Kelley woman has a right to be spooked by a blown protection—if that's happened—and to decide whom she'll trust."

Chris swore. "I don't believe it." He swung out of his seat and dumped his coat in the chair. He couldn't believe this sheer reckless disregard of the Marshal Service and a program that had safely relocated an overwhelming majority of its charges.

The truth was, though, that Chris admired the Feebs' ploy. If Eden Kelley were his witness—and if he were in Tafoya's shoes, already humiliated by a case that had publicly crumbled and left a witness marked to die—Chris would have done the same thing and to hell with the bureaucracy. The witness's life was paramount.

So, yeah. He understood Tafoya's reasoning—even admired the end result. A man who could think made a far better cop than a by-the-book drone. Tafoya was thinking.

Chris leaned against the black metal window casing and stared out the window, thinking. It didn't take a lot to imagine Eden Kelley's state of mind, either. Every relocated witness lived day in and day out in constant fear of being recognized by the wrong person. People began to see things. Imagine things. Get frankly paranoid—and justifiably so.

If Eden Kelley believed her life was in danger, if she made a run for it, or even if she decided to tell the system to screw off, that she'd choose another identity on her own, he couldn't fault her.

He didn't blame her.

He just couldn't afford to lose her, which would happen if Tafoya moved her too quickly. Chris had no choice now but to go straight from Paul Maroncek's office to that of Linda Desmond, who controlled access to all the files of relocated witnesses.

She owed Chris big time. He'd pulled her adult son out of some pretty desperate straits—twice, and without a ripple. If he hadn't, her kid would have been dead on the seedier streets of Boston—no one double-crossed bookies and drug dealers twice and lived to tell about it. So Chris had helped Linda, she owed him, and if he had any chance of learning Eden Kelley's alias and location, it had to be now, before Tafoya hid her someplace else.

Chris took a deep breath and picked up his coat, then turned to face Paul Maroncek one last time.

"Are you going to be all right, Chris? Let this thing go? The witness is Tafoya's problem. And Broussard is now an ex-con who's paid his debt to society."

"Yeah." Chris shrugged, tamping down his anger. Paul had made a leap of faith in telling him these things, and he knew his boss wanted to hear that his faith hadn't been misplaced. And wouldn't be betrayed, either.

Chris respected that. He respected Paul's intellect and his commitment to the job and his friendship. What Chris was going to do, what he had to do, was going to reflect badly on his boss. Very badly.

"Why don't you take some time off?" Maroncek said suddenly. "Go fishing. Get laid. Hell, get laid for both of us. Janna's been pretty hostile lately."

Paul didn't often say such things. Chris could have dealt with morality lectures, but not this.

He felt like his lungs had forgotten what to do. Like he'd just been knocked square and hard in the chest with a hockey stick. What he wouldn't give to go back to the early days when Catherine wasn't confused about what she wanted. Who she wanted. Times when she was straight with him. Times when Catherine was at home and alive and royally pissed off at him, because those were things he could fix.

She wasn't.

He swallowed. His voice barely worked. "Go home and make it up to Janna, Paul. Do it now."

Chapter Two

Eden woke when the sun rose these days. The early-morning chill always made her want to draw deeper into the cocoon of covers, but the old potbellied wood stove needed stoking before the embers died out. Judith's old bones didn't take kindly to the cold, even on an August morning like this when the temperature had only dipped to the forties.

She slipped from beneath the old quilt and straightened the bed covers. Removing her flannel nightgown, she quickly tugged on her jeans, then reached for a cotton bustier. The decision to testify so many months ago had cost her everything else she had ever valued in her life, but there was one thing they could never take away from her. The simple, private luxury of hand-stitched undergarments fashioned for her shape alone from the softest of imported silks and cotton fabrics. Camisoles and tap pants, old-fashioned chemises and bustiers she made herself.

She tied up the simple beribboned cotton bustier and pulled on a sweatshirt, then a warm pair of socks and sturdy shoes. The attire of a simple, mountain-dwelling woman, rising to stoke the home fires.

Home.

It was true, Eden thought, leaving her tiny room to perform the morning chores. Somewhere in the midst of her exile, she'd come to think of Judith Cornwallis's mountain cabin as home. Something primitive in it appealed to her.

The log walls encased four rooms, including Eden's bedroom, Judith's, a great room, which was both kitchen and living room, and a small bathroom. In back, the veranda was closed in to protect a pantry full of food Eden had canned herself this past summer, a thirty-year-old washing machine and a deep freeze. Their clothes had to be hung from a line outside to dry.

She'd sewn new curtains for all the windows. She knew the sound of the floorboards beneath her feet. She knew the next likely place the yellow jackets would invade. She could distinguish the bugling of elk from that of moose.

She bent now to open the stove and stir the coals, then poked in the firewood she had chopped herself. The months of backbreaking work had strengthened her, body and soul. Her blisters eventually hardened into calluses and the pine pitch staining her fingers became a badge of self-sufficiency. Eden Kelley, a.k.a. Lisa Hollister, needed to depend on no man to do for her.

Judith Cornwallis was an eccentric, cranky, demanding recluse, a British expatriate spinster who suspected she was harboring a fugitive of some sort when she took Eden in. Hard to get along with and proud of it.

To this day, Eden didn't know if Judith even liked her.

The old lady's crankiness, Eden had decided long ago, must have something to do with Judith's artistic temperament. The old woman wrote some of the most exquisite poetry Eden had ever read. Like W. H. Auden, only a woman's voice.

Unfortunately, Judith thought the same about her own writing as she did about other people's incessant jabbering, so if she was left to her own devices, her work ended up in the potbellied stove.

As Lisa Hollister, Eden was well paid by Britta Nielsen, Judith's New York agent, to conserve Judith's poetry. Eden had been provided with a state-of-the-art notebook computer along with a fax-machine link so she could type in and then fax out the poems before Judith destroyed them.

She and Judith fought many a tug-of-war over the papers, and in a real snit one night, Judith had tossed every item of Eden's scant possessions out the door. Eden had hurled them right back in the door and refused to leave in very explicit words.

"A good stiff upper lip, that's what I like," the old woman cracked mockingly.

Eden responded with some impertinent black-humored remark about a *dead* stiff's upper lips because Judith knew perfectly well that Eden's life depended upon staying here. After that, she had the old lady's grudging respect.

Now Judith pretended as if she didn't know what Eden was doing with the computer. She did. Eden often left the computer on because Judith wasn't one to resist a mystery right under her nose. She suspected the old lady even knew how to fax things herself—and access the on-line bulletin boards.

"Lisa!" Judith called out from the larger bedroom, snatching Eden back from her reverie. "Are you deaf, girl? Lisa!" She began to wheeze. Her chronic breathing problems weren't helped at all by living at this altitude.

"Give me a just a minute," Eden called back. She shut off the water tap and turned on the fire beneath the tea-kettle, alarmed that the old lady had awakened so early.

She found Judith already half-up, rising shakily from her feather bed with the aid of a cane carved from a twelve-point elk antler. Strands of her snow-white hair had escaped its braid. The room was lined with bookshelves on all sides save where her antique chifforobe stood. Surrounding even the picture window, which framed a view of the jagged Tetons, the shelves were crammed full.

Eden had heard Judith get up at least twice during the night, unsettled by something. She looked more fragile in the early-morning sunlight than Eden had seen in all these months. More frail . . . and deeply agitated.

Eden went to lend a steadying hand but the old woman swatted it away. "What is it, Judith?"

"Someone's coming!" she said, gasping a little for air.

Judith Cornwallis had an uncanny sense of when her privacy was being invaded. The mountains were far from silent. Birds began piping up at the crack of dawn. Water gurgled and flowed in the Snake River, echoing up from the floor of the valley. Pine trees crackled and popped, depending on the wind, and the aspen shivered.

The infinitesimal throb of an engine subtly intruded on all that and Judith was rarely wrong. But the sun had only just come up so Eden discounted the likelihood of visitors this early.

"Judith, it's only a quarter to six in the morning! No one's coming here. Please. Let me get your oxygen. Lie back down and—"

"I know bloody well what time it is, missy," Judith interrupted, rapping her cane on the wood plank floor. She drew a difficult breath. "My faculties are all intact."

Her hearing certainly was. "I know, Judith," Eden placated. Still, she pulled the small tank nearer on its dolly and opened the valve to begin the oxygen flow. "It's just that you can't breathe when—"

"I have a bad feeling, I'm telling you!" She took the mask from Eden and put it over her nose and mouth. Scowling as if Eden were an irretrievable moron, she inhaled as deeply as she could three times, then cast the mask aside. "A very bad feeling, and it's got nothing to do with my breathing or my not breathing."

Eden had never seen the old woman behave in this way. A nameless worry pricked at her. Judith didn't like intruders, but she didn't get "bad feelings." Maybe she'd suffered a small stroke during the night. Eden swallowed and shut off the oxygen valve. "What, then, Judith?"

Her lips pursed. "I don't know." She breathed raggedly again but her expression sharpened. She had been told that Lisa Hollister was a secretary to an English professor at the City University of New York, and that her family—a husband and child—had been killed in a car wreck. That she needed a job and a change of scenery and time to grieve.

Judith didn't believe any of it. She knew fiction when she heard it. Hard-bitten and testy by nature, she made up fanciful stories and composed bitingly emotional poetry. But Judith Cornwallis feared no one.

The only certainty was that she knew nothing of Eden Kelley's past. She couldn't. Her sudden uncharacteristic fright was very real, and it infected Eden.

Before Judith could say another word, they heard the clank of a car fender banging into a deep rut cast as hard as concrete by the sun and wind. The car had turned off the two-lane highway onto the dirt lane leading up to Judith's cabin.

"I'm sure everything is fine, Judith." She didn't mean to lie, but her fears had to do with having been Eden Kelley, not Lisa Hollister, and she couldn't give voice to them, even now. "Maybe someone just took the wrong road."

"Maybe it's the tooth fairy," Judith snapped.

Eden didn't really believe it, either.

Judith moved to her chifforobe. Eden darted to the window in Judith's bedroom. She tried to convince herself that this terrible fear was unreasonable. That Judith's bad feelings were hardly enough to justify this sensation of looming disaster.

But there was no one to protect her here, no bodyguards, no one safeguarding Judith's place as they had the house in Maine. Once her testimony was over, Witness Protection could only arrange to have her disappear. Her new location and identity were supposed to be known only inside the Marshal Service.

The chances of Web Broussard ever finding Eden in this life were exceedingly remote. But if he had, she would die.

Judith kept a 12-gauge shotgun on the back porch, but Eden had never learned to use it. Maybe the bad guys would die laughing at the way she handled the weapon.

But before she could move, the vehicle pulled into the clearing. The logo on the side was that of the county sheriff. Eden's heart thumped painfully.

"Who is it?" Judith hissed.

"Umm..." Eden swallowed. "The sheriff's department." Inside the four-wheel-drive vehicle were two men.

She wanted to feel relieved—and she was—that this wasn't Broussard or an assassin he'd hired to kill her. But something must be very wrong. Why hadn't her contact within the district marshal's office faxed her a message?

"Well, they're bloody well going to get a piece of my mind," Judith snapped, banging the floor with each stroke of her cane. "Bunch of self-important fascist bureaucrats."

Eden should have said something, or moved to prevent Judith's launching a misguided tirade, but she felt rooted to the floor, trapped by her need to stay where she finally belonged.

Suddenly, she knew why her fear hadn't abated at all. It had to do with feeling five years old again. With having been abandoned by her mother in the Boston Public Gardens like some hapless ugly duckling.

One of the park service men had taken her in his shiny pickup truck to Social Services, which took her in and then began to farm her out to foster families. Each time, Eden had tried desperately hard to fit in, and she'd succeeded.

Such a sweet, tractable child. Someone really should adopt her....

Or *Strong as a little ox, that one, hard worker....*

Or *Gets along with all the other children, even that little thug, Eddie Nichols....*

But a foster home was a temporary home where they weren't going to let Eden stay no matter how sweet, tractable, hardworking or congenial she managed to make herself.

Now the musty scent of Judith's old books plucked at Eden's heart. But the car engine outside fell silent.

The charm of a Kipling story or a John Donne poem or even a paperback romance from Judith's overflowing shelves had transported her many times. But outside, car doors opened and car doors slammed shut.

She felt a sudden panic. How would she cope if they had come to take her away again?

Do what you always do, she told herself. *This part you know by rote.* Turn off the thinking, shut down the feelings and remind herself of the stakes.

Eden Kelley had no home. Judith Cornwallis's cabin was only a place where she had grown stronger and more self-reliant. Strong enough to leave. Better to be uprooted than mown down.

The heavy footsteps of men came up the steps and a knock sounded at the door. Eden breathed deeply and crossed the bare plank floor.

Judith had flung open the door, but as she was already breathless from the exertion, one of the men got out a few words through the screen door before she could let them have it.

"Ms. Cornwallis, I'm very sorry for the intrusion—"

"You're sorry all right," Judith blurted, gasping a little bit.

"But it's imperative that we speak to Ms. Hollister."

"Well, you can just come back at a reasonable hour—"

Eden touched Judith's shoulder to calm her. "It's all right, Judith. I'll speak to them." By some miracle, the old lady deferred to Eden, but she scowled deeply while she turned away. Eden didn't recognize either man. One was dressed in the uniform of a sheriff's deputy, the other in a dark suit and lightweight summer trench coat. She stood behind the screen door with her arms folded. "Who are you?"

The thin, dark blond sheriff's deputy spoke first. "Lisa Hollister?"

Eden nodded. "Yes."

"Could we speak privately? Out on the porch?"

Eden grabbed a sweater from the old coat rack and shoved through the screen, closing off the heavier, solid, wood front door.

The deputy introduced himself, then the suit-clad man held up FBI credentials. "I'm Special Agent Dan Paglia."

"FBI?" Eden asked, not understanding. She wrapped the sweater over her shoulders.

"Yes," Paglia answered, noting her reaction. "I know such a visit must be very distressing to you. This is all very much out of the ordinary, but we don't have time to stand on protocol."

"I don't understand."

"Ms. Hollister," the dark, scrappily built FBI agent intoned, "your identity and location have been compromised, and we're—"

"Compromised?" Eden interrupted, disbelieving. "How? What does that mean?"

"It means," he went on, taking the tone of someone trying to explain higher math to a toddler, "that your life is in very grave danger and we have to move now. We don't have the luxury of time for explanations."

Eden shivered stiffly. Through the meadow she could hear a few elk bugling and knocking antlers. Resentment piled up in her like logs jamming the river during the spring runoff. Could Winston Broussard already be out of prison? Even if he had been released, that shouldn't have made any difference.

She had expected to be safe here. No one was supposed to approach her but her contact in Witness Protection, certainly not the local sheriff's department and an agent with the Wyoming FBI.

"I should have been notified," she insisted, feeling stupidly contrary for standing here arguing if her life was again in as much danger as they seemed to believe. "I want to talk to Dennis Shulander."

"He's out of the picture. The U.S. marshals are out of the picture, Ms. Hollister. There are important reasons for that, but—"

Her chin shot up. "I would still like to talk to Dennis."

"Listen," Paglia said, taking a softer, more reasonable tone, "I don't mean to scare you, Ms. Hollister, but the Bureau has taken over responsibility for your safety—

specifically Special Agent David Tafoya. Do you know the name?''

Eden nodded. Of course she knew the name. Tafoya had been the agent in charge of the investigation into Winston Broussard's illegal munitions activities. He had secured protection for her in the first place, and spent hundreds of hours working with her.

''Good. Now listen, because we really don't have any time.'' His brows rose for emphasis. ''Tafoya would have been here himself, but the weather in Boston has him socked in. I spoke with him a couple of hours ago. He said if you expressed any doubt about coming with us— now—'' he gestured emphatically ''—I should remind you of the day he came to see you in protective custody up in Bangor.''

Eden tilted her head. ''What about it?''

''He told you it was his daughter's third birthday, but his wife was leaving him and she split with the kid. Name was Jorie Ann.''

Eden remembered. These were details no one but David Tafoya himself could have revealed. He had passed them along to let her know she could trust the men he had sent and go with them. But her heart lurched in her chest. If Tafoya believed this couldn't wait a few hours until he could be here himself, then she must be in real danger.

She turned away and went to the railing. The sun shone brightly now, but warmth hadn't yet penetrated the morning chill. She had no choice to make other than to cooperate with these men.

To go on surviving despite Winston Broussard.

Though David Tafoya had drilled into her months ago that she must always be wary of strangers and unexpected events, he had clearly sent Special Agent Paglia here.

She didn't understand, but Tafoya would surely explain later what had gone wrong.

"Ms. Hollister?" the sheriff's deputy prodded.

She turned back to them. "What do you want me to do?"

"Pack a bag and make your farewells."

Of course. Eden nodded. "How much time?"

"Five minutes. Ten at the most," Paglia said. "We need to be out of here as soon as possible."

"What about Judith?" Eden asked. "If... will she be safe staying here?" The two men exchanged glances. Judith's safety was apparently not an issue they had considered. "I want your personal assurances that she'll be looked after."

"I'll do everything in my power to make sure nothing happens to Ms. Cornwallis," the deputy reassured her.

Paglia added, "Once you're no longer here, though, chances are she won't be in any danger."

Chances are. Eden wanted to laugh. Chance also dictated that her identity as Lisa Hollister would never be *compromised.*

She went back inside and closed the door behind her.

Tension crackled off Judith. "So?" she asked.

"So." Eden took a deep breath. What could she say? How could she tell this difficult old woman—who needed her whether she admitted it or not—that she must leave? With enough warning, she might have been able to come up with something more believable. "Looks like I've just won an all-expenses-paid vacation, courtesy of the U.S. government."

The old lady's lips pursed in a thin, taut line. "I don't wish to be humored, missy. I want to know what's going on."

That attempt at levity had felt lame to Eden anyway. "I know, Judith. But I can't stay and I can't tell you where I'm going. They don't even tell me."

Judith stared for a long moment, then nodded as if recognizing this was the way Lisa Hollister had come, and this was the way she must go.

"It would help me enormously," Eden said, "if after I've gone, you would fax a letter to your agent, to Britta, letting her know you're all right."

"How did you know?" Judith demanded imperiously.

"That you are perfectly capable of faxing things yourself?" Eden gave her a fond smile. It wasn't easy to find her voice. "Call it a lucky guess."

"My left foot," Judith cracked.

"Will you do it?"

Though for the briefest moment a crestfallen, helpless expression took hold of her, the old woman nodded. Then she straightened, cast her cane aside, and turning away to hide her watery eyes, she began to put together some fruit and graham crackers and a thermos of tea for Eden to take with her.

In her tiny room, Eden packed what she could in ten minutes and then went back to the great room to collect her needlepoint project and odds and ends.

Judith was sitting in the rocking chair, twining her hair back into its customary single white braid. She patted the ladder-back kitchen chair beside her. The old woman—whose affections Eden hadn't been the least bit sure of until this moment—was fighting back tears.

Eden didn't dare allow herself to feel this loss. "I'll be okay, Judith. So will you."

Judith said nothing, only examined her braid with a hand mirror that was almost two hundred years old. The back and handle were of one piece and made of silver etched in rose patterns. She held it out to Eden. Her hand trembled because the silver made the mirror so heavy. "I want you to have this."

Eden swallowed. "Judith, I couldn't."

"But you must, simply." Her British accent had never been so pronounced as it was now. "It's got quite a long history, you know. My mother before me, hers before her. Eight generations in all. I don't propose it should stop with me." She drew a labored breath and rose to tuck the mirror inside Eden's backpack, then, rather solemnly but with a twinkle in her eye, added, "I'd like to think the dear old bats might approve my rather belated maternal instincts, don't you?"

WHEN CHRIS APPROACHED Linda Desmond about the alias and location of the protected witness, Eden Kelley, it was already raining like hell south of Boston.

After Linda gave him access to the computer file, including names, dates and graphics precisely locating the remote mountain cabin, Chris made his flight reservation for Billings, Montana. From there, he would rent a cycle and drive the remaining three hundred miles to Jackson Hole. But the hurricane-force winds and torrential rains meant no flights would likely depart Boston for several hours before or after Chris's reservation.

He wound up on the last flight departing Logan International—or any other airport within several hundred miles—for the next few hours. The 747 was heading to Minneapolis, not Billings or even Denver, but Chris had one chance of getting out in time and he took it.

Minneapolis.

He had a lot of time to think, and after looking at all the angles, he realized Minneapolis would work in his favor. Sooner or later, Linda Desmond would have an attack of conscience, and she would find some backdoor way of telling Paul Maroncek that Chris had "somehow" gotten access to top secret relocation files.

Paul was smart, and Chris's biggest problem would be how to throw his boss off the scent. He trusted Chris. When it became known that Eden Kelley had disappeared, Paul would track Chris's movements and discover that he'd gone to Minnesota. Paul might be reassured for a day or two, convinced that Chris hadn't acted on his knowledge of the alias and whereabouts of Eden Kelley.

Since Paul had urged him to go fishing, Chris suspected the north woods might be as good a diversion as anything he might actually have planned.

He deplaned in Minneapolis in midafternoon, went to the car rental agency, leased a Jeep in his own name and with his own credit cards and confided he was heading farther north to do some backwoods fishing. He parked the Jeep in an immense lot at the airport.

Then he bought a ticket to Billings and paid cash. In Montana, he got hold of a used but powerful bike the same way. That and a sixteen inch machine pistol. He found an army surplus store still open at eleven-thirty that night and bought a bedroll and knapsack, tins of meat and powdered milk and Oreo cookies.

He didn't mind the bucks. The money came from Catherine's life insurance payout. She didn't have any use for it, buried on Chestnut Hill. Chris did. But the detour through Minneapolis and the time spent tracking down the Harley and pistol had cost him too many precious hours.

With all the lost time, he figured he had one chance in a hundred now of snatching Eden Kelley before Tafoya's men took her back into protective custody.

He took I-90 west to Livingston. Hauling ass south from there on U.S. 89 he crossed the Montana-Wyoming border at four in the morning.

He made it to Jackson in another hour and a half. His eyes stung. His body ached after almost six grisly hours in the bike saddle over some of the most dark and formidable terrain he'd ever traversed. His hands throbbed from relentless vibrations through the handle bars. The scenery was spectacular now in the predawn light, but he was too tired to care.

He stopped on the north side of Jackson to gas up the bike and get his bearings. In a national park area, maps were as common as houseflies. There was one under the glass on the counter in a convenience store. Aware that he was the lone customer in the store, marginally conscious of the painfully young doe-eyed clerk watching him as if he smiled at her he might make her whole day, he put a couple of packaged frozen burritos into the microwave.

He poured himself a large foam cup of freshly brewed coffee, then spent a few minutes conforming his recall of the computer graphics detailing Eden Kelley's location to the USGS map.

"Can I help you with that? With anything?"

The clerk's honeyed voice startled him—but not because she wanted to flirt with him. He encountered that with a tiresome regularity. Women came on to him all the time. Sometimes he thought the raunchier he looked, the stronger the come-ons got. But he was in his own little world and dead tired and hungry and the sound of her voice alone rattled his cage. He needed sleep badly.

He wasn't going to get it.

"No." He offered a smile so he wouldn't feel like such a bastard. It felt mechanical and condescending to him, but the girl smiled brilliantly back. "Thanks, though."

When the microwave dinged, he pulled out the steaming burritos and slid them into the pocket of his coat.

He finished off the coffee, then grabbed a pint carton of milk and half a dozen packages of little chocolate doughnuts to ease his sweet tooth. Tossing two ten dollar bills from his money clip on the counter to pay for the gas and food, he walked back outside and ripped into a burrito, downed it, then began eating the second one a little less ravenously.

Halfway through the doughnuts, he spotted a nondescript black sedan pulling over to the side of the intersection opposite him. Chris had tracked and captured and delivered hardened, streetwise, deadly fugitives, and he knew how they thought. What they saw. What niggling doubts arose to trigger their shifty little minds. He knew what the lowlifes would know. The man in the sedan was a cop. A Fed.

Undoubtedly, this one was the Feeb sent to collect Eden Kelley.

But why stop at this intersection?

A moment later, Chris knew. A county sheriff's four-wheel-drive vehicle drove up behind the sedan. The agent got out of the sedan, glanced around as he locked his car, then got into the county vehicle. Chris figured the FBI agent, who had to have come from central Wyoming, didn't know which of the roads farther up the canyon would take him to the mountain cabin where Eden Kelley, alias Lisa Hollister, now resided.

Chris polished off the two remaining doughnuts, wadded up the wrapper and tossed it into the battered trash barrel between the convenience-store gas pumps. Following them wouldn't be a problem, but he wasn't going to get to the woman first.

He threw his weight against the kick starter, thinking it could have been worse. The Feeb might have taken Kelley an hour ago. He might as well count himself lucky as not. But he wasn't into Pollyanna thinking. He had chosen a deadly course of action for which he needed Eden Kelley. He refused on principle to back off.

He would do what he had to do.

Chapter Three

Revving the engine, Chris shifted into gear, peeled out and accelerated onto the paved two-lane up the canyon. He formulated and discarded half a dozen capture scenarios.

The sheriff's deputy would have to drive Eden Kelley back down this same canyon road no matter which route out of Jackson the Feeb had in mind. Of all the possibilities, if it had been Chris's problem to solve, he'd choose flying her out of Jackson. He had to snatch her before then.

He narrowed the choices to two. He could either ambush the sheriff's vehicle at the old lady's cabin and take Kelley before she ever climbed into the four wheel drive, or he could set up some kind of roadblock on the way back down the canyon road. Trap them. Run them off the road. Blow out a few tires. Whatever it took to stop them long enough to grab the woman.

Leaning into a hairpin turn, visually scouring the high, shadowed, scrub-covered canyon walls, he knew there was no way trapping them would work. Not without risking Kelley's life—or a standoff he couldn't win.

He intended to win.

He accelerated out of the turn, going twice the twenty-five-mile-per-hour speed limit. He knew what he must do now, but not how it would come off. How the land lay. How he could snatch a woman from two presumably armed and able professionals. He had never yet fallen into the seduction of underestimating his lawless prey. He wouldn't start with men who were his peers.

He shivered hard, another indication of his exhaustion. When he spotted the turnoff at last, a good seven miles out of town and bearing north, he forgot how tired he was, and how cold.

He startled a couple of crows off the road. Avoiding a deep rut, he downshifted and took the rising slope slow and easy in order not to give the two men any advance warning of his approach.

Near the top of the rise, he angled off the dirt road and across a borrow pit to the cover of some scraggly lodgepole pines. He stopped long enough to arm the machine pistol he drew from the deep inside pocket of his leather coat. He had no intention of firing on innocent men but he had to be ready for anything.

He guided the Harley as quietly as possible off road, to the top of the foothill. The machine wasn't meant for offroad use, wasn't billed or built to be a dirt bike. He would just have to make do.

He turned off the cycle. Concealed by trees and scrub at the crest of the hill, Chris assessed the surrounding landscape. The old woman's cabin was nestled in a narrow valley, a couple hundred feet below Chris's position, and the mountain terrain rose as steeply opposite him.

He saw the deputy and the FBI agent standing on the porch. Neither woman was in sight. The Feeb dragged on a cigarette, pacing anxiously, then flipped the butt over the porch railing. The deputy dropped nervously down the stairs, heading in an impatient stride back to his four-wheel-drive vehicle. He opened the back window, lowered the tailgate and then opened both passenger side doors.

At last, for the first time since Catherine was murdered, Chris saw Eden Kelley emerging from the cabin. She came out the screen door, shading her eyes against the sun. Her long, straight, dark brown hair shone in the sunlight as she slung the strap of a backpack over one shoulder and stepped onto the veranda holding a suitcase in her other hand.

He noted for the record how pretty she was in even the most ordinary clothes, how his chest tightened, how much he resented her, how the bitterness clogged his throat. But now he had to focus on what must happen next despite the sexual awareness she triggered and the surge of anger at himself.

The movements of the trio seemed to play out in some surreal other world Chris knew from long experience. The way captures happened, every detail, every movement, every gesture registered in his consciousness, each one leading inevitably to the next, finally to the precise moment in time when he must make his move or sacrifice the capture or get himself iced.

It happened like that for him now. Still watching from his concealed place atop the hill, he knew where each of the agents were in relation to one another and the woman. He sensed their tension. Prepared to protect her, they were still unsuspecting.

Eden Kelley wasn't. She hadn't seen Chris. She hadn't even looked in his direction, but wariness pervaded her supple posture. Her hand went to her throat. She stopped at the top of the steps, dropped the suitcase from her left hand and looked uncertainly back.

At the same time, the sheriff's deputy got into the car and Chris dumped the clutch, then toed the Harley into gear, the engine noise coinciding with that of the four-wheel drive. Eden Kelley moved back toward the cabin door and hugged a white-haired old woman clad in a robe.

The FBI agent threw her bag into the back of the vehicle, then closed the tailgate and window, all the while urging her to hurry. Chris anticipated the agent would usher her into the back seat, then get in himself.

She stepped off the last of the creaking wooden porch steps with a fierce sort of determination, more quickly than Chris expected, almost convulsively.

In that split second, a rifle shot rang out from a position on the steep hillside opposite Chris. Eden jerked and spun and fell to the steps.

She'd been hit, high, Chris thought, too high to kill her, but he swore and exploded into action, full throttle, hurtling down the wooded hillside, crashing through sapling aspen and scrub oak toward the cabin. The rear of the bike slipped sideways, and Chris jerked hard to the right to correct the skid without stopping his downward trajectory.

He heard the old woman scream over the roar of his engine as another shot rang out. The sheriff's deputy shouted. Both lawmen dropped automatically to assault positions, their sidearms drawn and aimed away from Chris in the direction the shot had come from.

He saw Eden crawling, scrambling to get to the side of the porch stairs and to cover. The open door on the four-wheel drive had to be blocking the shooter's line of fire or he would already have gotten off a second round to finish her. But every inch she moved toward the side of the porch had to be bringing her back into the assassin's view.

The FBI agent must have anticipated the same deadly event. He flung himself from behind the car door into the line of fire. Another rifle shot cracked through the air. The agent crumpled silently to the ground and the sheriff's deputy took out on foot after the shooter. He didn't stand a chance against the shooter's rifle and high position.

Chris angled sideways to unleash a barrage of bullets way up the hillside, covering the deputy's wild, scrambling dash up the slope. Eden screamed and rose up and Chris barreled into the melee, the bike sliding within inches of her, spraying dirt.

She cried out again, screaming for the old woman to get to safety and send for help. She tried to run from him but he grabbed her by the forearm. She was strong, but by his size alone he had every advantage over her.

She knew that. He saw it in her desperate gray eyes. Shock would drop her like a rock in another few seconds. She had been incredibly lucky—the bullet had pierced the thick strap of the backpack before penetrating her flesh.

She'd survive, but she was losing blood and the adrenaline rush had already worn too thin.

He planted both feet on the ground and pulled the scarf from around his neck. Wadding the material, he crammed it beneath the strap to staunch the blood, then stuck her other arm through the opposite strap to keep the pack in place.

"Get on. Now!" he ordered.

Eden's gaze jerked to his face. His harsh voice commanded her splintered attention. The engine exhaust choked her. The god-awful noise of gunfire split her ears. The FBI agent, Paglia, lay dead, she thought, right in Judith's front yard, and the horror of his silent, lifeless body sprawled there played against the pain throbbing through her upper body. The air around the motorcycle trembled and the ground shook.

"This is it, lady," he shouted. "Get on. *Now.*"

There was no time to think. All Eden knew was that this man wasn't the maniac shooting at her, and she didn't stand a chance of surviving unless she went with him. She saw the flash of Judith's housecoat disappearing as the old woman got safely inside and slammed the door.

The searing pain at the front of her shoulder was like nothing she had ever felt before. Waves of nausea rolled over her, but she refused to give in to them. She turned back and flung herself astride behind the man who'd ordered her on.

"Hold tight," he shouted, but he didn't have to tell her. She clutched at handfuls of his leather coat and curled instinctively against him, pitting her forehead between his shoulder blades.

He opened the throttle wide. The powerful motorcycle burst forward, throwing him back as hard as it did Eden. She clung tightly, as much to keep herself from passing out as to keep from being hurled off.

A few muted shots rang out, followed by another lone rifle shot exploding through the thin mountain air. The bullet ricocheted off the wind deflector. Her rescuer swore and turned violently, letting his left arm swing out so his gun pointed up the opposite hill where the assassin's shots came from.

He fired again, another hail of bullets, then pulled in his weapon and roared off up the road this time, leading back to the highway.

She was cold. So cold. Her mind seemed to work at an agonizingly slow pace. The man's body heat comforted her. She couldn't figure out how this had happened. Where he'd come from. How he fitted into the picture.

Tafoya's men had come to take her safely away, some killer had been lying in wait, and *this* man seemed to come from nowhere into the middle of the deadly battle—as if that had been planned, too.

She could see him only in profile. His face was tanned. Weathered. Whiskered, with high cheeks and deeply set eyes and prominent, masculine brows. His hair was too long and black as coal. She knew him. Knew his face but now she couldn't remember who or where or when.

She gave up trying. She felt disconnected and wildly grateful for the solid body she clung to, for the strength and the warmth. It knocked the hell out of her vaunted certainty that she needed no one, no man to save her, but she was grateful.

They'd made it halfway back up the hillside when the shooter got off another clear shot at her back. The *thunk* preceded the impact by a fraction of a second. The blow slammed her body hard against her rescuer, making her head whiplash back then forward.

He swore again and called back to her. "Are you hit?"

The blow had knocked the breath out of her and she felt like she'd been hammered, but the bullet must have been deflected by her backpack or something inside it.

"Answer me," he commanded harshly over his shoulder. "Are you okay?"

"I think so. . . ." she breathed. If by okay he meant *not dead.* But her eyes fixed a moment too long on the ground speeding past below her. She groaned at the nausea roiling up inside her and her body started to slump sideways.

Throwing an arm back to keep her from falling off, he crested the hill out of the shooter's range, then slammed on the brakes, sending up another plume of gravel and dirt.

He steadied the bike with one foot on the ground. "Give me your other hand."

She didn't understand what he wanted. Her reaction time was so sluggish that he snarled at her and reached beneath his armpit and grabbed her other arm.

The sickness burned her throat. Distantly, Eden sensed her hands being drawn together around his waist. She thought he just wanted her to hold on a different way. But her arm reached a point when he was pulling on her that the bullet wound in her shoulder shot streaks of pain through her whole torso.

And when he clapped on a cold metal ring to first one wrist and then the other, Eden panicked and lost all control.

"No! Why are you doing that? I can't—"

"You want to fall off?" he demanded over his shoulder, over the noisy throb of the engine. "Because that's what will happen if you pass out."

Fear locked in her throat. She couldn't think which was more dangerous anymore—to fall off or be chained to a madman. Instinctively, she fought the cuffs, jerking hard, twisting her wrists to slip free. "Let me go!"

"Cut it out." Still balancing the bike by a foot planted on the ground, he grabbed both her forearms so she couldn't tear her own hands up trying to get free, then spoke harshly over his shoulder. "The cuffs. You got it, Eden? They *stay.*"

Eden. He knew her name.

"Who *are* you? What do you want from me?" But she knew he wasn't going to answer her. For her arms to reach far enough around him to be cuffed, her body was pulled tight to his. Her cheek rested on his leather coat. "Please . . ." she whispered, still gasping for air like some helpless fish out of water, still trying to pull loose. "You have to let me go."

"Not a chance." He quieted the engine, then spoke in low, terse, forbidding tones. "Any way but my way, Eden, and you die. It's that simple. Dead, you're useless to me, so that isn't going to happen. Now be still and shut up, or I swear to God I'll knock you out myself."

Eden trembled. He was a madman. The engine noise roared in her ears, and the seat throbbed beneath her. Blood began to seep again at the front of her shoulder.

He knew who she was.

What use was she to him dead or alive?

She believed he would knock her senseless, but the cuffs terrified her. Chained to him, she couldn't run away or do anything to help herself.

Her only hope lay in escaping him, or the slim chance that the sheriff's deputy would get the assassin and then catch up with them. "I won't fall off," she promised. "Please..."

"Right." He uttered a harshly disparaging sound. "You won't fall." Throttling up, he turned and guided the black Harley once more to the top of the hill overlooking Judith's cabin. He pulled the weapon from his coat pocket, extended his arm again and aimed downhill at the sheriff's four-wheel drive, its doors still gaping open.

"Don't!" Eden cried, helpless to stop him from eliminating any chance that the deputy could follow and catch them. Her cry was lost in the violent bursts of gunfire that destroyed both driver's-side tires.

Her captor's eyes narrowed and his whiskered jaw clenched. Satisfied, Eden thought, that he could not be followed. He turned back once more and sent the Harley plunging down the ungraded road toward the paved two-lane highway.

Eden shivered uncontrollably. She had no chance now of being rescued. She couldn't believe what he'd done. She couldn't understand how he could pull her out of danger and fire his weapon to cover the deputy... and then blow out his tires.

She had willingly climbed on his motorcycle, willingly put herself into his hands. When would she learn? She thought he was saving her neck, but if that was true, he would never have crippled the deputy's transportation.

The motorcycle slipped and skidded and bucked down the road. Her teeth chattered hard. Her body felt whipped about like a rag doll's. The surrounding trees and scrub and weeds and wildflowers seemed to fly by in a dizzying blur.

She shut her eyes tight and clenched her teeth against the queasiness and pain. The motorcycle hit the pavement and nearly skidded off the other side of the road before it was somehow brought back to the semblance of moving upright.

She breathed deeply, telling herself over and over again that she might die but she sure as hell wouldn't be sick. Wouldn't cave in to the ordeal of being taken hostage. Whatever he intended, she would fight him to her last breath.

"Where are you taking me?"

Scanning the terrain for signs of any nasty surprises, he called back, "I haven't decided."

"You'll never get away with this!" she uttered fiercely. "Never."

A harsh, mirthless laugh escaped him. "No kidding."

He had not underestimated his peers, but in his worst nightmare scenarios, he hadn't figured Broussard could already have gotten an assassin in place to take out Eden, which had to be what had happened.

But Chris knew he would get away with what he had to do. At least, long enough to see Winston Broussard burning in the fires of hell for what he had done to Catherine, who might have deserved a lot of things, but not to be murdered.

Still, Chris harbored no illusions. Hell was his own fate. His own destination. In the end, he wouldn't get away with anything. But then, neither would Broussard. Not ever again. Chris's own life no longer mattered. It hadn't for more months than he cared to remember. His soul had begun to shrivel away to nothing long before Catherine fell to Broussard's assassin.

He drove hard, back in the direction of Jackson, aware of Eden's womanly body tight against his own. Her cheek. Her breasts. Her thighs molding to his backside. He'd never been on a Harley with a woman, let alone a woman wrapped around him.

Hadn't been *with* a woman at all. Not in recent memory.

He wasn't going to deny, even to himself, that despite the grisly devastation that had gone on in the past hour, he was very much aware of the subtle pleasure of Eden's feminine form fitted to his.

He'd given up lying to himself for Lent three years ago, like someone giving up red meat. He never went back to it. So after that, he told himself the truth, and when it got too painful, he just drank and kept drinking—until he couldn't tell himself what day it was, let alone the truth.

So now he told himself the truth about what it felt like to have Eden wrapped firmly about him. And how pleasure hummed inside him. But he wasn't going to act on pleasures he'd almost forgotten. Real justice was all he could afford to seek or want. He had to figure out, and fast, what he was going to do with Eden in the wake of this disaster.

His best bet in most situations had been to lie low right under his quarry's nose. But now, he was the quarry. And given that Broussard's assassin had altered the balance and escalated the stakes to the point where a cop was now dead, *all* bets were off.

He swerved to miss a squirrel darting across the road and leaned into the tight curve of a hairpin turn. For the moment, the woman was riding quietly behind him. He set his mind to weigh the options in front of him.

He could take the bike off road and hole up with her in the mountains. He knew David Tafoya was absolutely committed to keeping Eden safe—which meant the agent would not risk a massive manhunt that would be guaranteed to keep Broussard alerted to the location of the woman he'd determined to silence once and for all.

But Chris couldn't count on such wisdom to prevail. Sooner or later, a manhunt would be launched, and if he chose to lie low in or near Jackson, getting out would become impossible.

He couldn't even take the risk that the sheriff's deputy wasn't already on a cell phone alerting state troopers in the four adjacent states to be on the lookout.

He downshifted to regain momentum on the other end of the hairpin turn. Passing an RV with a Jeep in tow, inching its way up the incline in the opposite direction, he asked himself why he had turned in the direction of Jackson at all.

The decision had been instinctive, and he knew from long experience to follow the thread of a gut-level choice to its conclusion, even if he had no conscious awareness of where it would lead him.

As they arrived at the east end of the canyon, he braked for the lone traffic light. The convenience store he'd gassed up at was to his left, a one-story real-estate building to his right. Across the street was a packaged-liquor store. In front of it sat the FBI sedan. Just this side of the street lamp was a square sign with an airplane graphic and an arrow.

Then he knew. His only way out was the way that Tafoya had planned to take Eden Kelley in the first place.

Chris's lips twisted into a grim smile. Like any law-abiding citizen, he waited for the green light and then turned onto the highway in the direction of the arrow.

Skyjacking wasn't likely to top the list of his felonies.

Chapter Four

Eden had no idea how she endured the hellish ride down the canyon. The pain in her shoulder never eased up. She should have passed out. She'd willed it. Her captor had figured that she would.

But maybe the threat of falling off had only been a ruse. He needed her. She was of some use to him. She couldn't grasp why, but he claimed to need her alive. He couldn't know whether, unshackled, she would make some death-defying attempt to escape him.

He wasn't taking any chances.

He didn't stop again until he'd ridden the cycle right up to the terminal building at the minuscule Jackson airport and into a space marked No Parking.

A couple of bystanders gave him dirty looks, and a family of five straggled past, the mother pulling a small child in a wide berth around the cycle. He ignored the looks, shut off the engine, kicked down the stand and pulled the key to the cuffs out of a pocket.

"I'm going to unlock these," he told her over his shoulder. "Try anything stupid, you'll regret it. Clear?"

Eden swallowed. She understood him, but only now did his inflection penetrate her awareness. A Boston accent, *clear* pronounced in two syllables, the *r* dropped. She looked up, eyeing him, stunned. Her hands were set free but she couldn't move.

He swung his right leg over the fuel-tank cover, stood and turned to face her for the first time. Her eyes opened wide and her jaw dropped. She stared at him as he unhooked his pack from behind her. Seeing him, *recognizing* him, eclipsed the pain in her shoulder.

"Oh, dear God. You're..." Eden reeled.

Paying no attention to her shock of recognition, he stripped the backpack from her unharmed shoulder in one swift, seamless move. She nearly went down in a sea of blackness. He shook her hand, tersely instructing her. He wanted the full weight of her pack on the injured shoulder to keep pressure on the wound—to staunch the flow of blood, which hadn't yet soaked the scarf beneath the strap.

None of that seemed to matter.

Not the light-headedness. Not the pain shooting through her torso. Not the aching numbness in her hands.

She didn't know his name, but she knew who he was. Impatient, dirty, windblown, unshaven, hell-bent, frankly exhausted, slinging his own pack over one shoulder, the man standing before her was the drop-dead gorgeous expectant dad whose pregnant wife Web's assassin had murdered in that parking garage.

He had seen her shock. She knew he had. But it made no difference to him. "Get off, Eden. Do it now."

She swallowed again. Her lips, windburned and cracked, quivered. Dread coursed down every nerve in her body. Did he want to kill her? How could he be thinking anything but that it should have been her who died that day?

He didn't tell her to get off a second time. He just threw an arm around her waist, plucked her up off the seat and started walking. "Move it."

She stumbled when her feet hit the concrete, but he still kept hold of her. He paused only long enough to steady her, then pressed on.

"Hey, buddy, kin you read?" an airport worker shouted, stalking over to demand he move the motorcycle, but when he got a closer look at the rider, the stocky attendant stopped dead in his tracks.

The bystanders melted away. The dead woman's husband looked like some upscale, deadly Hell's Angel and no one wanted to tangle with him.

"Please," Eden began, but he pulled her up short against him in warning, then turned a tired, sheepish grin on the attendant.

"Nailed, huh? Look, I'm flying out of here. You move the Harley," he offered, jangling the keys, "and it's yours. Deal?"

The attendant's jaw went slack. The locals were accustomed to jet-setters from both coasts flitting in and out of Jackson, and a hundred-dollar tip wouldn't have taken the attendant by surprise. The offer of a Harley did. If he'd even heard her plea, he'd forget it.

She tried again. "I need—" Her captor drew her closer, warning her.

The attendant missed the byplay altogether. "You serious, man?"

"You bet. Here." He tossed the attendant the keys, flashed a thumbs-up and shoved his way through the terminal door, holding her tightly to his side. In pain and teetering on the razor edge of shock, she wasn't in any condition to fight him. He had to know he didn't have to worry much that she could break away and make a run for it.

Dear God. The murdered woman's husband, bent on revenge.

Eden's knees buckled. Blackness threatened to engulf her time and again, but she was aware of his checking out the place in one sweeping glance. The ticket counter. The people milling around, the employees, the travelers. Outside, through an enormous picture window, she glimpsed a pilot pacing near a small private jet just like the one on which the federal marshals had flown her out of Logan International a year and a half ago.

She realized this jet must be what Tafoya had arranged to get her safely out of Jackson.

His abductor turned with her in the crook of his arm and headed straight for the door leading outside to the landing strip. He behaved as if he owned the place, so no one challenged him. No one.

She had to do something to stop him. God only knew what he would do with her, what he intended. No matter what that was, no matter if he never hurt her, he had no right to take her anywhere against her will.

She had to escape him. His hold on her tightened as if he knew she had decided she must try, whether she had a snowball's chance in hell or not.

If she were to salvage even that chance, she had to make a scene and pray someone would intervene.

She twisted in his grasp. "Stop, please! You're *hurting* me!" she cried.

"Darling, I'm sorry," he said, the regret in his voice sincere enough to convince a middle-aged man standing within a few feet and the woman joining him.

He used her twisting motion to bring her around into his embrace, till she felt herself drawn flush against him. The power of his lean, hard body embracing hers quelled her. She couldn't think what she'd been trying to accomplish, couldn't focus. He smelled of leather and dust and too many hours in the saddle. More man than she had ever come near. Stronger, harder, seasoned. And very, very angry.

He held her tight and with his other hand clasped her head against his shoulder. To the onlookers, his actions must have seemed intimate and caring. Eden wasn't fooled.

"Stop it," she cried, "just stop it!" But her voice was muffled against his broad, muscled chest, and unintelligible even to her.

He stroked her hair and made soothing motions and lowered his head to murmur softly, lovingly, in her ear.

What he said had nothing to do with how tenderly he held her. Or how he said it.

"Listen to me. Listen well. *Get this, Eden Kelley.* Try to remember. Innocent people die when you're around. If you keep this up, someone else gets hurt. You want that on your conscience, too, be my guest. Otherwise, my advice to you is to keep your smart little mouth shut."

Tears sprang to her eyes and her throat clamped tight. It wasn't her fault that his wife was dead or that Agent Paglia had been shot down in cold blood less than an hour ago.

It was even less her fault if Winston Elijah Broussard III had brokered every bullet that had ever killed anyone in the history of the world. She had given up everything, *everything* to stop him.

It wouldn't be her fault if this man chose to kill or maim or hurt whoever might play hero and step up to save her from Catherine's hate-ridden husband. But that's what it felt like to her.

Just as he knew it would. He stroked her hair.

"Don't touch me," she muttered.

"Don't worry." He let her go, dropped her cold, and Eden found herself clinging to him to keep from crumpling to her knees. She despised him for that, for making it clear to her how fragile she was.

He shoved open the door leading onto the apron of the runway, heading for the small jet. She fought desperately against the constant threat of fainting dead away. A gust of wind blew down off the Tetons, cold as ice. The pilot's coat collar whipped up about the time he drew a weapon and took a warning stance, both arms outstretched, both hands cupping the gun.

"Stop right there," he commanded.

But Catherine's widowed husband didn't even blink, much less stop. Propelling her along, his expression fixed in arrogant, grim determination, he produced a wallet that fell open on credentials Eden couldn't see but that gave the pilot pause. "United States Deputy Marshal Christian X. Tierney, Boston," he snapped. "Put the piece away."

Christian X. Tierney. A United States deputy marshal. Eden swallowed. Relief swamped her until she remembered what he had done to the county sheriff's vehicle.

The pilot, a brown-haired, ordinary man—of a build to be intimidated by Tierney—wasn't convinced and did not lower his gun. "I'm holding for Special Agent Paglia, FBI."

"I said put the piece away."

The pilot exhaled sharply and straightened from his shooting stance, lowering his arms. He jerked his head toward Eden. "Who's this?"

"The relocation witness you're waiting on. Your guy ran right into an assassination attempt. He's dead and the sheriff's deputy is either dead by now or still trying to take out the shooter."

The pilot cleared his throat, glancing nervously at Eden. "Then I'm required to report to Special Agent Tafoya and get revised orders."

"I need to talk to him, too," Eden broke in. "I—"

"What's your name?" Tierney interrupted.

"Haggerty. Agent Dan Haggerty."

"Well, do that, Haggerty," Tierney suggested in a lethal tone. "Report to Tafoya. Of course, every second of delay risks this woman's life. She's hit, she's bleeding, she's on your head. Add to that the possibility that the shooter makes it here and takes her out while you're getting permission to wipe your nose—"

"Look . . ." The pilot wavered, but Tierney reached out and grabbed him by the collar of his coat. "No, you look. You have two minutes to get this puppy off the ground or kiss your government pension goodbye."

THE PHONE RANG at ten-thirty Saturday morning.

Paul Maroncek sat at his kitchen table sharing a cup of coffee with his wife, Janna. Sunlight streamed through the fern-filled bay windows, the coffee was freshly ground, freshly brewed. None of this special-blend stuff, just good old-fashioned black coffee.

The rich aroma filled his nostrils. Pleasure settled over him like a favorite comforter. He'd taken Chris's advice and had a long talk with Janna where he'd done most of the listening. He couldn't believe the change in her attitude, how the hostility had faded. How just listening to her seemed to change everything. He had his wife back.

When the phone rang, she put down her mug, stretched out a hand and covered his. "Don't answer it, Paul. Let it go."

"Janna—"

"Just this once. Please. Let it ring. The nation won't go to ruin if you don't answer."

He felt a flash of irritation. He didn't want to spoil the rosy glow, but he had a life outside Janna's domain, too. Responsibilities.

He compromised with himself.

"I'll just see who it is and get rid of them." He rose swiftly and pecked his wife's cheek, intending to deliver on the second part of that promise. He lifted the receiver from the wall phone by the refrigerator.

Turning to wink at Janna, he stood leaning against the kitchen counter. "Maroncek here."

"Hold please," a brisk female voice returned, "for Special Agent David Tafoya."

Paul's level of alertness took a sharp climb. There was only one reason the Feeb would have to call Paul on a Saturday morning.

"Maroncek?" The Feeb's voice sounded accusatory from the start.

"Yes." Paul told himself to keep cool. To seem unwitting. He wasn't. "What's up?"

"I'll tell you what's up," Tafoya snapped. "I'm expecting a call this morning, no later than 9:00 a.m. from Wyoming. You know the call? The one that says my men have the witness safely in custody?" He didn't expect an answer and didn't leave time for one, either, but while he was yapping, Janna got up and wearily dumped the mugs of coffee down the kitchen sink. "Well, guess what, Maroncek? The freaking call never came."

Trapped between his wife's resigned disappointment and the Feeb's angry outburst, Paul snarled, "Gee, I'm sorry to hear about that, Tafoya."

"Yeah, well, sorry doesn't cut it! I'm gonna haul your ass—"

His wife banged through the swinging kitchen door. Paul only half listened to Tafoya's tirade. When the Feeb ran out of breath, Paul cut in. "How can the United States Federal Marshal Service be of assistance to you?"

"I want answers, Maroncek. Your *assistance* is the last thing I'm looking for."

Paul stared at the white-lacquered, six-panel swinging door. He couldn't even blame Janna. His promises were always predicated on demands of The Job. "Maybe your priorities are askew," he suggested, choking on the thick irony. "Have you thought about that, Tafoya? Maybe if you had let us handle the witness relocation—"

"Cut the crap," Tafoya interrupted angrily. "You should know this call is being recorded. You should know the attorney general is going to hear about this. You should know, in short, that your career is in the toilet. Now I want answers and I want them *right* now. What the hell's going on?"

Paul cleared his throat. "Maybe you should tell me what you think has happened."

"I got a fax at 9:53. My guy went with the county sheriff's department and ran into an assassination attempt on Eden Kelley. She's wounded and my agent is dead."

Paul swore. "I'm sorry, Tafoya—"

"I'm not finished," he went on in the same dire tone. "Seems some lone ranger on a Harley swooped in and snatched my witness and then blew out the damn tires on the county vehicle—*precluding* pursuit, *precluding* capture. Now who do you suppose this cowboy S.O.B. was?"

Chris Tierney. Surprise, surprise. Switching to the cordless, Paul walked over and booted the cat out the patio door. "How would I know that, Tafoya?"

"Because this whole deal was between you, me and the A.G."

"Granted. But you're assuming—"

"I'm *assuming* that the attorney general of the United States is unlikely to snatch a protected witness or even arrange such an event." Tafoya's voice rose a notch. "I had the full cooperation of the local sheriff's department in a perfectly controlled relocation, so—yeah. I'm making the leap and assuming you cowboys decided this matter shouldn't have been assigned out of your precious jurisdiction, and *you* interfered. So take this for fair warning, Maroncek. You can bend over now and kiss your behind goodbye."

The line went dead. Paul looked thoughtfully a moment at the receiver, then rang off himself.

He shook his head. The cat screeched to be let back in, but he ignored it. He would never grant the Feds *had* arranged a "perfectly controlled" relocation. Tafoya wouldn't be in this position if he had, but the point was moot. The witness was gone.

And a Feeb was dead.

Paul felt badly about that. In a perfect world, cops wouldn't get whacked. But Paul had taken what he considered an acceptable risk when he revealed the FBI position in this matter to Chris. Paul knew Chris wouldn't stay out of it, but his hands were essentially clean. Tafoya could howl foul play to the A.G. all he wanted. The herculean Christian X. Tierney was unlikely to be apprehended and less likely than that to betray Paul's confidence if he was. When the situation played out to its conclusion, Chris Tierney would be taken down a peg or two for his reckless interference.

He *needed* to be taken down.

Paul knew he didn't have anything to fear. The Federal Marshal Service position, his *own* position in the matter of Eden Kelley's relocation, clearly a matter of record, was hands-off. Chris Tierney was acting as a private citizen. He was decorated, celebrated and adored among the powers-that-be.

Paul Maroncek could not be held accountable if his ever-so-able and trusted subordinate had gone off the deep end. Besides, Tafoya was missing the most crucial point.

By the Feeb's own account, Chris had saved the witness's life.

EDEN BEGAN TO FEEL claustrophobic from the first moment she climbed aboard the federal government's Lear-jet.

After the near Arctic cold dumping into the Snake River valley from the Tetons, the air inside the jet felt hot and stale. Endlessly recycled. Like life in a coffin. Her skin felt tight. Beads of perspiration broke out on her brow and the nape of her neck and between her breasts.

Christian Tierney had his hands full making sure the pilot did as he was told. She heard them talking and she gathered the pilot was still resisting, but their actual words sounded garbled in her head.

She stared for a moment at the furnishings of the passenger compartment, feeling alternately hot and shivery and lethargic, as if her limbs were no longer taking orders from her. She told herself to breathe, willing herself to get a grip. To focus.

Bolted to the navy blue pile-carpeted floor of the compartment were twelve chairs arranged in conversational clusters, each covered in a rich burgundy tweed.

She should choose, before Tierney chose for her. She couldn't think why that seemed so vital. Pick a chair ... as if she were picking another destiny? As if she had some control? Deluded ... But making a decision, any decision, felt vital.

She eyed the nearest one and headed for it, but halfway there, after only a few steps, her head began to swim and she stumbled.

Tierney appeared to keep her from falling, of course. He swore, grabbed the collar of her coat, pulled her up and scooped her into his arms. The motion made her head spin all the more, but for that moment, cradled in his arms, she felt somehow safer than she had ever been.

She swallowed and shut her eyes to savor the isolated moment, then laid a hand on the warm, solid wall of his chest. His heartbeat comforted her. She momentarily forgot everything—her dizziness and confusion, the stabbing pain. Everything but the overwhelming sensation of her guard going down, her eternal vigilance slipping away... In his strong, masculine arms and against his body, she didn't have to worry.

But then the plane jolted forward and began to taxi. He dropped her like a hot potato into one of the chairs, and Eden knew the feeling of safety in his arms had only been a weak-minded illusion. Tears gushed to her eyes, but she would die before she shed even one.

Beside her on one knee, Tierney caught an arm to steady her and then raked his fingers through her hair, pulling it back from her face. She clamped her jaws tight, swallowed and stared out a miniature window, refusing to meet his eyes.

"Look at me, Eden," he commanded.

"No," she whispered. "No. Just leave me alone."

He swore softly and let go of her hair, but caught her chin in his hand, then laid his wrist on her brow. "You're flushed and warm."

"No kidding." She despised his gentleness and the concern in his voice. "Maybe I'll die and save you any more trouble."

"You're not going to die."

"I'd rather do that," she swore, her voice husky, "than be manhandled anymore by you."

"Don't be a fool," he snapped. His eyes narrowed, their thick black lashes fringing intense hazel. He rose and straddled her legs, then bent over her, digging along the seat cushion for the seat belt.

Eden stiffened. Pain shot through her shoulder and chest. Her head pounded and she felt disoriented and clammy all over. Still, she protested. "I can do that myself."

"Sure you can. But not fast enough to suit me, so just sit there and be quiet."

"When hell freezes over," she grated, grabbing one end of the strap from his hand. "I said I'll do it."

The bullet must surely be burrowing deeper with every move she made, but she didn't care. The throbbing never stopped. She would have welcomed a silly feminine swoon. After all this, it didn't seem likely she was going to be spared a single moment of this waking nightmare.

She gritted her teeth to stay strong. She no longer needed Christian Tierney to keep her on her feet and he was invading her space. His proximity unraveled her. His scent. The unruly, unkempt whiskers. The gentleness. The illusion of safety.

More than anything, the illusion of safety.

She didn't want him anywhere near her ever again. "Give me the other end," she demanded.

He hesitated—as if he were going to back off and allow her this one petty dignity—when an angry voice blared through the radio in the cockpit.

"Clearance for takeoff is rescinded, repeat, *denied*. You are to power down and deplane," the voice demanded, reciting the aircraft's specific call numbers. "Do you copy?"

Whatever slack Tierney had been about to cut her, he abandoned. He took her end, jerked the latch pieces together, crammed the male end of the buckle into the female and pulled the belt tight against her lap.

If he could have locked her in, Eden thought, he would have. Instead, he turned away and pointed a finger as he would his gun at the pilot.

"You tell them you're acting under the authority of the attorney general of the United States. If the FAA wants to take it up with her, more power to them."

Eden couldn't see the pilot but she heard him clearing his throat. "You'll have to tell them that yourself, sir."

Tierney grimaced and spared Eden one more warning glance, then covered the distance to the cockpit in three strides. Keeping a watch on her, he stood hunched in the doorway with the headset microphone cupped in one hand.

Eden couldn't make out what he said, only the commanding, preemptive tone. He never shouted or spewed off a list of ugly consequences if his demands weren't followed.

He never drew the gun concealed inside his coat pocket.

Still, FBI Agent Dan Haggerty began turning up the power. The jet attained liftoff speed and the rumbling wheels had barely risen off the tarmac when a burst of gunfire battered the underbelly of the fuselage.

The pilot swore. A few seconds earlier, a quarter mile back, and the bullets might well have struck more accurately or penetrated the fuel tanks in the wings, vaporizing the escaping aircraft into a ball of fire.

Over her dragging weariness, Eden saw clearly the kind of man Christian X. Tierney must be. Bulletproof. Clever and daring enough to steal her away under the noses of two lawmen and an assassin. Brutal enough to dictate her cooperation. Powerful enough to command a hijacking without ever drawing his weapon.

Tierney had saved her life twice in less than three hours, but Catherine's widowed husband terrified Eden.

Chapter Five

Sitting in the copilot position aboard the Learjet, Chris faced two immediate problems.

Pilot, and destination.

Chris hadn't actually pulled his machine pistol. The Feeb pilot, Haggerty, wouldn't doubt its existence, but so far, he'd believed Chris was who he said he was, and that he was acting under an authority that went beyond David Tafoya. Authority extending to the pinnacle of the Justice Department.

Haggerty's continued cooperation depended upon maintaining the illusion, so Chris never considered threatening the guy with his own machine pistol.

Haggerty gave him a sidelong glance. "You so sure *your* pension's gonna survive this stunt?"

Chris made empathetic noises companionably. A pension meant nothing to him. Less than nothing. He acted as though it did because he couldn't afford to lose the least credibility with this guy.

Sooner or later, Haggerty would know Chris had been acting without any authority at all. When that moment arrived, it would be far better if Haggerty believed that he was doing the right thing himself.

"I don't know about the pension," he said. "But no one's going to argue that we saved this witness's life."

The pilot shrugged and nodded, obviously willing to be counted a hero for saving a protected witness from an assassination attempt. "Hadn't thought of it that way—but I'm going to have to call ahead. Let Tafoya know—"

"Where we're taking her?" Chris interrupted. He shook his head.

Haggerty's gaze roamed his control panel. "You think the woman's in danger even now?"

"More than ever," Chris said. "The hired gun missed, but the lowlife who wants her dead isn't going to give up and go away."

Haggerty's expression hardened. "Probably add us to his hit list for good measure." The plane hit an air pocket and the pilot watched his flight indicators for a minute. "Hacks me off," he said, "firing at this aircraft. Whatever precautions Tafoya took weren't enough. He damn well better get his act together next time."

"There can't be a next time," Chris answered grimly. "I don't think even the director should know where we've stashed the witness until they nab the assassin and figure out how he got to her before we could."

"How do you intend to pull that off?"

Chris thought quickly about what it would take to keep Eden Kelley's whereabouts hidden not only from Winston Broussard, but all the cops in all the agencies of the United States Department of Justice. He might as well fly to the moon as undertake such a feat, but there were factors operating in his favor.

Right now he needed three things. He had to minimize Haggerty's involvement and exposure. He needed a place where it would be possible to hide Eden Kelley for a few days, preferably in the northeast, not too far from Boston, or too close. And he needed a landing strip that would accommodate the Learjet—both landing and taking off again—even if that had to be some mostly deserted stretch of highway.

Simple.

It wasn't, and Chris knew it. What he planned entailed taking on the vast resources of the entire law enforcement community. There had been nothing simple about any of this from the moment he first recognized that he wasn't going to get to Eden Kelley before the FBI. Broussard's hired gun only added one more deadly factor.

It was that, more than anything else, that cinched Chris's resolve in the face of all the daunting complications. Catherine was dead. Ending Broussard's lousy life wouldn't change anything that had gone down. Chris knew that. But the attempt on Eden's life this morning proved beyond any doubt at all that Broussard would not be content until the woman who had betrayed him was dead.

Chris grimaced. Winston Elijah Broussard III should have been content to serve his measly seventeen months and pick up where he'd left off—peddling death and destruction despite whatever unwitting innocents got in his way.

Chris couldn't ignore it. He couldn't let it happen anymore, not and live with himself. Broussard's immortal soul belonged to his Maker but his murdering, miserable hide belonged to Chris.

He thought then about the piece of land sixty miles inland from Cape Cod Bay that Winston Broussard himself had once owned. Chris knew the place. He'd been there. He knew it just as he knew Broussard's habits, his habitats, his vices—and it all went far beyond knowing Broussard had turned Eden's best friend into his latest acquisition.

The hangar and sheds at the intersection of highways near Ware, Massachusetts, had been heavily used to warehouse the illegal munitions Broussard dealt in. FBI forensics had found trace evidence of everything from gunpowder to the most exotic plastiques. That evidence had been tossed out of court on a search-and-seizure technicality.

Broussard's real-estate cronies had sold the property to a foreign cosmetics company as the site of a new production facility, but the investors and developers had been locked in some legal battle against the locals ever since.

The location was isolated and provided a landing strip. There would be no way to stash Eden there. Chris doubted there was even running water, but landing on the site appealed to his sense of dark poetic justice. And in practical terms, it put him close to the one place on the Eastern Seaboard where he knew he could take Eden and not be found.

His sister-in-law, Catherine's older sister, Margo, lived on an estate a few miles outside of Holyoke.

He'd grown up with Margo. Their friendship had gotten him through more troubled days in his marriage to her younger sister than Chris cared to remember. Her husband was a doctor, and such a cold, aloof, self-centered bastard that he barely knew Chris existed, or that Chris knew more about his wife's hopes and fears and dreams than he did.

Chris could conceal Eden in the guest house buried deep in the woods at the back of the Bancroft estate for days and the man would never know it. He knew Margo also had access to the closet full of sample prescription drugs Edward Bancroft kept at home for treating the children the minute one of them turned up with a runny nose or scraped knee.

Eden was going to need antibiotics to make sure no infection took hold. But Chris didn't know yet whether Haggerty would tumble to this strategy or not.

"Are you saying you're willing to duck Tafoya till I can get the woman stashed?" he asked at last.

"No." Haggerty shrugged. "But I sure as hell don't want to run into another ambush and end up like Paglia. I've got a wife and three little girls."

"Yeah." Chris's jaw cocked to the side. He knew the feeling. Or maybe he didn't. Maybe he just wanted the feeling so much that he'd blinded himself. "I had a wife."

Haggerty lifted a brow. Chris didn't want to get into it.

He outlined his plan instead. All Haggerty had to do was shut off his encoding transponder, fly below the positive control altitudes, maybe fourteen thousand feet, and follow his original flight plan. There wasn't much likelihood of drawing any real attention, and if the pilot deviated off course long enough to fly them into the private airstrip, he could continue on and then tell Tafoya he'd dropped them off somewhere in the middle of Kansas, maybe cuss and moan about the transponder failing.

"Is that all?" Haggerty mocked softly. "Tell me this. How can you be sure I won't rat out on you and tell Tafoya exactly where you are?"

"Because Eden Kelley's life depends on it." Chris looked Haggerty straight in the eye. Man to man. "Because you have little girls."

Haggerty breathed deeply and straightened a bit. Chris could see that his answer had hit Haggerty where he lived.

"Look," he said, "I'm not saying if you did call ahead to bring Tafoya up to speed that we would run into another assassination attempt. That would be pretty frigging unbelievable.

"I'm not saying Tafoya is a screwup, either. I think he's genuinely concerned for Eden's life—but her life won't be an issue much longer if something we do now somehow sets her up for the kill. Tafoya can raise hell, but in the end, all you've done is keep this witness alive."

Haggerty chewed on the problem for a while, then shrugged. "What the hell. It's just a pension."

EDEN SAT ON THE FLOOR of the passenger compartment, her back to the bulkhead, listening to the murdered woman's husband smooth-talking even the FBI pilot.

Chills racked her body. Her heart pounded and its beat echoed in her ears. Her right arm had gone numb from either the bullet at the top of her shoulder or the weight of her pack still bearing down. Or both.

She scarcely knew which way was up, which down. Christian X. Tierney, United States deputy marshal, a man sworn to uphold the law of the land, had sworn off instead and gone recklessly renegade. And if he'd saved her life, he'd also refused to release her afterward. Now, he'd convinced even this pilot to circumvent David Tafoya, the one man who had earned her trust.

Tierney needed her.

She needed her freedom. Some way out of this nightmarish experience. A trapdoor. An escape hatch. A stage-left departure and an unforgettable exit line.

It wasn't Tierney's fault that her choices had led her to this end, where she was more a prisoner of the system than Winston Broussard would ever be. She would never forget the agony etched in Tierney's features when he'd held his dead, pregnant wife in his arms a year and a half ago.

Her freedom had nothing to do with "nothing left to lose." Her life was at stake, vulnerable as the orchid blossom Winston Broussard had so crudely crushed and flicked over his shoulder.

She wasn't much better off in the hands of Christian Tierney. Though he was a lawman and a supposedly honorable man, he still considered himself above the rules. He hadn't saved her out of any noble intentions. The only scenario she could envision him needing her was if he somehow used her to find Winston Broussard to exact his own deadly justice.

Tears clogged her throat. She planted a foot and shoved herself to a straighter position against the wall between the cockpit and passenger compartment. She eased the heavy pack from her shoulder and the bag fell with a thud to her side.

Her entire right side prickled viciously as her circulation was restored. The pain in her shoulder splintered back to life. Tierney's black cashmere scarf slid to the floor caked in her blood.

He wanted Broussard's blood.

What she most feared was her own willingness to help Tierney exact his lawless revenge. She had no life so long as Winston Broussard lived and breathed and wanted her dead out of his need for revenge. But if her help was what Tierney was after, and she cooperated, she would have sunk as low as Broussard had himself.

She jerked the pack across her lap with her good left arm and shoved aside the covering flap, looking for her small pot of lip balm.

Chris ducked out of the cockpit and found her digging fruitlessly through her stuff. By some trick of light at whatever altitude this was, his shadow fell over her.

Shrugging out of his scarred black leather coat, he sank to his haunches beside her. "Eden, what are you doing here on the floor?"

She tried to ignore his effect on her. Everything about him unnerved her. His gravelly voice, his size, his body heat, the way his heavy, muscled thighs angled about her. He must know she'd been listening. "I want you to get me back to David Tafoya."

He shook his head. "That's not going to happen, sweetheart."

"Well, make it happen!" His mocking familiarity made her stomach clench. "And don't ever call me that again. *Not ever.*"

She couldn't breathe. Damn it, where was the lip balm? It wasn't as if she had brought so many possessions that it should take even five seconds to find any one of them.

"Let me help you."

"If you want to help me, get Tafoya on the phone," she snapped. "Otherwise, I think I've made it clear. I don't want your help." She still didn't look up at him.

He exhaled sharply. "Suppose you just admit that you need help whether you want it or not."

She shook her head and dug deeper. "I don't need it, either." Tears blurred her vision, and if the small pot of balm had leaped up at her she wouldn't have seen it. Her entire right side felt numb, and even her left hand trembled now. She gritted her teeth. Damn it, why was so simple an act beyond her? A tear spilled over her cheek. *Losing ground here...* She swallowed. "I just—" she cleared her throat "—my lips..."

He took the backpack from her lap. Peering inside, he came up with the miniature jar within a few seconds and opened it for her. "Here."

Though he held it easily within her reach, her hand trembled violently and she knocked it out of his fingers. He snatched it up off the floor before the small pot could roll away, wondering why he was bothering with the thing.

Jabbing his own finger into the balm, he scooped a dollop out of the pot.

Eden's already shallow breath caught in her throat. He brought his finger to her windburned lips.

She desperately needed the bullet removed from her shoulder. She needed the wound to be cleansed, antiseptics and pressure bandages applied and something to deaden the pain, and it was going to be hell enough to stifle her anger and determination not to submit to any man's help even for that.

But she needed the soothing balm on her lips like a parched and dying man craves water.

Everything in her cried out against allowing the vengeful widower to soothe her or ease her pain or act toward her with even so small a kindness as this.

Her protests wouldn't come. Her thinking was out of sync with her actions and she didn't turn her face away when she had the infinitesimal chance.

He didn't hesitate. He wouldn't. He wasn't the sensitive sort. He wouldn't ask her permission. He didn't care whether he had her consent or not.

He just began greasing her lips impatiently, like a man, intent only on slathering on the stuff to be done with it, but suddenly, he slowed. Eden uttered a low, witless sigh. Her eyes were drawn to his weary face, to his eyes. Lids lowered, his eyes followed the course of his fingertip.

He might have been ministering to a whiny child. This was nothing more than lip balm. Nothing half as intimate as he had forced in the small airport terminal. But he was still touching her lips when their eyes met and the kindness became something more, something very nearly dangerous, triggering a bolt of awareness between them.

His breath locked in his throat. Eden pulled back.

He exhaled harshly, stood and scooped her up in his arms as easily as if she had been a small child. "Haggerty says there are first-aid supplies in the head."

Carrying her, he strode the length of the passenger compartment to a lavatory three times the size of an ordinary aircraft washroom and put her down so that she was sitting on the countertop, nearly at eye-to-eye level with him.

He pulled a paper cup from the dispenser beside the soap, filled it with water and dropped a few ibuprofen tablets from the medicine cabinet into her shaking hand. "Here. Take these."

She didn't think he was surly again so much as exhausted. She managed to take a drink without spilling the cup and swallowed the pills by herself while he splashed his face and scrubbed his hands.

He found a first-aid kit. No sterile gloves, but there were a set of tweezers, gauze, peroxide, rubbing alcohol. "Can you get out of the sweatshirt yourself?"

Eden nodded. It was clear to her now that she did need help. That she couldn't even take care of dry and cracked lips, much less a bullet wound. As soon as she could, she would find a way to escape Christian Tierney, but this was not the time or place—with a bullet lodged in her flesh— for bravado or false modesty.

She held her right arm as still as if it were broken, and reached with her left hand beneath the sweatshirt. Easing the right sleeve past her elbow, down the length of her forearm and off her hand, she lifted the sweatshirt off over her head.

Her pink-ribboned bustier was soaked in her blood from the satin shoulder strap to the soft material covering the upper curve of her right breast.

She turned sharply away, closed her eyes tight and bit her lip but she couldn't keep from crying out. The pain was daunting, but seeing the damage, seeing her blood-soaked clothing was even worse.

Chris swore. Moving between her legs, he cupped her nape with his hand, drawing her head toward him to steady it against his and close off the sight. He held her, his jaw pressed to her cheek. He had seen far worse, but he also knew what it was to see the reality of one's own flesh ravaged and bloody.

Hot tears slid down her cheek and off his jaw. "Shh, Eden," he murmured over and over again, stroking her hair. "Breathe. That's a girl. You're all right. It looks worse than it is."

He felt silent sobs rack her body. He knew how close she was to hysteria, how badly she needed to get all the pent-up rage out of her system. He knew exactly how alone and traumatized, battered and vulnerable she felt. He suspected her tears had far more to do with being outraged at being unable to control anything happening around her.

The same sort of rage was a part of him, too. Or had been. Only this was Eden Kelley, a woman whose life he'd saved, but whom he didn't know and had no business holding.

He couldn't let her go. He held her, absorbing her anguished, silent cries.

"Oh, God, Eden. Don't cry." He whispered soft reassurances to her and stroked her back. "You're all right. You survived the bastard again." He brought his lips to her cheek and kissed her there—not for any reason but to comfort her, but it didn't stay that simple.

She turned her face toward his kiss like a flower strains toward the sun, seeking things so basic to survival as warmth and water and air.

He understood. She needed more. Something stronger, deeper, *human*. Eden needed his kiss as a matter of survival.

He was no less needy.

He kissed her again and again and, closing his eyes, inhaled the scent of her and dragged his lips over the soft, sweet texture of her cheek to her lips.

Eden moaned and clung to the back of his plaid flannel shirt with her left hand and took his kisses like balm to her ragged soul. The fullness of his lips pressed to hers, the warmth, the moisture, the wallop of conflicting emotions—desire and fear and anger and need—took her aback like a sudden squall. Like lightning crackling in the air, making it come alive, making *her* come alive, making her forget the pain and anxiety.

After a while, her tears stopped and she pulled back. Resting her forehead against his, she felt confused and uncertain. The pain intruded again, and the real world. The dull, constant hum of the aircraft engines. The stale air. Her heartbeat slowed. Her tears dried.

She couldn't remember a time in all her life when a man had given her a thimble's worth of comfort. Or when any man had kissed her and eased the soul-deep weariness inside her and then aroused her, too. This man, Catherine Tierney's widower, this dangerous, reckless, hell-bent, vengeful man had done both.

Her cheek still tingled where his whiskers had scraped her skin. She didn't know how to behave or what to say. Or even what to believe was the truth about Christian Tierney.

He didn't leave her wondering long. He cleared his throat and stepped back. The expression in his eyes hardened. Her crying jag was over, and so was his show of compassion.

Christian Tierney had his own agenda. The only thing that mattered to him was that she hang together long enough to fulfill whatever role was needed to further his intentions. His kiss, the hint of desire—even hers—were nothing but illusions.

She must have lost too much blood for her brain to function at all. Or else the constant, stabbing pain had short-circuited all her thought processes.

She swallowed and angled her head to look up at him again. His eyes were bloodshot and haunted and empty at once. He was beyond tired, beyond reaching. He still owed her an explanation. "I want to know what's happened. Why I have to be relocated again."

He dragged his gaze off her, plugged the drain and ran the small sink full. Ripping open a couple of packages of gauze, he soaked a couple of squares in the hot, soapy water. "This will hurt, Eden. No matter what I do, it will hurt. Are you ready?"

She clasped her hands in her lap and turned away, avoiding looking at the wound. "Is Broussard out of prison?" she persisted.

"Yeah." His jaw tightened. "They sprang him early last week. He served a grand total of seventeen months." He handed her a cloth towel he found in the cabinet below the sink. "Here, hold the towel. This will be messy. I don't want to spoil the rest of your... top."

He didn't know what to call her bustier. She felt embarrassed, caught in the not-quite-innocent pleasure of wearing such a garment. But she had never intended to be seen like this. By him. She nodded, clutched the towel to her breast and gritted her teeth, preparing for the worst. He brought the soapy gauze to her shoulder and held her hair aside with his other hand. When he touched the steaming hot, soapy cloth to her shoulder, it was all Eden could do to stay still and not flinch.

She caught her lower lip between her teeth and endured. It took him several moments of wiping and rinsing and drawing fresh hot water to clean away the mess.

He peered closely at his work. "It's a very small wound, Eden. The nylon on your pack strap must have slowed the bullet and your bone did the rest. It must have nicked the artery just below the bone to bleed so much, but you were very lucky."

Tears made tiny stabbing pains at the back of her eyes again. "I don't understand any of this. How could this happen?"

He shook his head, working steadily along. "A lot of big, bad coincidences."

She swallowed hard. Once, when she was in Sunday school with probably her third foster family, the teacher told them nothing happened except by God's will. There were no accidents. God sent tests sometimes. He must test the children's faith, else how would He know if they believed in Him?

She'd tried very hard to believe. After a while, it was easier to think there must not be any God at all. She focused on the door hinge behind Tierney's back. "Do you believe that?" she asked softly. "In coincidence, I mean?"

"No."

"Me, neither." She shivered. "How did Broussard know where to find me, then?"

He tore open more gauze and set to work again. "Did you ever contact anyone you knew as Eden Kelley?"

"Oh, that's good." Her voice trembled. "Blame the victim."

"I'm not blaming you, Eden," he grated. "But the facts are simple. In the huge majority of cases, when a relocation fails, it's because the witness couldn't take the isolation anymore. It's a fact, not an accusation."

"Well, I've had a lot more practice getting jerked around than most people."

His eyes met hers. "I know."

She lowered her gaze. She didn't want his pity. She already knew the extent of his concern. If he knew how many times she had been taken from one foster home to another, then he must know how experienced she was at shutting off her needs. "I didn't contact anyone. Ever. Period."

"You never sent a postcard or—"

"No."

"Made a phone call or—"

"No."

"Faxed anything?"

"Never!" Why didn't he believe her? "I knew the rules and I followed them! I didn't even call Dennis Shulander, not *once,* and I was told that I'd be safe."

"No one, Eden? Are you absolutely sure?"

"I faxed things to New York all the time—to Judith's agent, but—"

"Who was that?" he interrupted sharply, dumping a gauze near the sink.

"Britta Nielsen. But she only knew me as Lisa Hollister. She's a *literary* agent, Tierney, not some pipeline to Winston Broussard! She's a little old lady—a shark, but hardly a likely candidate." The towel at her breast was soaked. She folded it once. The warm water was beginning to feel good, but inside, she felt threatened. Uneasy. Where was he going with this? "What are you getting at?"

"Sheila Jacques, Eden." He straightened, stretching his shoulders, tilting his head from one side to the other, watching her.

"Sheila? What has she got to do with anything?"

"You tell me."

"Sheila is my best friend. Her parents were the closest thing I had to a family—but I haven't communicated with her since...well, since months before the trial. Did you think I called her?"

"Did you?"

"Of course not! Are you implying she had *anything* to do with this?"

Opening the bottle of peroxide, he ignored her question. "How did you communicate with her before the trial?"

"David Tafoya let me write her a letter. I understood that he was going to have it hand delivered. It was just...just a goodbye note, really. I wasn't even allowed to say that I was in protective custody." Eden hesitated. "I don't understand. *Are* you saying Sheila knew something? Anything? That she's somehow involved in this?"

"I don't know." He broke off and stood back, massaging his eyes with his thumb and forefinger. He stopped, crammed his hand into a pocket and blinked. "What I am saying, Eden, is that Sheila Jacques has become Winston Broussard's mistress."

Chapter Six

"Oh, my God, no."

Her cry took Chris apart more efficiently than the sight of her ravaged, creamy flesh. He couldn't begin to guess how he knew, but it wasn't the possibility that Sheila Jacques had betrayed her that made Eden cry out. It was dread for her friend, pure and simple.

She didn't doubt for a heartbeat the cunning of Winston Broussard to dazzle and win over to his side her closest friend. The malignant charisma would be dispensed like candy to a naive and innocent child.

Her dark brown hair, thick as a sable pelt, hung straight and true despite having flown wildly on his cycle, framing her face, making her seem even more pale, more delicate than her blood loss could warrant. Her wide gray eyes glittered with tears, like droplets condensing on a steamy mirror.

He couldn't take his eyes off her face. She dragged in a deep breath. "How do you know?"

He forced his attention back to her mangled flesh, but that only intensified his awareness of her. He could not deal with her wound and not see in his peripheral vision the swell of her breasts beneath what seemed to him a frankly erotic piece of clothing.

He registered this purely masculine reaction as the truth, but counted it reckless and irresponsible even to have noticed. All the same, closing in on the bullet wound, catching the nuances of her dismay, he found himself wanting to protect Eden Kelley.

To spare her.

To cushion the emotional blows.

She had already been treated to more death and devastation up close and personal than anyone should ever be. But the truth was an ugly check on reality. She had to understand that.

He told her how Sheila Jacques had resigned from her inner-city teaching position, about the forty-thousand-dollar silver sports car. He told her that the lease on Jacques's tiny garret apartment in an old house in the Back Bay had expired and not been renewed. He described the number and duration of visits Jacques made to the country-club prison where Broussard had served his time.

He described the way Eden's closest friend had dropped out of sight as only someone with money enough to burn can do, and then he drew the inevitable conclusion. "Your friend has gone over to the enemy, Eden. There's no way of getting around it."

He thought she did understand. She sat quietly, the delicate features of her pretty, heart-shaped face pinched, the dark lashes around her gray eyes damp with tears she blinked back.

She gritted her teeth when he touched a soapy swab near the bullet wound. "I don't doubt that what you said is true, but it doesn't mean what you think. You're wrong if you believe Sheila would betray me."

He wadded up a spent gauze and flicked it at the trash, hoping to shake off his growing aggravation with her along with it. "This is not something open to any innocent interpretation, Eden."

"You don't know her."

"I don't have to." He wanted to shake her. How could she sit here with a bullet riddling her flesh and still believe goodness and mercy were following her around? "Every living, breathing human being has a price. Sheila Jacques is no exception."

She swallowed. Their eyes clashed. The memory of their kisses wasn't far off. Her chin went up, unwittingly exposing more of her delicate neck. "What's yours, Tierney? Who else has to die for you to feel Catherine's death is properly avenged?"

He went deadly still. Shock coursed through him. He flashed on the moment of Catherine's death. Eden's biting response shouldn't have surprised him, but it did. He answered her question. "Only Winston Broussard."

"Then why aren't you tracing him? Tracking him down instead of me?" she cried. "Why drag me into this when you know Broussard will come after me?"

Chris didn't even flinch. It was exactly because Broussard would come after her that Chris had taken her first. The truth no longer pricked his conscience. He knew the man. He knew Broussard would keep coming after her no matter where she tried to hide. He'd keep sending his hired guns until all the failed attempts on Eden's life would goad him into coming after her himself.

When he did, Chris intended to be there. To see to it that Broussard paid in the most primitive and graphic terms for the lives he had destroyed.

For the hundreds or even thousands of nameless victims of the weapons Winston Broussard trafficked in.

For Catherine.

For the tiny, unformed life inside her whose very existence cleaved Chris's heart in two.

He couldn't guarantee what Eden would do, or ever hope to get the least cooperation from her, if he revealed any part of this to her. He ignored her "why me" questions and returned to the subject of Sheila Jacques's betrayal.

"Use your head, Eden," he warned in a flat voice. "People betray other people all the time." He knew from extensive personal experience that this was true. He paused long enough to look straight into her rainy gray eyes. "Even you."

Her lips clamped shut, he thought, to fight off the quivering. He knew it was a low, mean blow. She had betrayed Broussard, but she clearly counted it a different thing than real friends betraying each other.

"There's no way, Tierney, that Sheila Jacques would do or say anything that would hurt me."

"Oh, God, Eden! Grow up, will you?" The guilelessness in her blew him away. How she could have been exposed to such ruthlessness, such *evil,* and still have faith in anyone was beyond him. "Winston Broussard contaminated everything in your life. You think he's somehow sparing Sheila Jacques? You think he didn't pick her out with every intention of rubbing your nose in it?"

Her chin shot up. "What does it matter what his intentions were? He's a monster. That's not news. But he couldn't buy *me,* Tierney. Not the real me. The heart of me."

"He did, Eden, and you know it," he reminded her harshly. "For a while, you bought into everything—"

"For a while, yes…but not long enough! *I'm* still here, inside. I'm still fighting. I walked away from the purchase price and I testified even when I *knew* they couldn't put him away." She coughed, and her long, slender fingers gripped the towel clutched to her breast. "Maybe he gave Sheila the keys to kingdom come," she uttered fiercely, "and maybe she took them. Maybe she'll never wake up to what a monster he is, but I will never believe she would betray me."

"Yeah, and I'm sure there was a time when you believed Broussard would never harm you, either."

"That's not fair!"

"Damn straight it's not. You're right," he snarled, done with trying to spare her. He could quote her chapter and verse of the Book of Fair. He'd subscribed himself. He'd bought into God and country and Mom's apple pie. Truth and justice and . . . loyalty.

Men like Broussard perverted it all.

"Just think about it, Eden. Think about Broussard turning on that hot-blooded Cajun charm, making Sheila believe he's a changed man, making her think he's found her, but to assuage his freaking immortal soul, he needs to make amends to you. Think about him twisting what she knows and hopes to his own advantage.

"He *feeds* on people, Eden. Get this. Can you honestly believe for one minute that he wouldn't exploit her, too?"

Her lips tightened. She met his relentless expression. Her eyes roamed his face, looking, he thought, for a trace of compassion, settling a moment, then a pulse beat too long on his lips.

Her gaze flew back to his. Tension arced between them, magnified by the power of spent, reckless kisses. She broke off, lowering her gaze, and he could swear he heard her heart pound. "No."

"No. I didn't think so."

She reached distractedly with her right hand to shove her hair back from her face. Pain bit into her, reaching her eyes in a split second. A cry escaped her lips. Her hand dropped like lead to her lap. "I..."

He swore beneath his breath. She'd caused fresh bleeding. Applying pressure, he steadied Eden. And caught a glimpse of himself in the mirror behind the sink. It was an unnatural wonder she sat still for him touching her at all. "Just be quiet and let me finish this."

The jet hit a patch of turbulence and shuddered for fifteen or twenty seconds, but she held her body stiff and motionless—the level of her pain, he thought, ensured that—but she didn't stay silent long.

"It doesn't matter anyway. Sheila couldn't have betrayed me because she didn't know where I was."

"Tafoya believes she *did* know." Chris frowned, struggling to recall Maroncek's description of his encounter with Tafoya in the presence of the attorney general. Some fragment of that conversation was at odds with Eden's dead certainty that Sheila Jacques knew nothing of her whereabouts.

He tossed aside the bloodied swab and soaked another in peroxide. "Jackson Hole is a world-class resort area. A little rough around the edges, still a fairly well-kept secret. Just the kind of place Broussard seeks out—for the anonymity, if nothing else. Suppose he sent Sheila on a nice little retreat and she did spot you, walking down the street, or in a movie theater or a bar."

Eden winced, her expression pinched and hurting. "I thought you didn't buy into coincidence."

"I don't—but Tafoya is not a fool, and I can't explain how Broussard got an assassin in place if there's no other way he could have known where you were."

Eden's expression pinched. "There is another way."

"Yeah?" He picked up another towel and dried his hands. "What would that be?"

She adjusted the towel again. For a moment, Chris could see the sturdy wet fabric clinging to her breast and the dark shape of her nipple.

"Broussard's hired gun could have followed anyone." She swallowed. "He could have followed you."

Chris dragged his focus from her breast and looked up at her. "It didn't happen that way, Eden."

"How do you know? How can you be sure that you didn't lead him right to me?"

"Because I didn't even make it to Jackson until the time Paglia met up with the deputy. I saw him park and get into the deputy's vehicle at the corner across from the convenience store." He reached for a fresh swab. "I followed them. The shooter was already in place, Eden, and that doesn't happen without some serious planning."

She gulped. "You're saying Broussard's assassin was ahead of all of you?"

"Yeah." Chris inclined his head and doused the swab in peroxide.

"Yes? Just yes? What good are you people?" she cried. "What good are any of you? What kind of promises do you make? 'We'll keep you safe from harm, dear witness, right up until someone *really* wants to get at you'?"

Chris exhaled heavily. He knew the failure to adequately protect her was an ungodly fluke. He knew one failure couldn't impeach the whole of Witness Protection. But if he hadn't been there, hadn't snatched her away for his own purposes, their failure would have cost her her life.

"Look. Eden—"

"No." She shook her head. He didn't know where she found the grit to talk at all. "I don't want to understand you."

He decided to forget making any attempt to explain and drew the swab along the edges of the bullet wound. The peroxide foamed madly, trickling onto the exposed nerve endings and raw edges of her flesh.

A whimper seeped out of her. Still she didn't stop. "I don't trust you." Her voice broke. "I don't want you anywhere near me. I don't care if you saved my life. I don't even care if it was your fault that Broussard's assassin found me at all. I just want out."

He applied more peroxide, a soaking gauze this time, and she cried.

He forced himself to do what had to be done. He'd managed to shut off her tirade but he hated himself. Hated all of it. She had a right to blow off the steam, the anger. "I'm sorry. I have to do this."

She nodded and backhanded her tears. "Can you see the bullet?"

"Yeah. It's not that deep, Eden. I swear it." He squinted, so dead tired he could barely see anymore, focusing on the bullet.

"Can you get it out—without a scalpel or something, I mean?"

He nodded. "The bullet isn't deep, but it's lodged beside the bone and the tissue has swelled around it." Knowing if she was going to pass out at all, it would be when he pried the bullet from her flesh, he pushed her bottom along the countertop until she was tight against the side wall.

He picked up the tweezers, then put them down again and scraped at his whiskers, rubbing the back of his neck in a futile little gesture.

"Have you ever done…this…before?" she asked, her voice wavering, uncertain.

"Yeah." He shrugged. "Out of bricks. Wood. Doorjambs. Things like that."

"That's certainly—" her breath caught "—encouraging."

He glimpsed for the first time the hint of long dimples in her pale, too-thin cheeks and, for a moment, felt like he'd been slammed. He breathed deeply and blinked a couple of times to ease his itchy eyes, then took the tweezers and doused them in alcohol. Cupping her upper arm, he braced himself as well. "Ready?"

Eden clutched the wet towel. "Just do it."

She lasted through his pulling the bullet loose. She hung in there while he poured in more peroxide. He unwrapped a couple of small butterfly bandages and gently drew her flesh together with his second and third fingers.

When he was done, she scooted off the countertop, stood and turned to see how he had done in the mirror.

He stood behind her, a head taller, dragged out, beat. He met her wide gray eyes in the mirror, and then she passed out cold.

WHEN WEB BROUSSARD received the news that the hit on Eden Kelley had failed, he was sipping at a glass of Grand-Puy-Ducasse Pauillac, lying on a deck chair at the poolside of his private estate south of Marblehead on Massachusetts Bay. He had returned only hours before from the villa of a Cuban associate, where the living was easy and the heat reminded him of New Orleans, but the culture was oppressive and annoyingly melodramatic, even to him.

Broussard wished to live in joy. *Joie de vie.*

He clicked off the cellular to end the call, and in the next instant, the exquisite crystal containing his drink shattered in his hand. He took no notice of his own blood mingling with the rare, subtle wine.

Next to him, Sheila cried out, "Web, darling, what is it? Look at your hand! You're bleeding!"

"Take no thought of it, *chère*." His tone warned her against hovering or troubling him with further outcries. She sat very still, unnaturally constrained to silence and against her female instincts to minister to him.

He wanted nothing from her at this black moment, and she had been with him—though not long—long enough to back off at his command.

Naturally, Sheila Jacques had accompanied him. He found her accommodating in the extreme. She was an ordinary little creature, one that under most circumstances he would have given no more notice than he might a sparrow.

Still, her gratitude to him—for a thousand things, not the least of which was that he had rescued her from a lifetime of dealing with sniveling, brain-dead adolescents—knew no bounds. None that he had discovered anyway, and it wasn't as if Winston Broussard had ever been less than thorough.

She understood that the small humiliations he had occasion to subject her to were mere tests of her loyalty.

She understood the nature of his tests. She understood his need for complete and unquestioning loyalty. She knew her place in the larger scheme of things. There existed a universe of far more beautiful women who would also, for the gifts he bestowed, be as accommodating. Sheila knew he had chosen her, selected *her* from among the rest *because* of her friendship with Eden Kelley.

Sheila's idea of why this was so amused him greatly, but he was not amused now, and he was finding no joy, either. He was enraged. He had paid vast sums of money for his problems to be made to go away, and he had not gotten value for his investment.

True, all the other witnesses against him in that pathetic attempt by the Feds to stop his arms trafficking had been silenced. Two of the three permanently. The remaining traitor had been made to understand the lethal consequences of testifying against him, and that man, for one, had not valued his so-called honor over his life. And it was also true that the G-men had not seen fit to bring him before a grand jury to indict him on conspiracy to murder.

Eden Kelley, however, would not give up, but she had not been so accessible as the others, who could be sent very distressing messages while in prison themselves.

The Feds had managed to hide her away in a safe house long enough to get to trial. Her feeble testimony had been enough to send him away. He resented it bitterly. He loathed her. She would pay quite dearly. He hoped he'd made it clear how little her life was worth by the silent, eloquent gesture of flicking that crushed orchid blossom over his shoulder. He smirked. His hand bled on. He imagined Eden Kelley had no particular fondness for orchids anymore.

The bitch had managed to survive the assassination attempt, had eluded certain death.

He knew Deputy Marshal Christian Tierney, whose stunningly beautiful wife had died in Eden's stead, would murder him in his bed if he could. Since a Supreme Court decision had empowered the Marshal Service to track down and seize their quarry outside the territorial United States—without recourse to cumbersome treaties and extradition agreements—leaving the country no longer necessarily ensured a moment's peace.

They could not come after him without formal charges pending, however. Web had given some thought to the possibility that Tierney would goad the FBI into such a course of action—perhaps on murder charges, or conspiracy to murder—so Tierney would be sanctioned to track Web to the ends of the earth.

There were no such charges.

Tierney was a still a loose cannon, but such undisciplined behavior didn't faze Web. It would, in the end, be Tierney's undoing. And in the end, Web would be rid of them both—Tierney and Eden Kelley.

Twice, Web's hired assassins had failed. However much he would have liked to deal with Eden Kelley himself, to choke the life from her with his own hands, he determined to remain disciplined himself, unlike Tierney, and grant his associates one last opportunity. One more chance to send the viperous bitch to her rightful demise.

He would conserve Sheila Jacques's usefulness for another little while.

EDEN WOKE IN A SEAT aboard the government jet wearing a soft champagne-colored silk jersey camisole, her shoulders covered by a coarsely textured army blanket made into a shawl. Christian Tierney sat opposite her, slouched deeply in the seat, his eyes closed, arms outstretched, his long legs extending nearly to the base of her own chair.

Watching him through her lashes, she felt heat rise in her cheeks. He had to have unhooked and unlaced the bustier to take it off her. He had to have gone through her things to come up with the camisole and put it on her.

In the worst straits of her life, a captive in the hands of a man more immediately dangerous to her than Winston Broussard himself, she berated herself for caring that he had seen her, *handled* her, naked from the waist up.

But he had kissed her, and she'd let him, needed him to distract her from the pain. To make her feel human and still alive. Kissing had subtly changed everything, charging what went on between them with a sexual tension she didn't know how to combat.

With her eyes only barely open, coping now with a dull throbbing between her right breast and shoulder, she watched him for a long time. His eyes were closed. She didn't know if he was sleeping. She decided after a while that he was not—that he might be resting his eyes, but remained aware of his surroundings. Aware of her. Aware, even, that she had regained consciousness.

His raven black hair lay in damp curls, as if he'd stuck his head beneath the lavatory sink. He smelled now of soap. Starkly delineated against fair skin, his black whiskers created a dark, forbidding visage.

Her tummy fluttered. She drew a deep, panicky breath and opened her eyes, willing herself to see him not as a dangerously attractive, compelling man, but for the threat he represented.

If what he told her was true, then he hadn't known, any more than the sheriff's deputy or Tafoya's FBI stand-in, that Broussard's assassin already had her virtually in his sights. He had followed Paglia and the deputy, intending to kidnap her, to take her from them, nothing more.

He had saved her life, that much was true. She owed her life to him, but she couldn't allow herself to forget for one moment that beneath his heroics lay a reckless disregard for her welfare. He would use her for whatever purposes he had in mind.

Revenge was at the heart of his actions. She was sure of that much. And she believed deep inside that no matter how valorous he had proved himself to be, he could not exact his revenge against Winston Broussard without getting himself killed. Which almost certainly meant she would die, too—unless she managed to escape him and somehow get back to the protection of David Tafoya.

Observing him slouched low in the seat, resting his head back, she faced the fact that his pressing weariness touched her. That she sympathized with his deadly intent. Nothing would ease her own heart and mind so much as Winston Broussard's death.

To know that about herself gave her no comfort.

He opened his eyes then and met her stare.

Shuddering, she lowered her gaze to her hands, then looked at him again. Maybe, if she tried, she could reason with him. Maybe she could make him see that there was no way ever to get Catherine back. Tierney had to see that Broussard's life didn't begin to equal Catherine's and wasn't worth the risk to his own.

She had to try. She had to hope he would give this all up because even if he let her go and went on alone, it would cost him his life, too, one way or another. She couldn't bear to think of that happening.

"I'm sorry for what happened to...Catherine. To your wife."

"Yeah." He exhaled harshly. "Me, too."

"I know I wasn't directly responsible, but it...feels like I was."

He folded his hands over his flat abdomen. "No one's blaming you."

"I know. I guess that makes it easier to blame myself. If I hadn't testified, or if—"

"Things happen. Innocent people die every day."

She nodded, sensing the pain beneath his shrugging it all off. "I know." She watched his Adam's apple slide down at the opening of his green-and-blue plaid flannel shirt. "That can't be any comfort."

He didn't say anything or act as if he wanted to talk about his wife.

"You must have loved her very much."

He tilted his head and knuckled his eyes. "Are you going somewhere with this?"

"Yes." She remembered the shock on his wildly handsome face, the rank confusion, the horror of seeing his lovely, pregnant wife brutally murdered. In the few seconds it had taken to speed away from the scene of the violent assassination attempt, she had known such a brutal loss would deaden a man's heart forever.

"Where?" he prodded.

She scraped her hair back, to buy time, maybe. A few seconds to find a way to say what she thought Catherine might say to him. "Have you thought whether Catherine would want this?"

He shook his head. "What Catherine wants hasn't been relevant for a long time. You don't get to guess what she would have wanted."

His remark felt personal, like blame, whether that's what he'd intended or not. "But *you* can guess," she said, her voice low, urgent. "Do you think she would have wanted you to throw your life away?"

His looked straight at her and his lips curved, but Eden would not have called it a smile. "Catherine would have expected it."

Eden swallowed. "You can't be serious."

He looked away, sighing heavily. "I was in love with her. She would expect me to die of a broken heart. Or maybe to throw myself off a cliff."

His mournful response shocked Eden to her marrow. "People say that," she protested, "but—"

"But what?" he snapped, angry at her now. "*But* they don't mean it? They don't want to believe it will ever happen, *but* it would sure be one hell of a testimony to undying love?" He surged out of his chair and began to pace, rubbing the back of his neck in his agitation. He turned back to her, one hand cocked on his lean hip, the other pointing straight at her, his eyes shooting daggerlike warnings. "Don't presume to tell me what Catherine would have wanted."

Eden felt shaky again, and trapped. Caged by his anger, by emotions she couldn't fathom. By a kind of love she would never know, a love so powerful that neither person could imagine going on without the other.

She couldn't let his anger control her, or silence her. "Broussard is deadly, Mr. Tierney—"

"Chris."

"Mr. Tierney," she repeated, aware how very dangerous it would be to begin calling him by his first name. How the enforced intimacy of being his captive might begin to seem more rational and less a violation. "Listen to me, please! Winston Broussard has no conscience. He lives for the moment. His motto is loyalty, first, last and always, but he has no allegiance to anything or anyone but himself. He's an animal!"

"Are you saying I can't win, Eden?" Tierney mocked, smirking at her. He picked up his coat from where he'd left it near the bulkhead, and pulled a canteen from his coat pocket. "That even if I try, I'll lose? That I will have thrown my life away and changed nothing?"

"Yes! That's exactly what I'm saying. Winston Broussard doesn't care whom he hurts or who gets killed." Why was this so hard? Because deep within, she knew that if Tierney could contemplate revenge, he was more like Broussard than she wanted to accept? Because his beautiful hazel eyes were already lifeless? "I'm saying you're not . . . not like him. You're not ruthless enough."

He opened the flask and brought the opening to his mouth, drained it, then wiped his mouth on his sleeve and tossed aside the empty container.

"You're wrong," he said grimly.

Eden felt the color drain from her face. She knew then how hopeless it was to think she could persuade him to abandon his intentions. To forget, if not to forgive.

Christian Tierney loved his wife, Catherine, beyond life itself, but she was gone. He had faced the dilemma of what to do. How to go on.

His answer was not to go on at all, save to exact his revenge, which would cost him his life, but save him a lifetime without the woman he loved.

Eden fell silent.

He sat again across from her. "Look, Eden..." He started to say something she wasn't sure she wanted to hear at all, trying perhaps to find some way of putting his intentions into a better light, some way of justifying what he had set himself up to do, but he was interrupted by Haggerty calling back to him.

"Tierney. We've got trouble."

He looked once more at Eden, then rose wearily from the seat.

She sat forward, intending to get up, as well. She had to grit her teeth against the rush of pain and the stiffness taking hold of her body. "Do you mind if I hear what kind of trouble we're in?"

He fixed her with his stare. "I don't think that would be a very good idea."

Chapter Seven

He meant, of course, that she shouldn't know where she was. That he didn't trust her not to run, or to try calling for help. He would have to chain her to the seat to keep her from following, and she didn't think he was prepared to do that—at least not here. Not in confines she couldn't escape in any case.

The stiffness almost leveled her, almost made her sink back to her seat. Her chin went up. "I have a right to know what's going on."

He stared at her a moment longer, for what seemed a small eternity, then shrugged and turned away toward the cockpit. Eden shivered. It was a puny victory in a battle of wills she had no chance of winning. He could lock her in the lavatory if he chose, which meant that if he allowed her to listen to his conversation with the FBI pilot, it was because he figured she didn't stand a chance of escaping him anyway.

"*You're* wrong, Christian Tierney," she uttered fiercely, purposefully echoing his earlier harsh remark.

She pulled the coarse, scratchy blanket tighter about her shoulders and followed him.

She leaned against the hatch. Tierney occupied the co-pilot's seat and sat listening to the pilot, Haggerty.

"... is socked in with fog," Haggerty was saying. "Instrument landings only. I could do that at Logan, but not at a private airstrip. To get out of the weather, I'd have to go south damn near to New Jersey."

"What's the alternative?"

Haggerty tilted his head. From Eden's perspective, she could see a bald spot on top of it. "Looks like there's a break in the fog bank between the Berkshires and the Catskills. Saugerties, maybe."

"You know of any place you can put down there?"

"A couple. Fancy-assed private estates."

Tierney shook his head. "I'd rather not have to deal with any hotdog private security forces."

"We're not exactly long on choices here," Haggerty cracked.

"Pick one, then," Tierney said. "You can drop us and head for New Jersey."

Haggerty nodded. "It'll be better this way. I'll lie low, head up to Logan in the morning. Tell Tafoya I don't know where you disappeared to, only I really won't know."

Standing behind them, Eden battled a sudden dizzy spell. Glaring white spots appeared before her eyes. She shivered and focused on one of dozens of dials and indicators and switches at Haggerty's command. "How much longer?"

Haggerty glanced up at her and shot Tierney a look. "Twenty minutes, maybe. You all right?"

"Yes."

"Go back and sit down," Haggerty suggested kindly. "You'll have to buckle up in a minute anyway."

She nodded. "When you talk to David Tafoya—"

"Eden, go sit down," Tierney interrupted. "Do you need help?"

She recognized the warning, but what could he do to her in front of this man who thought he was such a damned hero? Maybe if she could push him into manhandling her, the FBI pilot would take a hint. She angled her head so it would stop spinning. "No, thank you. I just want David Tafoya to know that he shouldn't stop looking for—"

"Things will be taken care of, Eden," Tierney soothed, rising easily from the copilot seat, turning to her in the cramped space too short to accommodate his height. His eyes shot warnings only a fool would defy. "David Tafoya knows his job. He won't stop looking until the shooter is apprehended."

"I want him to know where *I* am," she shrilled, insistent, defying him to silence her, but it was all to no avail. The two of them exchanged glances.

"He will, miss," Haggerty said, taking the same patronizing tone, meant to calm a female bordering on hysteria. "Just as soon as they catch the guy who tried to kill you."

The white spots glared again in her vision. She had to try one more time. "You don't understand—"

"I think he does, Eden," Tierney said firmly, turning her from the cockpit. "You and I are going to have to reach an understanding, lady," he muttered beneath his breath. But as soon as he planted her back in her seat and got a good look at her, worry creased his forehead. He sank to his haunches before her. "Eden, your eyes are glassy. Are you hot?"

"If I am, will you take me to a hospital?"

His jaw tightened. "You never give up, do you?"

"No." She shook her head slowly. "This is wrong, Tierney. Please. Let me go. Let Haggerty call Tafoya."

He lowered his head for a moment, and for that few seconds, Eden prayed he was reconsidering. He wasn't.

She knew that when he looked back up at her and his expression seemed to her carved from granite. "Buckle up. Do it now."

SHE FELT EVERY FOOT of the descent in her stomach. She felt the wheels grabbing on the tarmac through her feet and legs, all the way to her chest. She had begun to grow hot, but as Haggerty applied the brakes, she shivered. Her seat was positioned backward, facing the tail of the jet, and the shuddering sensations as her body was drawn back were dangerously disorienting. She had eaten nothing all day. Still her stomach heaved.

Tierney was out of his copilot position and looking out the windows long before the jet came to a halt. The skies were a wintry gray though the trees on either side of the airstrip were a lush, rich green. Eden watched, feeling sick inside, while he shouldered both their packs and bent low to release her seat belt. He pulled her to her feet and eased her arms, the damaged shoulder first, into his heavy black leather coat.

Already opening the door, Haggerty lowered the steps. The two men looked at each other for a moment, as if reaffirming their agreement, then Tierney scooped her up into his arms. Angling her body feet first through the cabin door, he descended the stairs, then set her on her feet.

Haggerty followed long enough to gauge the remaining length of the airstrip, then shook hands with Tierney. "I didn't see them sending out the militia," he hollered over the idling jet engines. Eden thought he meant whoever owned the property.

Tierney's luck seemed to be holding. Holding her hair down, she cried, "Please, call Tafoya," but her voice was lost, and Haggerty, scrambling up the short flight of steps, never turned back.

If Tierney heard her, he ignored it. "Come on, Eden. Let's go." He took hold of her left hand and began running toward the chain-link fence separating the airstrip from a thick grove of trees. At the fence, he picked her up again and set her over the railing, then vaulted over it himself and took off running again, pulling her behind.

She heard the jet gaining momentum and rising into the air. They had no sooner cleared the fence and run several yards through the tangled undergrowth when a car screeched to a halt at the end of the airstrip where Haggerty had just lifted off.

Tierney paused at the thick base of an old maple tree, not because he was winded, Eden thought. Not for her, either, but to see if they had been observed. The two men getting out of the dark-colored car only stared after the plane, one of them with binoculars. Clearly bent out of shape, gesturing angrily, they weren't talking nearly loud enough to be heard.

Tierney gave a curt, satisfied nod. "They didn't see us get out." Through the haze and the swath cut through the trees for the airstrip, Eden could just make out the heights of the Catskills. Tierney readjusted both their packs on his left shoulder. He took her hand again and lit out through the grove of trees in a direction opposite the mountains.

The thick canopy of branches and leaves blocked out most of the scant, gray daylight. After a long time, maybe an hour, he let go of her and just led the way, beating a path through vines big around as her thumb, and dense undergrowth that made her footing treacherous.

She caught the toe of her shoe on something, stumbled and fell. It wouldn't have been enough to keep her down if she'd had any energy stores to draw on. Or if she had wanted to go on.

She didn't. Not with Christian Tierney. She huddled close to a tree trunk, leaning sideways against it, and kept quiet. It took him maybe a minute to circle back to her.

"What are you doing?"

She scraped her hair back and met his angry hazel eyes with defiance. It would help if her vision wasn't messed up, if she didn't see two of him, or if the white spots would go away. "Resting…no, that's not… I'm not going to go on."

His jaw cocked to the side. He shook his head, then dropped to his haunches and let their packs fall to the ground from his shoulder. Taking her face in his hand, he ordered her to look at him, and then he swore softly.

Scoping things out around them, he listened a moment for any hint of pursuit. He sank down beside her. He sat a moment, knees drawn to his chest, arms resting on them, his head bent low. "We can risk a few minutes, Eden. No more."

"Maybe you didn't understand. I'm not going with you anymore."

He ignored her. Lifting his head, he flexed his broad shoulders, then scrubbed away at his eyes with both fists. The childlike gesture caught her terribly off guard.

She swallowed hard. It would be so much safer not to notice the child in the man. Not to see his exhaustion. "You can't go on like this much longer, either, Tierney. You're in almost as bad a shape as I am."

"Yeah." He looked at her, smiling a little. That caught her off guard, too. "But we *are* going on."

She lowered her eyes, ignoring him.

He hauled his pack nearer and began digging through it. "I've got some bottled water in here. A tin of deviled ham."

A bird screeched and dive-bombed near her after some unseen quarry. She shuddered. "Water, please. My mouth is so dry."

"Yeah, well, it comes with the territory. Fever. Thirst. In a couple more hours, without something to stop it, you're going to have one hell of an infection going." He broke out the water and twisted off the cap. "Here. A little at a time."

She drank in small sips, then gulps, while he opened the tin of ham. He scooped some out with his fingers and ate it, then tried to hand her the tin.

"No." She made a face. "It smells vile." She shrugged at his look. "Canned meats make me gag. I'm sure I had more to eat than that when I was growing up, but all I remember are canned tamales and little weenies."

"What I remember is ketchup on macaroni." He smiled. She liked the look of his lips curved upward that way, liked it so much she turned away. He scooped out the rest of the small can and stuffed the seasoned meat into his mouth. "Guess I'll have to break out the Oreos, huh?"

Her eyes darted greedily back to him. "Oreos?"

He nodded, sucking the remains of the deviled ham from his finger. "A handful, Eden. Then we have to beat it out of here. If those two guys back there reported a trespass, it won't be long before someone puts two and two together."

Please, God, she thought. Please let Tafoya figure it out. She avoided Tierney's eyes and said nothing, but took a few cookies from the crumpled package.

Her prayers must have been excruciatingly transparent. She knew without looking at him that he realized what her silence was about. Trembling, she risked meeting his eyes.

His smile, *any* trace that he had ever in his life smiled, was gone. Her heart began to pound. She felt the throbbing above her right breast—and only then remembered that all she had on beneath his coat was her silk jersey camisole and gauze taped down to protect the wound.

She flushed and pulled the edges of the coat together.

He watched her trying belatedly to cover herself, when it was her transparent motives that most needed concealing. He closed up the bag of cookies.

"I'm not going to apologize for hoping someone can stop you, Mr. Tierney."

"You'd better hope no one does, Eden, because if they do you're a dead woman." He crammed the cookies back inside his pack. "You needed water. Fine." He shouldered both packs, then sank down on his haunches again to be right in her face. "But don't push me. I'm only going to say this once, so listen up."

He jerked the collar of his coat up on her shoulders. "You want to tell the United States Marshal Service to screw off, that's your right. If you want to put your life in David Tafoya's hands when this is all over, that's your business. But right now, *I'm* the only thing standing between you and sudden death." He grabbed her wrist and shook her. "Broussard wins. It's over. Are you clear on that? Are you?"

"I'm very clear on that point," she snapped, fighting back her tears, "since you're the one baiting Broussard to come after me." She jerked her wrist from his grasp, but she knew it was only because he allowed it that she broke free.

"Well, amen. We understand each other. Here's the other thing to keep in mind. I've seen people die of infections from gunshot wounds. Your blood gets infected and pretty soon every part of you is sick. You won't make it past tomorrow if you don't get some antibiotics. Now, get up and move it, or so help me, I'll drag your sorry little butt all the way back to Boston.''

He stood. He gave her one more look, then turned and began making his way farther and farther away from the mountains.

She threw aside the cookies and stumbled along after him silently for what seemed hours. Her mouth and throat grew dry as dust again. Sweat poured off her in the sweltering heat and humidity. Birds startled and squawked and chattered angrily. They terrified her, the way they swooped so near her and then darted off. Tierney paid them no attention.

Intent on getting somewhere else, ultimately to Boston, he paid her no attention, either, trusting that she would follow where he led.

He was right. She couldn't go on much longer without medicine. The spots before her eyes were now as common as the bright green leaves on branches slapping her in the face every few feet. No matter how much peroxide he'd dumped into the wound, she'd gotten blood poisoning from the bullet.

She had no idea how he planned to get prescription drugs for a gunshot wound without drawing the attention he didn't want. It didn't matter. Tierney would do what he had to do to keep her alive. She wouldn't put it past him to knock over a pharmacy.

She tripped over an exposed tree root but kept going, promising herself that Tierney would have to take her to a doctor and then she would get away from him. Promising herself anything just to keep going, to get out of this sweltering maze teeming with raucous birds and mosquitoes and gnats and moths.

She knew now, at least, that he intended to take her back to Boston. She had to keep her wits together until she could find a way to let Tafoya know that he could find her somewhere between Saugerties and Boston.

She paused long enough to pull the wrinkles from her socks, then plunged back after Tierney. She had gotten used to the forests in Wyoming. Used to pine needles, not ground-hugging vines. In Wyoming, even at the height of summer, the heat was never so intense as this.

But maybe it was her own fever. Shoving her way through a tangle of bushes, she nearly ran into Tierney, who had stopped. When she looked up, she saw why. They'd reached the edge of the private property, only now, abutting the densely forested grounds, they were confronted by a solid brick wall ten or twelve feet high.

Eden slumped to her knees on a mound of rock covered with moss, barely registering Tierney's muttered curse. She wanted to make some disparaging remark about the poor planning, but her mind wouldn't work that way, barely worked at all. She shivered violently and pulled his coat tighter around her shoulders. The army-blanket shawl had fallen and she'd lost it somewhere.

She watched him hoist himself into the branches of an old oak. He climbed the tree until she could no longer see him. At last, she caught sight of him again, making a leap for the top of the wall. Somehow he made it. Poised there, crouching down, he looked in both directions, then started to duck walk along the cap until she couldn't see him anymore.

Panic swept through her. "Tierney, don't leave me here!"

An interminable minute passed before he came back into view. "Eden—"

"I mean it. Don't leave me here." She hated the pleading tone in her voice, but she couldn't help it.

He stared down at her and spoke softly. "Eden, I'm not going to leave you anywhere."

She knew that, suddenly. Knew he wouldn't have gone to these lengths to grab her and then just abandon her, but her mind wasn't working. God, how she hated him for bringing her to this! Tears spilled down her cheeks.

She dashed at them with the sleeve of his coat and nodded. He leaped back from the top of the brick wall to the tree. Birds screeched and flocked out of the tree. A squirrel landed at her feet and ran over her shoes. Tierney crashed through smaller branches coming down, then sat on one high over her head.

"Listen now and do exactly what I tell you, Eden. Button up the coat." She tossed her hair back and did as he instructed. "This wall goes on forever. It might take hours to get around. I want you to give me your hand so I can pull you up after me. Come on. Try it. You can do it."

Nothing she had ever faced seemed so daunting to her as the brick wall. Nothing. Not the glassed-in cubicles of Social Services where the man in his park-service truck had taken her; not walking out on the enormously powerful Winston Broussard; not the witness box. She'd been lucky to put one foot in front of the other, and now she would have to climb. She clapped a hand over her mouth to stifle a choking cry.

"Come on, Eden. You can do it," he urged.

She pushed herself up from the soft moss. Staring at the tangled vines hanging from the tree branches, she shoved her hair back again and took a deep breath.

"That's a girl. Don't think. Just do it. I'm right here."

His voice worked on her like a salve. He wasn't her enemy now, wasn't even the man who'd gotten her into such desperate straits.

He was the man who would get her out of this if only she could manage to do what he told her.

She reached for his hand. He grabbed her wrist and began to pull her up to the lowest branch where she could put her feet, but as she was finding a foothold, her shoulder brushed a vine and a cloud of moths flew out at her. She gave a small cry and turned her face, then planted a foot on the branch.

All the way up, he spoke to her, crooning praise and encouragement, pointing to the limb that would be her next foothold. He moved up and they repeated the process.

Smaller branches snapped. A jay nearly flew in her face. She couldn't lift her right arm at all, even to protect her head. Tierney made her think she could keep going. From the time she started to the time he pulled her up beside him, daylight had faded to near dark.

He hauled her up at last using his coat as a hoist. Straddling the thick tree branch where it forked off from the main trunk, he lowered her down into the circle of his arms. The top of the wall was only a few feet away. Eden collapsed against him. Tears streamed down her face now that she had made it. Her whole body trembled.

He cradled her close, holding her head to his chest, and rocked gently from side to side. "Shh, Eden. It's over. It's over. You made it."

She couldn't seem to stop shaking. If he weren't holding her together, she would fly apart into a million little pieces. His whiskers caught in her hair. His heart beat strongly beneath her cheek. He thumbed away her tears until they had dried.

After a while, her trembling eased off, too. "How's your shoulder doing?"

His lips were close to her ear. His breath felt cool to her. She coughed. "It's on fire."

He exhaled sharply and swore. "We're going to have to go. Now, before it's too late."

A car drove slowly by on the winding road below, its headlights piercing the night, making her aware how dark it had become. For the first time, she saw what lay on the other side of the wall. Or, what didn't. The brick wall ended in what seemed a sheer drop to the road, twice as far down as it had been to climb up the tree on the inside of the barrier.

She swallowed hard on the knot of fear in her throat, and sat up. "How?"

"I'm going to lower you down. You'll have to hold tight, then drop off, but it won't be bad. Have you ever seen anyone rappeling?"

"In the movies."

"Do it just like that, right before you drop. Just a little shove with your feet against the wall, then let go. You'll fall into more bushes and undergrowth." He paused and took her chin in his fingers, turning her face up to his. "Think you can do that?"

Tears sprang to her eyes again. She nodded quickly, lowering her eyelids so he wouldn't see them glittering. She wished he wouldn't be so kind, so patient. She needed a reason to fight him, not to admire him, not to feel as if he might really care what happened to her.

She didn't want to leave the safety of his embrace, either, but she couldn't sit on this branch like a ninny all night. Or allow herself his comfort. "Let's do it."

"Fine." He straightened and let his arms fall away from her. They moved to the top of the wall, which was wide enough to sit on. He shoved their backpacks over the edge and heard them land with a soft thud. He showed her how to get on her knees, then to lie flat on her torso and let her legs down over the other side of the wall. "I won't let go of you before you're ready. You say when, okay? Can you do that?''

"Do I have a choice?"

He smiled at her, proud of her for hanging on to even a shred of humor. "None."

"Then what happens?"

"When I do let go and you fall, curl up and try to relax. I'm going to lift you up now by your good arm so your body clears the top of the wall. Then I'll lower you till I can't reach any more. Got it?"

"Yes." She hadn't really. It all seemed somehow too much to comprehend. She would have to trust him as much as her own instincts.

"Okay, Eden. Take it easy now."

He stood on the narrow ledge, bent over and clasped her left wrist. Her hand was nowhere near big enough to encircle his wrist. She clung to him as best she could and brought her right arm and hand in near to her body. He lifted her easily by her arm and leaned out so her body cleared the wall, then began slowly to lower her down.

She felt him controlling her weight, shifting his own, getting to his knees, crouching, finally lying flat as he lowered her, straining hard to take the brunt of the task. "Eden, that's it. That's as far as I can reach. Kick out from the wall now, curl up and drop. Easy. Real easy."

"Easy for you to say," she mumbled. She took two deep breaths, raised her knee, placed her toes against the wall, then consciously made herself take her lower lip from between her teeth and shove off.

Chapter Eight

She wished at the instant that Tierney released her that she'd eaten those cookies.

To make herself do this at all, to leap from a wall in the dark, she promised herself she wouldn't have time to feel the terror, that her landing would be into a feathery bed of leaves and compost and soft, willowy branches, that her shoulder wouldn't hurt any more than it already did.

She was lying to herself and she knew it. She felt every harrowing second of the drop, from the mind-numbing horror of falling to the bone-jarring crash into harsh, stabbing brambles.

She heard Tierney make the leap, then fall to the ground. His landing was no easier by the sound of it, but he had collected the packs and made it to her side before she could get any air in her lungs again.

"You okay?"

She couldn't do anything more than nod.

A car came roaring down the twisting road. He crouched low beside her. For an instant, the headlights caught them and she saw his face, the implacable set of his chin, the raw determination.

The car sped past. She doubted the driver had time to notice them at all. Tierney slung both packs over his shoulder and took her hand. He pulled her to her feet and then angled down the steep roadside slope to the pavement. They crossed to the other side of the road.

For what seemed to her hours, she managed to trudge along beside him in the soft night air. The downhill side of the road leveled off. Her fever continued to rage on. She could hear Tierney encouraging her for a time, but after a while, the dull roar of her heart pounding and her blood rushing drowned out his words. All she could hear then was the vague impression of a deeply resonant masculine voice.

Perspiration soaked her. She couldn't think or reason. She clung to Tierney. Half-carrying her, he kissed her damp brow and urged her on. "Another few steps, Eden. That's all, baby. Just another few steps."

Without him, she would die. For a few seconds, her mind fixed on that one thought. Without him, she would sink to the cold, damp ground and surrender to the fever engulfing her.

Something inside her wouldn't let go. Something inside her began overriding every nonessential function so that she could keep holding on to him.

Haltingly, she began to see things in a different light. He wanted her alive. She wanted to live. Stumbling blindly along beside him, she dimly recognized the truth about Christian Tierney. He only wanted to live again, too. He needed desperately to be free of the demons that possessed him, heart and soul, mind and body—like the fever that had her in its grip.

She had to survive.

She willed herself to put one foot in front of the other, again and again and again, endlessly, until they rounded a bend and came upon a deserted intersection. The road they had followed dead-ended. A green neon light glowed in the window of an old tavern built of stone.

Only three cars were parked in front. Tierney stopped, then ran a hand through his hair. Standing concealed in the trees, he pulled her into his arms and rested his head for a moment on the top of hers.

CHILLS CONVULSED her slender body. She shivered violently. Chris drew her closer for another long moment, murmuring softly to her. He couldn't believe how incredibly hard she'd fought, how she'd stood up to him and doggedly followed him. How she'd climbed up that tree against all odds and then let him drop her over the other side of that brick wall. He knew men, good men, who would've folded.

Her grit all but shamed him.

He knew she couldn't win this battle. The infection would spread, the fever only get worse. In the end, without immediate medical attention, she could die.

Indecision rankled in his head. He knew enough to fear that more than anything. He hadn't slept in three days, couldn't keep a clear thought in his head. He needed to get her to a hospital or to Margo's place in Holyoke. The first required only that he get her across the road and make a call to an ambulance service. The second meant stealing a car, driving a minimum of three hours, praying he wouldn't fall asleep at the wheel or get stopped along the way.

He had no choice. He couldn't risk her life. Broussard had found a way to get to her, and if the assassin's bullet hadn't done the job, the resulting blood poisoning would. Chris's own plans had gone so seriously awry that they no longer represented a viable option.

His heart pounded painfully in his chest. The heat coming off Eden Kelley's body felt scalding to him. He couldn't indulge his indecision a moment longer. He swallowed, stroked her hair, murmured something he wasn't even aware of thinking, then picked her up and carried her across the road. He had to put her down long enough to open the heavy door leading into the tavern, then picked her up again.

The inside was nearly dark. All the tables were empty. Only a few patrons sat at the bar. The barkeep glanced up and saw Chris carrying Eden. His eyes widened to the size of saucers. He put down the glass he'd been polishing. "Holy cow, man! What's going on?"

Eden had already lost consciousness.

"Get an ambulance up here," Chris croaked. "Now. Please."

THE LOCAL EMERGENCY ROOM admitted her under a Jane Doe.

Drawing on mental and physical reserves he hadn't plumbed in years, Chris followed the paramedics in, past plastic-laminate chairs filled with sick and hurting kids and shaken parents. He calmly refused to take a seat or be denied entry beyond the swinging doors at the admissions desk. Once inside the large, brightly lit emergency room where the paramedics had taken her, Chris refused to let anyone but the head of the ER come anywhere near Eden.

Her vital signs were very poor. Respiration shallow at thirty-seven per minute, temperature 102.6, blood pressure low but not critical.

The attending physician, having taken Eden's vitals from the ambulance paramedic and already put out with Chris's peremptory behavior, took one look at the wound beneath his patch job on the front of her shoulder and ordered a shot of penicillin. She snapped shut the curtain hanging from the ceiling around the gurney, closing off the rest of the busy ER.

A slight, wiry, gray-haired woman with horn-rimmed glasses and the intensity of a war-zone surgeon, she fixed Chris with an angry glare. "I want to know what's going on here. This is a gunshot wound. Is this woman a Jane Doe because you don't know who she is or because you shot her?"

He pulled his wallet from his back pocket and flashed his badge. "This woman is a protected witness. She's Jane Doe because I said so."

The doctor's expression became pinched. "It doesn't appear that she *was* protected, now does it?"

He drew a deep breath and agreed that it didn't. He relied on his instincts about people, on intuition so deep it went to his core. He knew that, for himself at least, he could not survive in this job in any other way.

His gut feeling about this doctor was that he had only won a temporary reprieve. He would have to satisfy her questions, but if he could do that, if he could make a believer of her, if he could convince this doctor that he was legitimate, she might be persuaded to bury altogether the admission of a gunshot victim to her ER.

Seeing that the doctor was competent and that she cared, he knew his own best bet would be to get the doctor to see him in the same light.

He asked for and received permission to stay with "Jane Doe" while the doctor worked on her. Clearly concerned for the safety of the emergency-room employees, the doctor asked directly if there was any threat of harm to her staff.

Chris shook his head. For whatever reason, the doctor believed him. She asked if he was armed and nodded curtly when he answered that he was.

She called for the supplies necessary to sterilize Eden's wound, and a local anesthetic. She ordered her staff, at Chris's suggestion, to conduct themselves as if this woman had never been admitted at all. The doctor administered the shot of penicillin and then grilled Chris for the length of time it took to anesthetize Eden's flesh and place the stitches.

Watching Eden, seeing her wide gray eyes flutter open now and again as she drifted in and out of consciousness, he indicated to the doctor that his witness was still very much a target of the man who had hired an assassin to kill her.

He lied when asked where the shooting had taken place but told the truth as to the number of intervening hours. He admitted that he was not only without a means of leaving the hospital, he was also without the necessary transportation to get his witness to safety.

The doctor grimaced. Her brow furrowed thoughtfully.

He held Eden's thin, pale hand. His eyes were drawn again and again to the dozen or so small scratches from tree branches catching her in the face. He described the man who wanted her dead and the prodigious efforts of the Justice Department to defend her life.

The doctor placed the last of five stitches, then dumped the forceps and hook-shaped needle into a metal bowl. Stripping off her gloves, she discarded them into a bio-hazard waste container.

"Exactly how is it that this man, this . . . *assassin*," the doctor demanded angrily, "got to this woman if she was a protected witness?"

Chris shook his head wearily. "I don't know."

"That's not a very satisfactory answer, is it?"

He agreed again that it was not.

"Well." The doctor stood back, removed her glasses to massage her eyes, replaced them, then breathed deeply. "I take it you do not trust your cohorts and the *prodigious* resources of the Justice Department at this point."

He shook his head. "No."

She nodded. Turning back to her patient, she examined Eden's pupils with a penlight. Apparently satisfied, the doctor reached for a crushable ampule and snapped it near Eden's nose. The scent of ammonia exploded in the air. Eden coughed a couple of times and squinted as her gray eyes opened.

Inclining her head toward Chris, the doctor asked Eden point-blank, "Do you know this man?"

Eden rolled her head on the pillow away from the doctor toward Chris, and stared at him. She blinked and coughed and kept staring. Agonizingly long seconds passed. He knew this was her best chance to escape him. All she had to do was let out a piercing scream. A whimper would do. A frightened swallow.

The doctor would give any such reaction every benefit of the doubt. He had no doubt that if that happened he could draw his machine pistol and, without ever firing a round, make his escape from the ER with Eden. But if she cried out her name or his, Chris would be screwed. Tafoya would be on to them in less than twenty-four hours. Who knew if Broussard would beat Tafoya again?

So here was Eden Kelley's big chance, and he knew that despite her fever, she knew it, too.

"Well?" the doctor prodded.

He held his breath. He couldn't remember a time when he gave a solitary damn whether another human being trusted him. Whether a *woman* trusted him. He hadn't gone out of his way to endear himself to Eden, but he'd done what he had to do to save her life.

And he'd kissed her. Held her. Her gaze went to his lips, reminding him. He couldn't breathe. Worn to her limits, sweaty with fever, fragile and dirty and scraped up and stitched, she struck a chord in him so deep he wanted to bolt.

She shut her eyes and turned her head away and murmured tiredly, "Yes."

He shivered hard.

"Is he responsible for the gunshot wound to your shoulder?"

"No."

"Has he harmed you in any way?"

"No." Eden seemed on the verge of fading out again, but she rallied for another few seconds. Her whisper was nearly inaudible. "He saved my life."

He stared at Eden, a little in awe. He wouldn't exactly call it trust or faith in him that motivated her, but whatever it was, if Eden Kelley still meant to escape him, she'd passed up one hell of an opportunity.

He felt somehow... pardoned, and dared breathe again at last.

The doctor sighed and pinched the bridge of her nose, then fixed Chris with her stern look. "Is your badge legitimate?" she demanded.

"Yes." At least it had been before all this began. He thought the doctor would as soon not hear that reservation.

"Then I'm releasing 'Jane Doe' to your protective custody and purging all records of her admission to this facility." She opened the curtain and pointed to a hallway clearly marked Authorized Personnel Only. "Follow that hall to an exit off the next hallway to your left." She took a clump of keys from her lab-coat pocket and began twisting a set of car keys off the solid-brass dolphin ring. "Outside you'll find an '85 Mustang. Maroon. See to it you don't mar the paint job."

Chris took the keys and stared numbly at the doctor, not sure he understood her correctly, or if he had, that she meant what he took her to mean. That she was offering him a way out. "Why are you doing this?"

She looked down at her aging hands a moment, then met Chris's disbelieving gaze. "Your Jane Doe deserves a break." The doctor stuck her hands into her pockets. "God forgive you if she comes to any more harm."

CHRIS PLANNED HIS ROUTE to Holyoke to avoid the toll roads and the Mass turnpikes. He stopped at a convenience store a few blocks away from the hospital for coffee, then headed north before crossing the Hudson River and going east toward Massachusetts, sticking to the secondary highways.

The coffee kept him functioning.

The drive kept him sane, soothing his jangled, caffeine-hyped nerves.

Eden Kelley kept him feeling.

He'd avoided that state of affairs for a very long time. The last thing he needed was to feel anything for anyone, least of all a witness to his wife's murder, a witness whose life was in his hands. A witness he intended to set up like a sacrificial lamb to lure a mercenary, cold-blooded murderer. But in keeping with his determination to tell himself the truth, he knew it was already too late. He admired Eden Kelley and he cared what became of her.

He looked over at her sleeping fitfully in the passenger seat. The dash lights didn't adequately illuminate her face, but he knew by the fine sheen of perspiration on her brow that the penicillin had not yet begun to work.

Killing off the infection would consume hours, perhaps days, even with the antibiotic, hours in which Tafoya would either track them down or lose their trail altogether. The same hours in which, Chris had to assume, Broussard would be furiously tracking her, as well. His assassin had failed to kill her—assuming Eden pulled out of the life-threatening infection—but the attempt had succeeded in flushing her out into the open.

Broussard had his best chance now, before Eden could be relocated. He wouldn't waste the opportunity.

Chris pulled off the road at Great Barrington and sought out a public telephone not far from the main drag. He found one to the side of an automated teller machine and got out of the doctor's maroon Mustang, leaving the engine idling. He dropped the necessary coins in the phone, then dialed Margo's number in Holyoke.

If Ed Bancroft, her yuppie doctor husband answered, Chris was out of luck. Or one of the kids.

The phone rang once, twice. Half a dozen times before voice mail cut in. Cursing under his breath, Chris hung up, dropped in more change and dialed again. Someone was on the line, ignoring the Call Waiting.

He tried twice more, then went back to the car, thinking he would try again in Otis. He found Eden awake, sitting sideways in the seat, curled up like a child, her face resting against the seat back, her eyes fixed solemnly on him.

Her lips curved, the barest shadow of a smile. He didn't know what to think or say. Didn't know how to respond because his chest tightened and because, exhausted and unguarded and like a child, she was looking at him with unutterable trust. She blinked a couple of times before her eyelids fluttered closed again.

He wanted to kiss her. The need came on him just that fast. He wanted to reach for her and cradle her sweet, battered face in his hands. He wanted to feel her warm breath on his wrists and touch his lips to her fragile eyelids.

He had rarely regretted his vow of self-honesty as much as he did in that brief moment because the feelings sapped his will to answer violence with violence. To deliver real justice to Winston Broussard.

Instead, Chris found himself wanting to make both their worlds right somehow, his and Eden's. He wanted to create a space in each of them that all the ugliness and violence and tragedy would never taint.

He wanted to make love to Eden Kelley.

He exhaled. Hadn't even known he was holding his breath. He rubbed his eyes and clenched his jaw. His body hummed in the wake of the swift, fierce desire.

He shoved in the clutch and backed out of the parking area and picked up Highway 23 heading east. In Otis he stopped again to phone Margo. Parking where he could keep an eye on Eden, he left her in the idling car. His sister-in-law picked up on the first ring.

His shoulders sank in sheer relief. "Can you talk?"

He knew she would recognize his voice. She hesitated less than a second. "Let me get rid of my other call."

She clicked off. Chris stood there waiting. He watched a state trooper cruise by going in one direction, then a local cop heading the other way. His gut feeling was that they had nothing to do with him, but for the first time in his life, he had something to hide. Cops had a radar for fear like that. He took a deep breath and transformed his body language from the hunted to the hunter.

Margo came back on the line. "Chris? God, it's good to hear your voice. Where are you?"

He could hear her lighting a cigarette. "Knock off the smokes, Margo. They'll kill you."

"No. Ed is going to kill me. He's on one of his quiet little rampages."

"Again?" Chris's hold on the receiver tightened. "Why?"

He heard her dragging on her cigarette. "Over the kids, of course."

He flicked the receiver to the ends of his fingers, making himself loosen up. He had to get a grip. He couldn't remember ever being so rattled.

Local cops cruising by had nothing to do with him.

Neither did his sister-in-law's husband's tirades.

But Chris was dangerously tired and he had Eden Kelley's life in his hands and he couldn't afford mistakes, so every scrap of information entering his head filtered through the possibility of real danger, however remote.

"I need a place to crash, Margo. Somewhere no one knows to look for me."

"Are you in trouble?"

"There is that," he said, breathing out.

"Hurt?"

"No—but there's a woman with me who is. I'm going to need some of Ed's stash of drugs. Penicillin."

"My God, Chris! Can you get here? Should I come get you?"

"No." God bless her, he thought, for not requiring endless explanations. "I can get there. I'm just not sure how to get to the guest house without coming through the front drive."

She lowered her voice. "Remember the private road— the rear access to our property? It's . . . let me think. Half a mile past the sign that says Holyoke Five Miles if you're coming north. It's paved but hard to see. I'll have to shut off the alarm system zone. How soon will you be here?''

"Inside an hour." He thought about making sure he didn't run into Ed or the kids. He was crazy about Tiffer and Jake. He was the one who took them ice-skating for the first time, the one who gave them their first hockey sticks. But the boys were only eleven and five and Chris couldn't risk their knowing he was there. "Margo, I don't want you to have to get into it with Ed over this—there'll be hell to pay if he finds out—"

"There's always hell to pay with Ed," she interrupted wearily. "I don't even care anymore."

"I know, Margo." He stared at a beetle plodding along on the sidewalk under the street lamp. Neither one of them had made the most brilliant marriages, but Catherine was dead and Ed was very much alive. Utterly capable of making Margo's life even more miserable, Ed Bancroft wouldn't hesitate for one heartbeat to rat on Chris, either. "Still—stay away, okay? If you haven't seen me, you haven't seen me, you know?"

"Okay." She dragged on her cigarette again. "I'll bring some groceries and pills in the morning. Shall I just leave them on the porch?"

"That'd be great, Margo."

"Chris, are you okay? You sound terrible."

He swallowed and asked himself for the first time how likely it was that he'd succeed without getting himself or Eden Kelley killed.

Chapter Nine

"I've been better."

"I hear you." Margo gave a troubled sigh. "In case I can't make it down to the guest house, the key is under the mat."

Chris shivered. His eyes felt gritty. If he had ever been more worn out, he couldn't remember the time. "Might as well leave the key in the lock, Margo." He knew she would take the rebuke for teasing, which might reassure her that he really was all right.

He would be, once he got there. The periphery of the estate was wired into a high-tech alarm system. And for a while, he would be able to keep Eden Kelley alive.

He hung up and got back into the Mustang. Eden was sleeping. He followed secondary roads for another twenty-five miles and found the back entrance to the Bancroft estate, though the wild foliage nearly concealed the turnoff. He doused the headlights and drove by the light of the moon. He parked the Mustang at the rear of the small brick guest house beneath a canopy of oak and ash trees and satisfied himself that the car could not be seen from the main house.

The cottage was dark, and as Margo had promised, he found the key beneath a welcome mat with a goose on it.

He vetted the place in under two minutes without turning on any lights, then returned to the car and lifted Eden out.

She snuggled close, curling into him. He shoved the car door shut with his foot and told himself that it was the fever. That she didn't know what she was doing. A part of him wished she did.

"Where are we?" she murmured.

He could feel her warm breath on his neck. "Somewhere safe, Eden." Carrying her, he strode into the house, over the hardwood floor to the bedroom, and put her down, praying she'd fall asleep again. She got up to use the bathroom, washed her face and came out wearing only her panties and camisole.

Chris managed to get her tucked in beneath the covers, then went off to take a cold shower. He shaved for the first time in several days, then fell onto the bed beside her and finally—finally—slept.

Eden floated in and out of consciousness for almost forty-eight hours. Margo brought him a plastic bag of penicillin tablets and a sack full of groceries the first morning, after Ed had gone off to the hospital and before the kids were awake.

Eden had small chunks of time when she was lucid, when she remembered vague images of what had gone on after they went over the wall. The wail of the ambulance. The antiseptic smell of the emergency room. The pricking sensations. The smell of the leather seats in the doctor's maroon Mustang. If she remembered telling the doctor Chris had saved her life, she didn't speak of it.

The first time she woke for more than a few minutes, Chris had been sleeping on the bed next to her for several hours. He came instantly alert, helped her to the bathroom again and got her to swallow a couple of the penicillin tablets.

She lay back down in bed, watching him for a moment as he sat sprawled in an overstuffed chair, then put her hands together like a pillow beneath her cheek.

"What does the *X* stand for?"

He'd answered the question countless times so he knew she was asking about his name. "Xavier."

Her eyes were still too bright. She smiled and murmured something that sounded more like "savior" than Xavier, then "fitting." He felt sucker-punched.

She drifted off and slept another five hours. Chris paced. He knew how to sit still for hours on end. How to keep a vigil without going nuts. How to put a thing, even a woman, out of his mind, how to keep his nerve intact, his attention pitched and his goal in mind.

Watching over Eden Kelley shredded all that. He couldn't sit still for more than an hour at a time. He'd forgotten how not to go nuts. He didn't remember how to put everything nonessential to the moment from his mind.

Or maybe he did remember, and it was that Eden Kelley wasn't nonessential.

The notion scared the hell out of him. He couldn't get centered in the way he'd come to expect of himself. Couldn't help returning to the way she'd soaked up his kissing her like a dying desert flower soaks up rain.

When she woke again, moonlight was filtering through the trees surrounding the guest cottage, spilling through the picture window in the bedroom, and Eden was back to *Mr. Tierney*—not in a sarcastic way, but after "savior"...a little distant.

He shook his head. *What the hell are you thinking, Tierney?* He reheated a saucepan of beef barley soup and coaxed her into eating a few spoonfuls.

She wanted a hot bath. He didn't want to take the chance that a light might be seen by Edward Bancroft up at the main house, so he lit a thick candle he found in the pantry and ran the hot water for her. She insisted she would be all right on her own.

He sat in the dark outside the bathroom door in case she passed out. She did fine until she needed to rinse shampoo from her hair. He didn't know what was wrong, but he heard her sniffing and he couldn't make himself stay out of the bathroom.

In the candlelight, she looked as bedraggled and defenseless as a half-drowned kitten—from the neck up. She grabbed a washcloth, trying to cover her breasts.

He gritted his teeth and started through the door.

"Don't come in here, Tierney."

The cloth didn't come close to covering her. "How are you going to get out, Kelley?" he snapped, tired of *Tierney* and *Mr. Tierney* and feeling his groin tighten. The situation was just too damned ridiculous. The woman was on and off death's door. What he knew of her he knew from government-witness documents, but he was half in awe, half in love with the woman no dossier could reveal by half.

His blood pooled painfully at the sight of her bare breasts.

The washcloth clung to her shape as faithfully as a second skin and the glow of the candlelight only heightened his awareness. He hadn't been with a woman in nearly two years—not Catherine, not any woman, and now the pent-up sexual energy made him hostile.

"How are you going to get the shampoo out of your hair? Huh?"

Her chin quivered. Her gray eyes filled with tears. She swallowed. He watched her throat muscles move in her slender, long neck.

"I don't know."

"Me, neither." He shrugged, dismissing the standoff, picked up a bath towel and stood over her, offering a hand. "This is crazy, Eden," he murmured. His voice was thick. "Let me help you."

She breathed deeply, then took his hand and stood. He couldn't help seeing her breasts or the deeply feminine lines of her torso and bottom or the slender length of her leg. He wrapped her in the bath towel for his sanity as much as her modesty.

He pulled the drain and stripped off his jeans, then stepped into the tub and sat in his boxer shorts on the side. Laying her across his lap, her head in the crook of his arm, he rinsed the lather from her hair with the spray attachment so the warm water flowed off her hair into the tub. By the flickering light of the candle, he saw that the stitches were doing fine, that her flesh had begun to heal.

She had on one of Margo's expensive discarded bathrobes, a thick white terry cloth embossed at the breast with a coat of arms, when she climbed beneath the fluffy goosedown comforter on the bed. Chris sank into the chair. Eden stared for a while at the LED numbers on the bedside clock. "How long have we been here?"

"Two nights." Wearing only his boxer shorts, he lay back and put his feet up on the chintz-covered ottoman. Holding her in the candlelight wrapped in nothing but a bath towel, rinsing her hair, combing out the tangles, carrying her against his body—had worn on him like coarse sandpaper on a fine patina.

"Two nights? You've been taking care of me all that time?"

He nodded. "Nearly." Enough hours that he'd begun to expect pursuit. But he hadn't seen Margo at all, and she would have come to warn him if there was news of a manhunt in search of a kidnapped protected witness. Tears suddenly glistened in Eden's eyes. He cursed the moon for scattering enough ambient light that he could still see the glitter of her tears in the darkness. And cursed himself more for allowing her tears to matter. His throat tightened. "What is it, Eden?" *Why ask, you fool?*

The silence was so complete he could hear her swallow. "Nothing."

"Did you think David Tafoya would have rescued you by now?"

"No." She stared at him. "I wasn't thinking of David at all. I was thinking how lucky Catherine was. Not... I mean, not when she died, of course, but to have you to take care of her... to be there for her."

"Yeah," Chris answered, but he flinched inside.

"How do you bear it?"

"What?"

"The loneliness. Being without her."

He shoved himself out of the chair and walked to the window. He stood there staring out, fending off reactions, harsh responses he might make. "It doesn't concern you, Eden." He wanted her to be quiet, to go back to sleep.

She didn't seem inclined to do either. Instead, she was wakeful now, and talkative.

"With Broussard," she said, "I was lonely all the time. I just didn't realize it. He had this way of making things seem exactly the opposite, you know?"

Chris turned back and leaned against the window casing. It was easier to face her even in the dark when she wasn't on the subject of Catherine. The sash bars on the windows cast shadows in the moonlight on the bed. "A real stand-up guy. And then he gave you the boutique."

"He wanted to give me the boutique," she corrected, "but I drew the line there. I would only accept a loan. I needed the boutique to be mine.'' She fell silent for a few seconds. ''David Tafoya said that was my fatal mistake, trying to have something of my own. Why Web started wiring money and orders and invoices through *Eden's!* accounts.''

''It wouldn't have made a difference,'' Chris said softly, ''whether Broussard gave you the boutique outright or not. The business he did through your channels represented less than a percentage point of his operation.''

''I know.'' She nodded and lifted herself up on one elbow. ''Tafoya told me the FBI believed Broussard had been arming terrorists, citizen militias and mercenaries for a long time before I met him.''

Chris gnawed on the inside of his lip, thinking there was some element to Broussard's motives she hadn't begun to touch upon. ''You're saying Tafoya chalked Broussard's action up to arrogance—that he used your international connections because they were there.''

''Yes.''

''But you think there was more, something else?''

Eden blanched. It wasn't as if Chris could see any color in her face by only the moonlight coming in through the window, but her cheeks seemed to go translucently pale and he felt a level of panic coming from her.

''Tell me.''

She sat up and drew the covers with her. ''It doesn't really matter why he did what he did. It only matters that in the end he used me and I betrayed him.'' Her voice strained, fading to a whisper. ''He would forgive anything but that.''

Chris cleared his throat. It turned him stone-cold inside to think Eden Kelley would die if Broussard succeeded in exacting his pound of flesh. ''You didn't betray him. You only tried to stop him from dealing death without a backward glance.''

"But that came later." Her fingers idly went to the stitches the doctor had put in beneath her collarbone, exploring, massaging. "I don't know why I couldn't see how much power Broussard had over me. How controlling he was. He didn't try to dictate what I did or where I went. I would never have gone along with that.

"Instead, little by little, he gave me things—everything I had ever wanted in my life—even the loan to start the boutique. I guess I wanted it all too much. And I believed he loved me."

Chris sat again in the overstuffed chair. He couldn't fathom why she hadn't seen the trap coming, either, but he had none of her life experience at being a ward of the state, never belonging anywhere, never having anything of her own. "It felt safe, I imagine. Secure."

"I suppose." Her expression hardened, and she shivered.

"What went wrong, Eden?"

Her shoulders slumped. "I knew. Somewhere inside me, I knew that it was all wrong. I knew there would be a terrible price to pay for letting Broussard take care of me. But I had spent my whole life mistrusting people, and after Monique took me in, I wanted to believe that was all behind me. I thought what I had with Broussard was extraordinary. Sheila thought so, too—and I wanted to believe that I didn't have to mistrust everyone all the time. That I finally belonged." She sat cross-legged now, clutching one of the pillows to her middle. "That's all I ever really wanted ... just to *belong* somewhere."

His chest tightened. Catherine hadn't wanted a safe haven or a place to belong, hadn't wanted what Chris had to offer her. He'd wanted to believe otherwise himself, but even before Broussard's assassin mistook her for Eden, the time for lying to himself was over. He'd seen it coming at him like a freight train out of control. He'd thought he could still avert the disaster with Catherine, but he couldn't.

"I was very wise, you see," Eden was saying. "Or at least I thought I was. I thought I'd seen it all. Awful things go on in orphanages. Not so much now, I guess, but twenty years ago they did. And I'd lived in foster homes where the dad would...come after me." Her voice quavered. She breathed deeply, then plunged ahead. "Twice I was sent away—thrown out, really—because those foster dads said *I* was behaving inappropriately. Because *I* was coming on to them."

Chris grimaced. He hadn't grown up knowing there were men who preyed on children, but he'd known better for a lot of years now. "Did the Social Services people believe them?"

"They didn't know what to believe." She shrugged. "I was only ten the second time it happened. They had no choice except to move me." She took a deep breath. "Somehow I dodged all those bullets. Years went by. Then I went to St. Anne's—you know, on the North End?"

The Boston parish ran an all-girls school and boarded homeless adolescents. Chris knew from her witness profiles that Eden had attended St. Anne's. He shifted his weight in the chair. "Is that where you met Sheila?"

Eden nodded. "We shared a room for four years with two other girls. I learned to sew and I became good enough at it that when I graduated I was hired as a dressmaker's assistant to Monique Lamareaux at her bridal boutique in Cambridge."

"*Treasures?*"

"Yes. You know it?" she asked, surprised.

"Yeah." He'd read about it in Eden's witness profiles, but he'd been there, too. "Catherine bought her wedding dress there." He switched subjects. "Isn't Monique Lamareaux a cousin of Broussard's?"

"Yes. They're first cousins. It seemed everywhere I turned there was another cousin or aunt or uncle—family of some description. Cajun, you know, but very upscale, very different. They all had the attitude that home was home but not nearly grand enough to embrace their passions. *Petites pommes de terre, chère!* Broussard would say. Small potatoes... A mixed-language joke." Eden gave a shake of her head. "Anyway, Monique took me under her wing and I moved into the fifth floor of her brownstone."

"Which is where you met Broussard?"

"Yes. At a party Monique gave. He was so respectful and so gallant—more of a gentleman than I had ever met. I began to see him. He took me out for several months, and in all that time, he never touched me except to take my arm crossing the street and once in a while to kiss my fingers.

"After a year or so, he made the offer of my own boutique. Not long after that, he asked me to marry him. I... he never expected... anything... from me."

Chris felt the surprise, the shock, invade him. "Are you saying he never touched you?"

"Yes."

"You're kidding."

She met his disbelief straight on. "No. I'm not."

"Did you think that was normal?"

Her chin jutted up. "Normal? No. It went against everything in my experience with men from the time I was old enough to understand what they wanted from me... from women. That's why I thought Winston Broussard was extraordinary. I thought his gallantry, his restraint, proved that he loved me.''

Chris straightened in the chair. Alarms began to go off in his head. ''What did he want, Eden?''

She didn't answer for a moment. Her eyes fixed somewhere beyond Chris. ''I didn't know. *Eden's!* began to flourish. I was working very hard. I thought he approved of my success, but I know now he'd only expected it to be an interesting little diversion. A hobby to keep me occupied with something other than *bonbons* when he was busy. When *Eden's!* became more than that, he began to get more and more distant. A little ... cold.''

Chris had the sudden urge to smash something. He knew he hadn't heard the worst of it yet, nor did he want to, but he couldn't shut her down. Couldn't not listen to her. He gnawed on the inside of his lip. ''Were you concerned?''

She looked at him, then looked quickly down. ''It was terrifying. I confided in Sheila. We ... I thought he was getting impatient with me, that he was waiting for me to make a move, to indicate that I wanted ... him. So I made the grand gesture. I chose a night when Monique was to be out and invited Broussard to dinner. I made a special Cajun-style meal for him. A quail dish and a *crème au café* for dessert.

''I had sewn a beautiful old-fashioned corset. It took days to complete. The stays alone ... then the ribbons and lace.'' Her voice thickened with emotion.

Chris's jaw tightened. The garment, he thought, was everything to her. Something beautiful she'd created. A piece of herself. Everything she was in her heart. Heat spread through his chest. He knew what she looked like in such a garment. He'd seen her. The image of her breasts came readily to his mind. His own sex thickened. He didn't want to hear what Broussard had done.

She wasn't sparing herself though. "After supper we went to the living room and I began to unbutton my...blouse, to reveal the corset I had made. It was... He stared at me. His face grew—" her hands fluttered "—*mottled*...with anger. He told me to cover myself. I was confused. I never expected such displeasure. He looked at me and said I must not cheapen myself—as if what I'd done made me somehow dirty. He said I must keep myself pure for our wedding night. But he refused to set a date." Tears welled in her eyes. "He said he'd know I was ready to marry, to 'take him to my bed,' when *Eden's!* assumed its proper place in my life again.

"God, I hate this!" she cried. Swiping angrily at a tear on her cheek, she climbed off the bed. Still clutching the pillow to her chest, she began to pace. "I hate the way it sounds. Like if I had two brain cells to rub together I would have known what he was! But he never treated me with anything less than the utmost respect. He never did or said anything to make me feel sordid or ashamed of myself—until that night."

And then, Chris thought, Broussard had shown his true colors. He sat watching her pace in the dark, stunned to his core, indecisive. He wanted to get up and take her into his arms and hold her. To comfort her and kiss her and make her know what a sick bastard Broussard was. But she knew that now, and he knew she hadn't told him any of this so he could fix it for her.

He didn't know what to do. She stopped a small distance behind him by the window. He turned sideways in the chair and slung his legs over the armrest. Still holding the pillow to her chest, Eden was watching thin streams of wispy, insubstantial clouds floating across the face of the moon through the canopy of maple leaves.

He wanted to take the pillow from her. He wanted to see the shape of her body silhouetted against the moonlight. She turned her head and looked at him, and though he couldn't see her eyes, he felt caught out with his thoughts, with wanting her. Rationally, he realized it was impossible that she knew his thoughts, but a mighty awareness hummed between them and she didn't turn away.

He took a deep breath. "Why didn't you leave him then, Eden?"

She breathed deeply, as well. Weariness pervaded her. She combed her fingers through her hair and held it back that way for a long time. "I should have. I knew that night that Broussard was not the man he pretended to be. That Cajun charm, the respect he showed me, the courtesy, the kindness—was all a sick game with him. I knew what I had suspected all along was true. There were strings attached to everything. I had just refused to see them. But I thought I could save *Eden's!*"

Chapter Ten

Winston Elijah Broussard III wasn't sleeping well. He paced the length of the veranda off the master bedroom suite, sipping at a fine, aged brandy, listening to the waves lapping against the beach below. Well sated as all his appetites were, he should have been soundly asleep by now. Instead, inside himself he felt this constant buzz ever intensifying, a foreboding that rode through his nerves like too much electricity humming down too few transmission wires.

He blamed Eden Kelley. She haunted his every moment. His little garden of secret delights had concealed a viperous nature he still couldn't fathom having overlooked.

Like some vengeful wraith, her visage rose from out of his dreams to persecute him at every turn. He didn't know why this should be so. Hidden away, terrified for her life, she represented no realistic threat to him.

And yet, she consumed him.

What to do with her? How to make her image cease plaguing him? He was tempted by his Cajun roots to seek out a black-magic remedy. Voodoo. Potions.

Evil spells.

She had twice escaped certain death.

She, along with the self-styled smoking gun, Christian X. Tierney, had eluded capture, as well—for nearly seventy-two hours now. Web had not been content to sit back and let the FBI do its job and apprehend them. His resources were not more extensive than those of the government, only more sophisticated, and more motivated.

In his organization, among whom he numbered a good many of his extended Cajun family, heads would roll should Eden Kelley escape again with her life. Such sanctions were not possible on the other side of the fence. The government couldn't go around exterminating its failures.

Agent Daniel P. Haggerty, for instance. Veteran of numerous government positions, a first-class pilot, a man with a family, a stalwart believer in Mom, apple pie and the American way. He should not have thought he might get away with aiding in the escape of Eden Kelley. Brave almost to the end, he had finally been persuaded to reveal the nature of the Hudson Valley estate where he had left Eden Kelley and Christian Tierney.

Broussard made a mental note to have flowers sent to the grieving widow and daughters. A nice, civilized touch in the wake of an admittedly harsh judgment.

He took immense satisfaction in certain niceties and civilized amenities, and considered himself for the most part extremely genteel and civilized, only ruthless as in the case of those like Agent Haggerty, who could not be left alive to tell his tales to his compatriots in the FBI.

No, Broussard thought now, pulling a cheroot from a box and lighting it. He was only *necessarily* ruthless. Left to his own devices, he wished only to live in peace and joy, savoring the company of one beautiful and compliant woman after another, imbibing a superior wine and enjoying a cleverly prepared meal.

All such predilections put him several notches higher on the evolutionary scale than those who bought his deadly armaments, which would be bought in any case from someone. It might as well be his own coffers that overflowed as someone less . . . civilized.

And, as with Eden Kelley, he liked things nicely sewn up.

She represented an intolerable loose thread in his scheme of things. She could not be allowed to live on.

He puffed on the cheroot and returned to the wrought-iron table where his cellular phone awaited his use, reflecting on the absurd ease of his endeavors to date. It had been a simple matter of phoning the Jackson Hole airport to determine the identity of the hijacked jet and its pilot. Easier still to locate the man himself, after what must have proved an unsatisfactory debriefing with his superiors.

And once Broussard knew where Haggerty had dropped his passengers, the hospital was only a few logical deductions away. There were certainly enough disgruntled hospital employees these days to find one willing to sing to the scandalmongering media of an admission purged from hospital records.

He knew, then, that Tierney had Eden Kelley stashed somewhere between Saugerties and the Atlantic. Broussard took a moment to salute the ingenuity and persistence of Christian X. Tierney, who did not yet understand that in Winston Broussard, he was not dealing with some half-witted fugitive from the laws of chance.

In truth, Broussard had now, tucked away in his safe, a dossier so complete on the formidable federal marshal that Broussard could reasonably surmise *exactly* where Tierney had gone to ground with Eden Kelley.

Broussard's decision at this moment was whether or not to inform the FBI clods and leave it to them to flush Tierney and Kelley from their lair, or merely to send in yet another assassin and be done with it. There was a certain appeal to the latter, but he found the buzzing inside his body somehow less intense when he considered prolonging the chase.

He could more happily envision the unfolding scenario in which the FBI cornered his quarry. David Tafoya, a prince among fools and a desperate man, must be frantic by now, covering his ass, making sure he would be the first to get to Eden Kelley.

Broussard smiled. He could almost see the horror in sweet Eden's eyes when she learned of the tragic fire in which Judith Cornwallis expired, and of Agent Daniel P. Haggerty's demise.

Broussard could almost smell her subsequent desperation. People had died in her wake, and because she was a smart little cookie, too smart for her own good, she would understand that so long as she lived and breathed, others would die and never breathe again.

Because he knew her so well, Broussard could comfortably predict Eden Kelley's choices now. She would shake Tierney and elude David Tafoya's protection. She would come back to Broussard, crawling. Begging him to put an end to it all. Her conscience could not tolerate more deaths, all because of her.

A virgin sacrifice. How touching. How rare in this debauched day and age. His decision came easily. He would not call the Federal Bureau of Incompetence. David Tafoya would happen on the information himself sooner or later, just as, sooner or later, Eden Kelley would selflessly give herself up to him.

To that delectable end, Broussard could afford to wait. Her personality virtually assured him the guilt of so many dead would consume her.

The buzzing inside him fizzled to an end. His nerves, by contrast then, felt as light as spider silk.

He crushed out the cheroot and put down the cellular on the glass-topped wrought-iron table. Returning to his bed, where Sheila Jacques had left behind her scent, he dreamed the dreams of the hunt.

EDEN STOOD SILENTLY at the window, holding a little less tightly to the pillow. Chris exhaled. For an instant, the sky lit up with lightning, and in the distance he heard the crack of thunder. The air seemed charged.

Eden shivered hard. "I just had the worst sensation." She turned to him. "Tierney, I need to know if Judith is okay."

Chris nodded, sensing this was not a request she considered negotiable, or one, for that matter, that he could refuse her. "In the morning we'll find out."

Her head tilted. "Do you promise?"

"I said we would," he answered. "You can believe what I tell you, Eden, without asking for promises."

She stood very still, then gave a reluctant nod. "All right."

He nodded back, feeling somehow better than her hesitancy to trust him warranted, but it was a start. "Will you go on? Tell me what happened when you tried to save *Eden's!*"

She turned back to stare out the window. Rain began to pelt the windowpanes. "There's not much." She shrugged. "I worked very hard, and when I took a closer interest in the business end of *Eden's!*, I began to discover wire transfers routed through my accounts, incredible amounts of money and long-distance charges that appeared to be mine but weren't."

"Broussard must have believed that you would never understand what he'd done, even if you uncovered the proof," Chris guessed.

"Of course. He didn't go to much trouble to conceal what he'd done, so at first I didn't think any of what I found could mean what it seemed. I thought if he were really into criminal activities, he would have been more careful."

"Then you didn't know that it was guns and munitions?"

"No." Lightning streaked through the sky and thunder cracked, nearer now. Wind began making the tree limbs flail and scrape at the windows. "I had no idea what it was until I went to the FBI—and of course, David Tafoya knew instantly."

"Did Broussard know you looked for other financing? To pay off your debt to him?"

Eden pursed her lips and shook her head. "I didn't want him to know until I had an offer in hand. And he didn't give me that much credit. I don't think the thought entered his bigoted, chauvinistic brain that I would ever try to make a go of it alone."

"What a disappointment you turned out to be."

"Yes," Eden reflected, giving a bittersweet smile that Chris could see only in shadows. "He intended to rub my upstart, ungrateful little nose in the harsh realities. If he'd wanted to, or if he'd thought I might try to get out from under his thumb, he could have called in the note and shut *Eden's!* down in a day." She buried her chin in the pillow a moment before going on. "He wanted me to see the 'full measure of the error of my ways,'" she quoted, her inflection imitating Broussard's thick New Orleans drawl. In profile, Chris could see her lower lip was trapped between her teeth. "The first time he said that to me, *the first time,*" she uttered fiercely, "I went to the FBI."

Chris let his head fall forward. He had believed there was no way he could despise Winston Broussard more than he had when Catherine had died in his arms and when he'd buried her in that cemetery on Chestnut Hill, and certainly not after all these months with rage and resentment festering inside him.

He was wrong. Eden's story made it all just that much more squalid. Broussard had virtually dared her to defy him. To betray him. "Would you go so far as to say he made no effort to conceal what he was doing?"

"Almost none," she agreed, "right up to the moment I left. The last person I saw with Broussard was the assassin he sent—the man who killed Catherine instead of me." Eden sighed and straightened as if the burden of her secrets had fallen off her slender shoulders. A tear brimmed over onto her cheek. She brushed it away and gave him a wry smile. "Please don't take this the wrong way, but . . . you know what they say. Whatever doesn't kill you makes you stronger."

Chris swore out loud. The platitude made him want to shake her. "You know he won't quit until you're dead. You know it won't matter how strong you've become."

"It does matter!" she returned fiercely. "I never gave up. I would have gotten financing and I would have paid him off. I wasn't helpless. I knew what he wanted by then—and when I uncovered all those transactions, I knew what I had to do and I did it. I got stronger every day, Tierney, and I haven't stopped yet. With or without you, I will survive, so don't you dare count me out!"

He sat there wanting to get up and soothe her, but he already knew not to count her out meant not patronizing her, either. If she were another kind of woman, he thought, she would have flown at him, lashing out in her anger till he took hold of her and trapped her flailing fists and stopped her angry cries with his kisses—all because of some female genetic code expressing a subconscious desire to get herself taken care of.

Cynically, he expected it. He was no genius when it came to women, but he understood this much. He even got the not-so-flattering opposing side of the male-female picture. He'd goaded her into flying at him—with his own you-won't-survive-out-there-without-me-babe attitude—so he could play the big hero, take her in his arms and comfort her and then take her to bed and keep her there.

But Eden Kelley was strong enough to resist this unwitting female response, and Chris was awed. He found he wanted nothing more than to be the kind of man she could trust to treat her as an equal if . . . *when* he took her in his arms again.

If he took her to bed.

"You mean it, don't you?" he said quietly.

"Yes." She shifted the pillow in her arms. "I mean it. I don't want to be taken care of, Tierney. I won't. I want more than that or nothing at all." She stared out at the rain battering against the window. "You can't kill him, Chris," she said after a while.

It didn't escape him that she'd used his given name for the first time, but he didn't want her to misunderstand him. "Watch me."

"No. I won't watch you and I won't help you do it." She shivered hard, as if the fever and chills had reclaimed her. "It will make you into what he is."

He turned away from her and sank heavily back into the cushions, making himself soften his warning tone. "I've heard the argument before."

"Then maybe you don't understand—"

"I understand."

"How can you say that?" she persisted, her voice cracking with emotion. "How can you say that you understand, when in your heart you must know that what you're planning to do will make you a monster?"

"Just drop it, Eden." He wanted her to drop the discussion cold. If she could stand there having had a bullet in her that had missed her heart by less than six inches and still believe that taking Broussard out put Chris in the same breed, then he couldn't change her mind.

But she wouldn't leave it alone. She came to him, shoved the ottoman out of her way and knelt down before him. "Chris, listen to me. Please. Everything in my memory of the day that Catherine was killed is just ... brutally clear.

"I was in this sort of emotional wasteland. Right there in open court, Broussard crushed an orchid blossom and flicked it over his shoulder. I *knew* then he intended to kill me. The judge was furious and kept banging his gavel, and every time it hit I flinched inside. I left the witness stand and it took everything I had not to run. I was escorted out of the courtroom surrounded by half a dozen marshals and I flashed on how many times I'd been down halls exactly like that with the Social Services caseworkers." She paused, then let go of the pillow and laid her hands flat on his bare thighs just above the knees. "Chris, more than any of that, do you know what scared me the most?"

His gut tightened. "No."

"I turned that corner and there you were, spilling into the hallway with Catherine and your friends. You were laughing and joking and carrying on." Her voice went low and tight. "I was so scared because I knew that nothing Broussard could ever do to me, even if he succeeded in tracking me down and killing me, *nothing* could hurt so much as never *belonging* with someone else like that. Like

Catherine belonged with you. Like you all belonged together."

"I grew up with Gary Dilts, Eden—"

"But don't you see? I didn't grow up with anyone! And I knew I would die without ever having had that, without ever being part of a couple who loved and respected each other like you did."

Chris went cold deep inside, finally certain of her meaning. She hadn't said "belonged *to.*" She'd said "belonged *with.*" He didn't know where the line was that he'd crossed over between telling himself the truth and telling someone else, but suddenly it mattered that Eden Kelley get it.

"If you believed, Eden," he said carefully, "that when Broussard's assassin killed Catherine he destroyed a storybook relationship, a man and a woman who—how did you put it?—who loved and respected each other—"

"Yes, exactly."

"Then you were wrong."

Eden blinked, then swallowed. "But you said you loved her—more than life."

"That's true. I did."

"You loved her... and then you didn't?"

"Nothing is that simple, Eden." Nothing was ever half so clear. Now he knew better, but then? "Then I didn't know."

"How could you not know? She was your wife. She was pregnant!" Eden protested. "I heard you laughing and joking about it. I saw your friends congratulating you. Are you saying now that you don't know if you really loved her?"

He sank deeper into the chair as if he were sinking again into the morass of emotions he'd felt the day Catherine was murdered. The hopelessness, the sense of her terrible betrayal, the rage. And the guilt. His feelings had been no more sophisticated than those of a child who wished someone would die, and then they did.

A flash of lightning revealed her look of perplexity. "Eden, you know things are not always what they seem."

"Some things, yes, but—"

He held up a hand to forestall her argument. He wanted her to know the truth. "What you saw and the sense you made of it is not even close to the way it was between and Catherine and me."

Doubt suddenly stilled her expressive features. Tiny baubles of light and shadow cast by raindrops on the window played at her parted, dampened lips. "How was it, then?"

"The truth," he answered, "is that I didn't know Catherine was pregnant when she came into my office that day."

"But what a lovely surprise!"

"Eden, don't!" he commanded harshly. "Catherine didn't take me aside. We didn't go to lunch. We didn't go look at baby things or maternity clothes at Filene's. I heard about the baby at the same time my whole unit heard." It wouldn't have been a lovely surprise even if any of those things had happened, but he stopped short.

Eden stared up at him, then bowed her head. The sky lit up again and silvery rays glinted off her hair. He'd thought he could give a fair recital of this much without betraying the pain, but the quality of Eden Kelley's silent empathy proved he was wrong.

"Tell me the rest," she urged softly.

He took a deep breath. He would rather have sat there and laced his fingers with hers on his thighs, but he got up and began to pace. Even that wasn't enough. He knew he ought to walk away from this conversation. What had gone down between Catherine and him had nothing to do with Eden, nothing to do with Winston Broussard or Chris's own intentions now.

He didn't owe Eden his life story. He had no right to burden her with it, either. But the fact that she'd asked, that she recognized there was more he'd left unsaid, that she could even think beyond her own immediate, life-threatening problems to his . . . all of it disarmed him.

He cared for her in some slowly spiraling and inexplicable way, but he hadn't expected it to be returned. Not from her, not after all she'd been through at his hands.

"Catherine was having a fling," he said before he could change his mind. "An affair. Her third that I know of. I went along with the smiles and congratulations just like she knew I would. She died before I could ask her if the baby was mine."

Chapter Eleven

Long after Chris had stunned her with the truth of the way
things were between him and Catherine, Eden sat watching the rain patter against the window. He slept uneasily,
but he slept. She had promised him she would not try to
run away.

Why was it so hard to know the heart of another person? Of all people, Eden reflected, she should have known
that things were not always what they seemed to be.

It had seemed to her that her mother had loved her. Her
father had abandoned the two of them, sure, but she didn't
think things had ever gotten so bad that her mother should
have abandoned her, too. She had.

It had seemed to Eden many times between finding herself alone in the Boston Public Gardens and the time she
went to work for Monique Lamareaux that no one was
trustworthy, not the Sisters at St. Anne's, not the priest,
not her classmates. Only Sheila Jacques had managed to
worm her way through Eden's stiff defenses.

And it had seemed to Eden that Winston Broussard was
trustworthy when he was not.

All delusions. But she'd made the mistake of placing
herself at the center of the universe, believing she was the

only deluded one. That she was the only one who repeatedly failed to see into the dark motives of those around her.

So she had left that courtroom, done with the testimony that would put Broussard in a country-club prison for a minimum term. She'd rounded that corner in the federal building in Boston, frightened to her deepest being. She was stiflingly familiar with being all alone. She knew the routine of being shuffled from one place to another, one so-called home to another, as well as she knew the North End streets and the cell-like room she had shared for four years with Sheila Jacques and two other girls.

Going off to a witness-protection relocation seemed remarkably in keeping with everything she knew so well and hated so much. How to be alone.

Seeing in that moment what she imagined was an intensely joyous moment was in reality Christian Tierney making happy over a baby he wanted more than anything but knew in his heart was not likely his.

Lightning cracked again, so close the thunder reverberated within only a few seconds. Eden hunkered deeper into the massive chair. Chris kicked the comforter off and groaned in his troubled sleep. He lay there on the bed wearing only a pair of thinly striped boxers. Dark hair covered his legs and chest and jaw.

Eden swallowed. He attracted her. His high Slavic cheekbones gave him a haunted quality that spoke to her. As did his warm hazel eyes, his thick, overly long black hair and eyelashes, even the stubble slashing across his angled jaw. His muscled shoulders and arms had both held her against her will and supported her when she would have collapsed.

She noticed now, when lightning pierced the dark, that his long legs were powerfully formed and his feet were as big as gunboats.

Maybe it was because she'd been sick and delirious and sleeping so much, but he seemed almost like a figment of her imagination, a man her subconscious had conjured up to satisfy and tempt every feminine instinct kept so long under wraps inside her.

But she could no longer disown her attraction to Christian Tierney, or chalk it up solely to infatuation or a physical appeal. She trusted him. She believed what he said. She wanted him to kiss her as he had on the jet he had hijacked for only one reason—to save her life.

She knew very well that he intended to kill Winston Broussard and that he would not be dissuaded from trying. She understood his dark desire to take justice into his own hands because God's justice was just too slow. Broussard sold guns and bullets and had killed and would kill again. Would kill her.

But where she had failed to see Broussard's sullied, self-serving motives, she saw Christian Tierney's clearly. She knew his were somber reflections of a deeply honorable and truthful man betrayed by the woman he loved more than life and offended by the license of Winston Broussard to murder without answering for it.

She swallowed hard yet again, overwhelmed by Christian Tierney, by the man he was. She admired his strength, his kindness, his capacity to love too much, even the driven recklessness of what he stood for, the lengths he would go to stand up for someone.

To stand up for her.

The minute Chris had committed to protecting her from Broussard's paid assassin, his plans to use her for bait, to lure Broussard from his evil, protected enclave, had gone up in smoke.

Unless he was certain she was again alone, Broussard would not come after her himself. He was too much a coward, too arrogant and dependent on his hireling thugs to risk exposing himself. Chris would have to go after Broussard, only Chris wasn't a killer, so Broussard would win.

Chris would die.

She got up from the chair, suddenly aware of hunger pangs gnawing at her stomach. She stood for a while watching Chris Tierney thrashing now and again, softly snoring.

She straightened and gave a quick shake of her head. Her hunger wasn't only for food; she realized it was far more complex than that. So complex it was impossible. U.S. Deputy Marshal Christian X. Tierney was still in love with the woman who had betrayed him. And still determined to kill Winston Broussard.

She put the pillow back on the bed and tiptoed into the small kitchen. She found a can of hearts of palm, her favorite, and half a loaf of crusty French bread, but when she'd eaten it all only her stomach pangs were eased.

Rain poured down from the eaves, overflowing the gutters. Restless now, she spied her backpack on the floor by the bed and sank to the floor beside it to search through her things for the mirror Judith had given her. She needed to look into its glass and find herself, the woman who needed no man, who was capable and strong and getting stronger every day.

Groping blindly in the dark through the pack, she stabbed her hand on a shard of something horribly sharp. She smothered a cry and plucked out the mirror. More jagged shards spilled into her lap.

Lightning crashed through the sky again and she saw what had happened. The butt end of a bullet protruded from the sculpted silver backing. The impact had shattered the glass. Judith's mirror had stopped the bullet, but it was ruined.

Judith's heirloom mirror.

Eden's throat closed and she began to shake. Blood dripped from the base of her thumb. Rage bit into her, then the memory came rushing back, the horror of the blow, its force knocking her into Chris as she clung to him on the back of his Harley. She clenched her teeth and forced herself to breathe, to think, to stay in control and be strong.

She had to get out of here. She had to escape Chris and find David Tafoya and get him to help her. Broussard would kill her, or he would kill Chris and let her live because if he caught them together he would somehow sniff out that she was in love with Catherine Tierney's husband.

And he would know the worst he could do to her would be to let her live after Chris was dead.

She scrambled to her feet and shed the luxurious white terry robe with a savage, determined calm. She heard the steady downpour drumming over Chris's uneasy breathing. She wouldn't look at him. Couldn't—not if she wanted to leave him.

She never questioned the fact that she was in love with a man she had known less than seventy-two hours and under the ugliest conditions. She would trade her life to save his on the spot, which was all she knew and everything that mattered.

She sucked the blood from the base of her thumb and wrapped it in a dish towel from the kitchen. As quietly as she could manage, she pulled on her only pair of jeans and a cardigan she usually wore over something else. The stitches beneath her collarbone felt stiff and tight, but her skin was healing.

The only other clothing in her backpack was an extra pair of socks. She yanked them on, then began to search for her shoes. She blinked back sudden hopeless tears when she realized Chris hadn't half trusted she would keep her promise. Or if he had, he'd already long since done something with her shoes to prevent her running away.

Panic gnawed at the edges of her determination. She took a deep breath and exhaled silently. Fear was good, panic was not. She had to keep herself under control or she would never manage this escape.

Where? Where would he hide her shoes? Maybe he hadn't hidden them at all. Maybe they were in the car. Maybe she'd taken them off herself. She shook her head and made her way silently over the hardwood floor to the door leading outside from the kitchen.

The sound of the rain was so much louder, so much more intense when she opened the door that she bit her lip and scooted through it before the noise awakened Chris. Shaking now, she almost tripped over her shoes, which sat alongside his boots on the stoop, protected from the rain.

She bent and started to put one on, then jerked it off and went back for her pack, for the shattered mirror that would serve as a constant reminder of what would happen if she didn't leave and leave now.

Crouched at the foot of the bed, she heard his troubled breathing. The scent of him on the bedclothes sapped her will to go. Her eyes darted to his powerful prostrate figure. Her heart twisted painfully in her chest. Her lungs seemed not to work.

She wanted to stay.

She wanted to know, for once and the first time in her life, what it was to make love with a man. What it was to be in love with a man like Christian Tierney and what it was to have such a man in love with her.

But she could not indulge such fanciful and dangerous desires. Recklessness was in her now, too, and she would have made love with him whether he loved her back or not, but *this* recklessness was born of needing more to do something, anything, to prevent him from putting himself in the line of fire again.

Winston Broussard would kill him.

Tears pricked at her eyelids. The thought of leaving him, of going it alone terrified her, but the consequences of staying terrified her more. She dared not risk another second of delay.

Her knees cracked when she arose. Holding her breath, praying Chris wouldn't wake, she grabbed up her clothes from the bathroom floor and stuffed them into her pack. She took several bath towels to cover her head and shoulders, then slipped through the back door again, this time closing it behind her. Sitting on the stoop, she put on her shoes and eyed the dark-colored Mustang.

Why hadn't she thought of it earlier? She didn't know.

She clamped down hard on the temptation to go back and find the keys. Every moment she delayed, every chance she took digging through Chris's things to find the keys while he slept, was a gamble she couldn't afford. All she needed was to get to the road, hitch a ride to a telephone and put in her call to Tafoya.

A few hours at most. She couldn't hide in the car, and by now, the authorities must be on the lookout for it. And if anyone knew to look for the Mustang, so did Broussard.

No. She would be far safer, far more likely to make it on foot.

Ignoring the fact that she was weakened from hours in bed, from the blood loss and having eaten almost nothing, she stood, flung her pack on her left shoulder and the towels over her head and shoulders, then plunged down the brick steps into the drenching rain.

She followed the heavily treed paved lane leading away from the house. Even though she kept to the side of the road under the partial protection of the trees, the going was brutal. Despite the barrier the leafy branches provided, the persistent downpour had saturated the grass and ground cover.

Every slippery, claustrophobic step defied her. Her heart pounded. Her calves burned. Thunder rumbled far away, but she could still feel the electricity in the air. And within minutes, the rain spilling through the cover of trees had drenched the towels covering her head. They became a leaden weight bearing down on her without giving her any protection.

She shivered hard, then cast them off and kept doggedly jogging.

Level for the first few minutes of her run, the grounds began to dip and climb in the rolling way of backwoods Massachusetts. Over and over again, she stumbled and fell, unable to see where she was going in the black night and dense, smothering rain.

Time and again, she got up and pushed herself on. Her clothes were soaked and heavy with mud. Whatever advantage she might have had from living at a higher altitude had vanished with her blood loss.

She lost track of the road. It had to be to her right, didn't it? Yes. It must. It had to be. She hadn't crossed the pavement, so the road must still be to her right. But that was only if her course had followed the road. Confusion came close to overwhelming her. She felt panicky and uncertain, disoriented and perilously close to tears.

She pulled herself together with a jerk and plunged to her right, crashing through a tangle of brambles and undergrowth. A deer startled from behind her, bolting within a few feet of her. She cried out, then lost her footing and took a treacherous slide down the steep terrain toward a brook swollen now to the edges of its banks by the hours of rain.

The jarring slide knocked the breath out her but she fought back and managed to grab and keep hold of a small shrub, then pulled herself back up a few feet from the cresting, roiling brook and clung to the trunk of a young tree.

Shivering so hard that her teeth chattered, she wrapped her arms around the tree and rested her forehead against its smooth, wet bark. Soaked to the skin and badly battered by her fall, tears welled in her eyes, hopelessness in her heart, and she began to cry.

She badly needed a break, but the rain kept coming down hard. Shoving her dripping hair out of her eyes, she wiped her face with the soggy sleeve of her sweater and forced herself to buck up one more time.

The more hopeless things became, the harder she would fight. Grit filled her. She would not give up. It would take more than the wretched cold or rain or black of night or all the mud in the commonwealth to keep her down.

She would have to climb back up the bank.

Then she heard it, all but obliterated by the swollen brook crashing against its banks. The low thrum of a car engine.

Her head came up, and she struggled to listen, to find its direction. A bird screeched and thunder rumbled far away, but she managed to hear the distinct sound of car tires splashing through the water on the road.

Relief coursed through her. She would make it now. Somehow, she would make her way to the roadside.

Eden stood and turned. Almost blinding her, the rain fell in sheets over her face, but she ignored it. She was going to make it. Hand over hand, ignoring the now-familiar pain in her shoulder, clinging to undergrowth and branches, she scrambled up the steep incline.

She would have made it, too, but either she misjudged the ledge or it collapsed beneath her. As her feet slid out from beneath her, she fell hard to the ground on her stomach. Crying out in shock, she lurched for a handhold, missed and began to plunge down the treacherous bank again when something clamped hold of her.

A man's hand. Chris Tierney's hand.

She screamed and jerked hard but he kept a firm grasp and sank to his butt on the ground. Planting his feet against oak saplings, he held on to her tightly enough to haul her back up the slippery slope between his legs. He had on nothing but his jeans and boots.

The solid, muscled wet wall of his chest mocked her heart. In the midst of the fiercest storm and black of night, in the midst of running from him so Broussard wouldn't kill him, all she wanted to do was give in to him and lay her head on his chest. Once. Just once.

"Let me go!" she cried fiercely.

"You promised, Eden."

Lightning split the sky again and thunder exploded, but neither matched the storm of fury in his eyes or the anger in his voice. He lifted her as if she weighed nothing at all and planted her hard on her backside with her body braced against a sturdy sapling.

His jaw went rigid. Steam rose from his back and shoulders. "You gave me your word."

Her heart hammered. "I changed my mind! Tierney, you have to let me go!"

"Tierney again?" he grated. "Lady, you are one cold-hearted selfish little bitch."

"You idiot...bastard...stupid man!" she cried. Rage tore through her, and lightning fast, she slapped his face. "Don't you dare judge me! Broussard will kill you," she shrilled, bordering so close to hysteria now that she hardly knew what she was saying. "He'll *kill* you!"

"No." He grabbed her wrist as fast, far more in control of himself than she was of herself, and he shook her. "No. He won't." His eyes glittered with a dark passion so furious it terrified her.

"Then someone else will! They *will*. His underlings...and if they don't—"

"Do you think I care? Do you think I give a good goddamn what happens to me afterward?"

"That's what you want?" Water streamed off her face, but whether tears or rain she couldn't tell. Her skin felt afire with her anger at him. "That's it?" she shrilled again.

"Eden, stop it!"

"No!" *She was completely, desperately, madly, profoundly in love with him when all he really wanted was a way out of his own pain?* "That's what you want, isn't it? To take out Broussard and get yourself murdered so I'm the one left alone again? You *miserable* excuse for a man!" she cried, tears streaming from her eyes. She tried to get to her feet, to lash out at him and escape, but he jerked her back down and cupped the back of her head with his hand, tightening his fingers in her hair.

"What are you saying, Eden? Spit it out."

"I'm saying I won't have it, Tierney! I'm saying I won't be left alone by you. I'm saying—" She broke off. His were fixed on her, staring at her as if he were seeing her for the first time. His brow was creased, almost in pain.

His beautiful dark eyelashes were wet with rain and she thought they were tears. Her throat constricted and she began to shake.

"Say it, Eden," he urged, his voice low and strained.

Her knees slid in the mud and she clung to him, but she was not so suddenly helpless as to refuse to meet his eyes when she laid herself bare.

She took off the backpack and hurled it under a bush. Her heart thundered, louder now in her ears than the real thing. "I'm saying…Christian Xavier Tierney, that I want to make love with you and I don't ever want to stop."

"Oh, my God, Eden. Eden." He shut his eyes, and the groan that came from deep in his chest stirred her blood beyond any sound she had ever heard. He fell back against the drenched undergrowth and pulled her down with him. "I want you, and want it never to stop."

Mouth open, he kissed her, drew her in, stroked her lips with his tongue, and Eden thought she would die with the keen, smothering pleasure of that kiss alone.

He held her face in his hands and moved his lips over every part of it, kissing her eyes, her forehead, sucking the rain from her cheeks and chin and neck, and when he brought his lips back to hers, her heart lurched painfully with sensations too new and intense and sharp and inciting to bear.

"We've only begun, Eden," he uttered harshly. She knew that what he said was true when he only had to stroke the side of her breast before her nipple puckered tight in a rocketing swell of pleasure so shattering and exquisite that it bordered on pain. "We have only begun."

In the torrential downpour with the roar of the swollen brook in her ears, she returned his kisses. Heat flared between them and the bitingly cold rain on her back and bottom and thighs made her crazy with need. She seemed driven, toward seeking to get closer, toward willing herself to be consumed in Christian Tierney's fire.

Kissing her, absorbing her, he slid his hands down her sides, lingering at the flattened swell of her breasts, but he wanted more and reached to pull off her sweater, to have no barriers between them.

"Let me." Her idyllic, sterile dreams of candlelight and violins and satin paled, fading to nothing. She pulled back and sat up, alive, electric with need and instinct and the power of her choice, to make love with this rugged, reckless lawman in this fearsomely elemental and primitive forest, beneath storm-blackened skies opening up in thunder and lightning and in torrents of rain.

She stripped the clinging, sodden sweater from her body. The drenching rain poured over her bare back and her small naked breasts and the ugly black stitches. Her nipples tightened into hardened buds, in the cold of the night air. She didn't know just how sensitized they were before he raised himself up on one elbow, touched her face with his fingers and then sipped the rain from one and then the other of her beaded nipples.

When his lips closed over one of them, desire exploded in her. Deep inside, her muscles clenched and throbbed, making her cry out. Her pelvis began to rock unwittingly and Chris drew her rhythmically deeper and deeper into his mouth, stroking her with his tongue, knowing now for himself that what she'd said was true.

Eden Kelley was untouched . . . and already, so soon, so sweetly, on the brink of her first climax.

His sex burgeoned painfully against his fly. His body hummed with incredible tension. She held his head to her breast and cried out again when the powerful sensations took her over the edge.

He grabbed the sweater she'd shed and laid it out before turning her on her back. Frantically, she lowered her jeans till she could spread her knees. Just as needful, he lowered his. When he entered her for the first time, when the pain receded and the pleasure washed over her in torrents, when he brought her again and again to spiraling, soaring heights, Eden was still mindful of the exquisite moment when she knew what it was to be taken care of and treasured and to know that wasn't necessarily a bad thing.

To know that once, she had belonged to Christian Tierney and he had belonged to her.

TIFFER BANCROFT was messing with the VCR, playing his little brother Jake's Power Rangers tape. At eleven, he thought they were as lame as all get-out, but Jake would whine his head off when the tape wasn't in the right place and that was just fine with Tiffer. Jake wasn't all that bad, but a little guerrilla action their mom would never believe Tiffer had done anyway wouldn't kill the little rug rat.

But when Tiffer heard his dad come in the back door off the garage, he grabbed the remote control, shut off the VCR fast and changed the channel to the morning news. His dad walked through the family room to the kitchen where his mom was making breakfast. Tiffer acted as if he was listening hard to the news, the only acceptable reason for the TV to be on in the Bancroft prison, and the only reason for not standing to attention when his dad walked into the room.

He didn't know what made his dad such a creep, but it didn't matter. Tiffer just steered clear. He was always teed off about something, especially when he came back from having been called out to the hospital in the middle of the night—like now.

His mom had been real jumpy since the day before yesterday. Usually, he didn't catch her puffing on a cigarette and he could never come up to her and make her jump out of her skin. He knew she didn't have eyes in the back of her head, but lots of the time, he could swear she did. But not in the past two days.

His old man was yelling about the alarm system being turned off at the eighth zone when the TV newsman started talking about that hospital in western New York. The news graphic snagged Tiffer's attention. It was the FBI seal superimposed over the federal building in Boston where his Uncle Chris worked. Tiffer paid attention because it was just like his dad to demand a full account of the news stories he'd seen over their meal. Something stupid about how what was good enough for the Kennedys was good enough for the Bancrofts.

Tiffer tuned in.

"The story just keeps growing more and more interesting. The hospital has been under a great deal of scrutiny in the past several weeks—first for the transfusion of a unit of donated blood to the wrong patient, then again ten days later when an elderly patient was found dead in a whirlpool bath. Now, as we reported on the ten o'clock news last night, a woman was admitted with a gunshot wound under a Jane Doe alias, which admission was then itself purged from the records of the hospital emergency room. For more details, let's go live now to our reporter on the spot. Thea?"

Yeah, Thea! Tiffer thought. Enough of the old fart....

"Last night, the FBI apparently took an interest in the bizarre claims made by an anonymous caller. This morning, the ER chief physician met with agents of the FBI. It's clear now that our first reports of last evening concerning

*a Jane Doe gunshot victim were accurate and provoked
this joint statement by the FBI and local police:*

*"'We believe that the identity of a witness relocated in
the Federal Witness Protection Program has been compromised. That witness is, in all likelihood, the Jane Doe
treated and released by this hospital for a gunshot wound
almost forty-eight hours ago. In the hopes of protecting the
witness from further incident, the physician in charge
made the decision to purge all records of her admission
here. We appreciate that gesture.*

*'However, the witness is now believed to be in the cus-
tody of United States Deputy Marshal Christian Tierney.'"*

A photo of his uncle flashed on the screen. Tiffer sat up,
excited. "Mom, listen to this!"

His dad raised his voice, something lame about Tiffer
coming to the kitchen if he wanted to talk to his mother.
Secretly, in his lap, he flipped his dad the bird. It was apparently all right for *him* to yell. But Tiffer went from
thinking it cool that his uncle was on TV to being freaked
out when he heard what Thea-the-babe newswoman said
next.

*"Tierney is believed to have taken this witness hostage
after a shoot-out in Jackson Hole, Wyoming, where he
appropriated a U.S. government jet to make his escape
with the witness. He is acting outside his authority and is
urged to return the witness to protective custody and face
the unofficial charges.*

*"An all points bulletin has been put out for a 1985 ma-
roon Ford Mustang. Tierney must be considered armed
and dangerous. Information leading to his whereabouts
and/or the whereabouts of the Jane Doe gunshot victim,
is being sought and a reward offered."*

"Liars!" Tiffer snarled, totally disgusted they would say those things. His uncle would never do anything like they said. Tiffer turned off the set and threw down the remote control. His mom called him to breakfast. He didn't know what to do. He didn't believe those creeps on TV, but he didn't know what to believe.

He went to the table and jerked out his chair. His mom shot him a warning look while she put a plate of toast and another filled with scrambled eggs on the table.

He glared at the food. He didn't even want to eat. He hated eggs. He wanted to go kick his soccer ball through the stupid garage door. How could they say that crap about Chris? He ought to sue their pants off.

His dad didn't even notice how pissed Tiffer was. *He* was still going off about the alarm system being useless if people couldn't remember to keep it turned on . . . which was when he knew why his mom was so jumpy.

She had turned it off on purpose.

He choked down a few bites of egg and asked to be excused. He had to get to his uncle Chris before his dad figured it out, too.

Chapter Twelve

Chris awoke from the best sleep he'd had in two years to the most gut-sick, hollow feeling he'd ever known. Curled against his body, Eden was shaking him, her beautiful sleepy-eyed face frozen in anxiety.

He stiffened. "What is it?"

"Listen."

Stock-still, he heard a pinging sound, a pebble striking the window.

He swore, trying not to overreact, trying to convince himself that in these few hours of letting down his guard, he hadn't sealed his own and Eden Kelley's death warrants.

He touched her face. If he never saw that kind of resignation in her wide, stormy gray eyes again it would be too soon. He murmured softly, encouraging her to roll off the other side of the bed and stay there. Another pebble hit and bounced off the window.

He went for his gun, rolled off his side and slipped on his boxers. Crouching low to the floor, he moved into the kitchen, then rose slowly in the corner beside the door. Twisting the doorknob, he shoved the door open so that it banged against the wall.

He sank down against the other wall. Crouching on the cold tile floor, he worked the action on the Mac 10 and aimed with both hands. He stretched out his arms and waited.

He heard footsteps approaching warily. The first thing he saw was a sneaker, then a stick-thin leg, finally a knobby knee.

"Uncle Chris?" came a scared voice. "Is that you?"

Relief poured through him and his eyes fell closed for the briefest interlude. An assassin was hardly likely to announce his presence or intentions with pebbles bouncing benignly off the windows, but Chris couldn't afford to take anything lightly.

He disarmed the automatic and came upright in one swift, effortless motion. Tiffer Bancroft stood on the stoop, trying to see in. Relief swam through Chris and he let out his breath.

"It's all right, Eden," he called softly. Then, "Tiff. You scared the crap out of me, kid."

"Chris!" The boy's face lit up when he heard Chris, and he grinned widely when he saw him, but then the pleasure disintegrated. He bounded over and gave Chris a fierce hug. "Chris, you gotta get out of here. There's stuff on TV. Is there some lady here? There's this hospital and the cops and they know you ran away a couple days ago and they're saying—"

"Whoa, wait a minute." Chris took his nephew by his narrow shoulders. Tension knotted the boy's small, immature features, and the tendons of his thin little neck were stretched tight. For a moment, Chris felt violently angry at himself for exposing his nephew, this *child,* to this sordid mess. "Tiffer, listen to me. Does your mom know you're down here?"

His dark eyes wide, Tiffer swallowed and shook his head. "No, but—"

"Your dad?"

"No," Tiffer said, "but Chris, he's pissed about the alarm system being off, and then I heard on the news—"

"What's on the news?"

"About you and that lady, and I figured out that Mom turned it off on purpose and if my dad hears that—"

"Tiffer," Chris interrupted, giving his nephew's shoulders a small shake. "What are they saying on TV? Exactly. Can you remember?"

"I don't . . ." Tiffer gulped and he stared at Chris, too scared just then to remember.

Wrapped in the white terry-cloth robe, Eden scooted around the door into the kitchen. "You're scaring him, Chris."

His head jerked around. His eyes swept over her. Memories of their lovemaking made his chest tighten. She looked pale but no longer scared . . . and incredibly lovely.

He knew she was right. He knew his voice sounded far harsher than he meant it to be, but Tiffer was eleven and he could go off half-cocked for twenty minutes without getting to the point. Right now, he was afraid of what his dad might do.

Chris couldn't afford to ignore Ed Bancroft's ire, either. He would assume the worst-case scenario and turn his knowledge of Chris's whereabouts over to the authorities in a New York minute. But Chris and Eden were in an even more deadly position if, because of the news reports, Winston Broussard had any idea where to find them.

But Eden was right. He was upsetting Tiff, and that was the last thing he wanted to happen.

"Tiff, this is . . ." His eyes met and locked with Eden's. "This is my friend. This is Tiffer Bancroft. My nephew.

Catherine's sister, Margo, is his mom." He watched Eden's eyes widen, watched her glance uncertainly down at her hands. He wished he could tell her how it was between him and Margo, but that would have to wait.

"The gunshot lady?" Tiffer asked, his eyes darting to her.

"Yes. But I'm better now," she answered softly.

Tiffer blew out a breath, calmed a little, Chris thought, by Eden's gentle reassurance. His child's lips were still pressed thin.

"Tiff, man, I need to know what they said on television. Start at the beginning and just say what you remember. Better sit down now."

The boy nodded and went over to a chair. He had on one of Chris's old hockey-club shirts, and it covered his shorts.

He recited what he could recall of the news clip. "They said the hospital had a gunshot lady and that they let her go. They said it was good the hospital didn't blab about it 'cuz she's a protected witness—like in the movies. Is that right?"

Chris nodded. "Yeah, like that. Did they say which hospital, Tiff?"

The boy nodded. "I can't remember exactly, though." His brow puckered. A lock of his dark brown hair fell in his face. He shook it back. "Western something? In New York?"

Chris bit back a curse. Dragging in a deep breath, he exchanged glances with Eden. "That's right, Tiff. They got it right."

"But not all right," Tiffer objected. His freckles stood out and his fists clenched. "That bitch said—"

"Lady, you mean," Chris warned.

Tiff's little jaw tightened. "She isn't a lady, Chris. She said—"

"You know what I mean. Men don't call women things like that, or hit them or—"

"Chris, leave it be," Eden interrupted softly. "I'm sure Tiffer knows that."

Tiffer looked from Chris to Eden, then back. He was old enough to pick up the vibes between them, probably old enough to figure out what they meant, as well. He wasn't allowed to comment on things like that in his father's presence, even Margo's, but he'd always had the straight poop from his uncle Chris—one of the myriad reasons Ed Bancroft detested him.

So Chris could see the question lurking in his nephew's eyes. "Tiff, look." He glanced at Eden. "Neither of us knows how things are going to work out right now. I'm in some serious trouble, and there are people trying to kill this lady, so a lot of problems have to be ironed out before I start thinking about...other things. You following me?"

"Yeah." Chris's answer seemed to put that whole guy-to-guy female issue to rest for Tiffer. "But they've got things screwed up. They said you're acting out...I mean...like, on your own, and that you took her hostage." His head bobbed toward Eden. "They say you're armed and dangerous." He snorted. "Sure. Dangerous for wise guys. What do they know?"

"Yeah, what do they know?" Chris gave Tiffer's head a Dutch rub and the two of them roughhoused for just a minute—another one of Bancroft's pet peeves violated.

Chris drew a deep breath and Tiffer sat back on the chair. Eden leaned against the doorjamb, watching him interact with Tiffer with a longing so naked it hit Chris like a blow to his chest. But there were also deep shadows beneath her eyes, and the implications of what Tiffer had heard were not lost on her.

The guest house was surrounded on all sides by dense woods, and every window covering was drawn. Nevertheless, Chris was unnerved. Given the news reports, if Broussard didn't know exactly where they were, he must still have it narrowed down now to the radius of a few hundred miles.

But while Chris had that to consider, it wasn't right that Tiffer had to hear or deal with this. That he had to take sides and feel as if he had to warn Chris about his dad. The boy's loyalty touched Chris, but Tiff needed to understand that even Chris didn't believe what was happening and what he was doing were the way things should be.

"Tiff, listen. I didn't take this lady hostage, but I'm not doing things the way they should be done. That's because I don't want to see her or anyone else get hurt. And it's not the way things should be done for your mom or you to lie to your dad."

"But—" Tiffer's hands flailed "—just because he doesn't like you—"

"I know," Chris said. "But that's for your dad and me to solve when somebody else isn't going to be hurt by it— so I'm going to ask you a big favor."

"What?"

He shouldn't have put it like that; his nephew thought he was going to get to do something exciting to help. "You need to go to school, Tiff, and act as if you never saw us. As if you haven't seen me in a long time."

"Who cares?" the boy demanded. "I—"

"Somebody might, Tiff," Chris interrupted firmly. "They might get the idea I was here, and that could be real trouble." In a school yard, it was vastly unlikely, but there were no certainties with Winston Broussard. "You don't talk to strangers and you act as if you never saw me, okay?"

Tiffer's neck bowed. He didn't say anything.

"Is your dad still at home, Tiff?" Eden asked.

The boy looked at her, then shyly, self-conscious, turned away. "Nah. He's gone. I turned off the zone again, but he left already."

Chris socked him man to man on the shoulder. "Are you going to miss the school bus?"

Tiffer nodded. "If I don't run." He looked at Chris's gun. "Uncle Chris, can't I stay? I could help you—"

"Tiff." Chris grabbed him up in a bear hug and Tiff clung hard to his neck. "I need you to cover my butt here, buddy. Is your lunch outside?"

"In my pack." The boy's chin quivered, only barely, but it embarrassed him. "I gotta go." He bolted out of Chris's arms and through the door, but he ducked back in. A tear was running down his face. "They know about the Mustang," he warned fiercely. "And they got an APB out."

Then he was gone.

Chris slumped against the wall, staring down at the terra-cotta tiles, his jaw clenched. Eden swallowed the lump of emotion in her throat.

"He idolizes you, doesn't he?"

"Much to his father's disgust."

"He's wrong."

Chris cocked a brow. "Tiff or his dad?"

She gave him a warning look, but she had to smother a smile. "You know what I mean, Chris. Does Tiff have brothers or sisters?"

"One. A baby brother called Jake. Not much of a baby anymore. The little kid's on hockey skates."

"And they belong to . . . Catherine's sister?"

Chris nodded. "Margo." He met her gaze. "I have a lot of friends, Eden—"

"I didn't mean—"

"Margo is the only one who knew about Catherine's little flings." He smiled bitterly. "She told me the day I married her little sister that I was setting myself up for one killer heartbreak. I was just . . . cocksure enough, I guess, to think I could keep Catherine happy all by myself."

Eden didn't know what to say. She couldn't imagine how different her life might have been if she'd had Catherine's choices instead of her own.

Chris had made love to her with every part of his being, with his mouth and his large, square hands, with his heart, his sex and his soul, and if the devil himself had offered her the chance to marry and be faithful to this man and to have his babies and raise them on skates, she would surely have made any bargain.

But all she could have of him was what he had given her last night because Catherine still lurked in his heart . . . or the memory of what he'd wanted her to be.

She couldn't dwell on that, or even regret it. Christian Tierney was the man he was, and the lover he was, because of what he'd been through. And the gift he had given her last night, the sensation however fleeting, of *belonging,* was all she had ever wanted.

She took a deep breath and looked straight at Chris. "Do you think Broussard knows all this by now? About the hospital and the car?"

"He knows," Chris answered grimly.

"Then we have to get out of here, Chris. Before we put that child's life in danger. And Jake's and Margo's."

"I know."

"Even her husband." A sudden thought struck her and she shuddered. "What chance is there that if Tiffer heard the news and put two and two together, that his father won't do the same?"

"None." Chris scraped his whiskers with his knuckles. "He spends ten to twelve hours a day in surgery, but if he figures it all out and calls the FBI between cases and tells them he believes we were here..." He didn't finish the thought. Eden knew as well as he did that Broussard was imminently capable of biting the hand that fed him the information. Of killing them all in punishment for harboring Eden Kelley, of aiding and abetting the flight of his property.

Chapter Thirteen

"I'm going to have to talk to him. And we need to make your call to see if Judith Cornwallis is okay."

Remembering the shattered mirror and the bullet lodged in the silver backing of Judith's mirror, Eden's chest tightened. Blinking back tears, she nodded. "Let's do it."

She dressed in her still-damp jeans and sweatshirt, then, along with Chris, plunged into thoroughly cleaning the Bancroft guest house, which included wiping fingerprints off every imaginable surface. Her damp, dirty clothes were a constant annoyance. She longed for a shower and fresh clothing. But there was a mood between them that sent her heart soaring. An intimacy in sharing domestic chores together. Occasional, not-so-accidental touches. Lingering looks.

A fierce and tender awareness that made soggy, filthy clothes unnoticeable.

When they were done restoring the small guest house to order, Eden showed him Judith's heirloom mirror and the bullet lodged in the silver frame. Grimly, he searched for the bullet hole, and found it concealed by a side-to-back seam and the natural folds of the supple leather. The bullet had also torn through a piece of linen that Eden had been working in a needlepoint design.

She behaved matter-of-factly, as if none of it really counted. He called her on it.

"It matters, Chris," she admitted. "I ran away last night because I found the mirror like that, all broken to pieces."

He let her off the hook. She'd had no more than a few moments back in that old woman's cabin to gather together the things that were important to her, so he wasn't fooled about the other things, either. He knew these were her prized possessions. A set of thimbles, needles. Her needlepoint. The mirror.

And a few delicate, exquisite pieces of underwear.

He replaced the mirror in the pack and put it down on the kitchen counter. He turned and, leaning against the edge, caught her wrist and pulled her into his arms.

Eden stilled. The experience was still so fresh, their lovemaking still so keen in her mind that the scent of his skin and warmth of his body made her insides ache with longing. Her eyes were at a level with his Adam's apple. She wasn't tiny but she felt delicate and womanly in his arms.

She let her gaze wander slowly upward, over the shadow of a cleft in his chin and his unshaven whiskers to his lips. Her mouth watered. His breath warmed her nose. Her hands lay flat on his pectorals and she stared at his parted lips. She rose up on tiptoe and touched her mouth to his.

He growled fiercely and pulled her hard against his body. The power of his response swept through her like wildfire, lit by her, consuming them both. He wanted her, loved her, and knowing that inflamed her more than even his kiss.

More than when he opened his mouth and tasted her lips and her tongue.

More than the arousing sensation of the edges of his teeth gently raking her lips and cheeks and the flashpoint of the tender flesh below her jaw.

"Eden. Eden," he murmured thickly. "Feel what you do to me."

Her pelvis rocked back, seeking him. His hands were all over her, beneath her sweatshirt, cupping her breasts, his thumbs flicking her sensitized, hardened nipples. A tide broke loose inside her and she cried out. She never noticed that when Chris stiffened, withdrew his hands and held her hips it wasn't to torment her with pleasure in some other way.

"Banging a protected witness now, Tierney?" a man's voice taunted. "That's got to be a new low, even for you."

Dazed, confused, Eden turned her head toward the furious voice. In the kitchen doorway stood a tall, impeccably dressed man with razor-cut hair, razor-sharp creases in his slacks and a mean, razor-slashing look in his eyes. And he stood there aiming a double-barreled shotgun.

Chris closed his arms protectively around her. "For an educated man, you have a filthy mind, Ed."

"You stupid son of a bitch," Ed Bancroft sneered nastily. "You kidnap a woman, hijack a plane, steal a car, come onto *my property,* proceed to shack up with her, and *I'm the one with the filthy mind?*"

The look that came over Chris's face frightened Eden. Before he could respond, she touched his biceps and stepped back, facing Ed. "Everything Chris has done has been to protect me, Dr. Bancroft—"

"Does that include the screwing?" he inquired, exuding a terrible disrespect.

In one lightning movement, Chris's left hand darted out and grabbed the barrel of the shotgun, disarming his angry and spite-filled brother-in-law. "Watch your mouth, Ed, or so help me God, I'll rearrange it for you."

For an instant, fear played in Ed's eyes. "Fine, Tierney. Add felony menacing to your laundry list. I'm going to go call the authorities." He turned on his heel and nearly collided with a small, out-of-breath blond woman who appeared suddenly in the doorway behind him.

Margo. Chris's sister-in-law looked so much like Catherine Tierney that Eden's heart plummeted. Her fingers flew to stifle the cry on her lips.

"Margo." Chris conveyed a hundred apologies in his voice. He turned. "This is the woman I told you about. Eden Kelley."

She gave a wavery, stunted smile. "Ed, please," she begged. Her eyes darted to Eden, then back to Chris. "I'm the one who's sorry. I tried to stop him, Chris, but—"

"And I asked you to stay in the house," Ed snapped.

"If you would just listen—"

He waved a hand dismissively. "I've listened to your excuses for Tierney for fifteen years, Margo. This is beyond the pale—"

"That's true, Ed," Chris interrupted. "And I'm sorry. But I'm going to have to ask you not to make any calls."

Ed gave an icy stare. "Ask, Tierney, but what you want has very little to do with what actions I take." He took Margo by the elbow. "Turn around and leave here with me right now," he ordered her. "I have a civic obligation to fulfill."

"Think again, Ed," Chris warned softly.

His brother-in-law turned back. "What did you say?"

"I said, think again, Ed," Chris repeated. "I don't give a damn what else you do, or when you do it, or if you file suit. Just don't make that call."

"You *have* completely lost it, haven't you? What is there to prevent me? What will you do, Tierney? Shoot me in the back with my wife looking on?"

"Oh, Ed, stop it!" Margo snapped, jerking her arm away from him. "You selfish prig! Isn't there even one compassionate bone in your body? Why won't you just leave it alone!"

"Dr. Bancroft, please," Eden interceded. "You'll put yourself and your family in terrible danger."

"What danger?" he demanded.

"The man who wants her dead is not a forgiving sort, Ed," Chris answered reasonably. "Winston Broussard. Remember the name? He deals illegal arms, Ed. He hired an assassin to take out the only witness against him, and the assassin got Catherine. He kills without compunction."

Chris droned relentlessly on. "I don't like it any better than you, Ed, but you'll have to swallow your fancy-assed indignation and trust me." He cracked open the shotgun and emptied out the cartridges, then handed the weapon back to Ed. "You don't want this man to know she's been here, and sooner or later, if you've told the cops, he will know about it."

"Fine." The blood had all but drained from Ed's face. He raised a finger and pointed at Chris. "But I want you to stay away from my son. I want you to stop calling my wife. And I want you off my property inside an hour."

THEY TOOK OFF THROUGH the backwoods of the Bancroft estate for three or four miles. Beyond the junction of 202 and 20 in Westfield, holding hands, ducking through back alleys, they walked another couple of miles to the place of an old colleague of Chris's.

J. J. Gelham was a former legal counsel in the Boston district U.S. marshal's office whose chief delight in life had been finding a way to let the marshals do what they had to do without running afoul of the letter of the law.

A small man, blond, with a wide brow and balding head, Gelham lived alone in an isolated spot on the outskirts of town. He wrote opinion pieces for periodicals now, and repaired and renovated vintage Karmann Ghias as a hobby.

The former attorney was wheelchairbound. Chris had told her that Gelham had lost the use of his legs in a car bombing. He despised most lawyers. He knew more ghastly lawyer jokes than any stand-up comedian. According to Chris, after the bombing, Gelham had decided that life was too short to spend the rest of his life facilitating criminal arrests. He'd quit, and mostly he wasn't much for company, even old friends.

Or maybe, especially old friends. But he was more than happy to sell Chris a little hunter green Karmann Ghia that Eden liked for a couple thousand bucks, which was about all he had left of Catherine's life-insurance payout.

Eden offered to show Gelham how to make some repair stitches on an original piece of upholstery he'd been working on when she and Chris had arrived. Chris went inside to call Margo and make sure things had gone okay between her and Ed after their encounter.

When Chris didn't return for a while and the repair was done, Gelham rolled to the miniature refrigerator in his impeccable garage and pulled out a couple cans of root beer and gave one to Eden.

She cracked hers open gratefully and sat on a tool chest. In peaceful moments like this, it seemed almost impossible to believe that somewhere out there, Broussard was just waiting for one more chance. And remember that he would never stop coming after her.

Gelham looked at her. "It appears the two of you are in some serious doodoo. I don't imagine you would deny that."

Eden swallowed. "No. We're in a lot of trouble on my account."

"Winston Broussard...unless I miss my guess?"

She shivered, then met Gelham's flinty gaze. "You know who I am?"

"I do."

"How long have you been gone from the Marshal Service?"

"Six years. However, I keep abreast of things. Tierney got drunk here with me one night not long after he put Catherine in the ground. Told me about her. I doubt he even remembers the occasion. He never spilled his guts about her before that night. Not once." He took a slug of his soda. "Tell you what," he went on. "I've got a fairly good idea of what Chris intends to do. I'd kill the S.O.B. myself were I in Chris's shoes. Although I believe there are better ways of handling such things."

Eden looked down at her hands. Gelham seemed to be expecting her to say something, maybe confirm for him what Chris was planning, both to kill Broussard and get out of the "serious doodoo." She wouldn't betray Chris's trust, and so she said nothing.

Gelham swallowed the rest of his root beer in a single long pull and crushed the can in one hand. He nodded slowly at her, as if approving her allegiance as much as her silence. "Personally, I'd rather see Broussard do hard time in a maximum security pen where he can get a substantial grip on what it is to be preyed upon."

Eden cleared her throat. "Did he have anything to do with the car bombing?"

"No." Gelham wheeled around and lofted the remains of his can into a recycling bin, then angled back. He blinked. His brown eyes gleamed. "At least, nothing that I know of, though he may very well have supplied the terrorists with their nasty little hardware." He reflected silently a moment, then smiled faintly and went on. "It does not require a personal vendetta, Ms. Kelley, for me to wish quite fervently that Winston Broussard experience that particular brand of powerlessness every day for the rest of his miserable, offensive life. And I think it can be done."

Eden crossed her arms over her chest. "How?"

"The best defense is always a good offense, Ms. Kelley," the former legal counsel answered. He let her ponder his reply before continuing. "As we speak, Broussard is doubtlessly smiling himself sick he's so enamored with the chase. The more you run, the harder you run, the better he likes it."

Eden said nothing, but her expression must have conveyed her certainty that what Gelham imagined of Broussard was more than likely.

Gelham leaned forward, his voice harshly urgent. "*Don't wait for Broussard to come after you.* Go after him. Enlist David Tafoya to your cause. Go in wired and get him to admit he paid good money to incompetent fools to kill you once and for all."

Eden shook her head. "Broussard is too smart to make such a foolish mistake, Mr. Gelham. Much too smart."

"I'm certain he believes he is."

"But?" she prompted.

"He is not a fool, but you have an edge. An...advantage he cannot overcome."

"What's that?"

"Winston Broussard is a moral cretin." Gelham threw an arm over the back of his wheelchair. "He believes in voodoo. And he's obsessed with you, Ms. Kelley. Surely you can find opportunity in such twisted passion."

Eden shuddered. The thought of going anywhere near Winston Broussard again made her stomach clench painfully. But perhaps that was exactly Gelham's point. So long as she ran from him, Broussard was in power anyway. "If you believe this will work, Mr. Gelham, why aren't you trying to convince Chris?"

"Because, Ms. Kelley," Gelham responded, "Christian Tierney is not in love with me."

AFTER CHRIS'S conversation with Margo, he came to get Eden to place her call to Britta Nielsen in New York.

She went with Chris to J. J. Gelham's study. Done in native rock and stained hardwood, the interior of the house was darkly handsome. The mahogany desk gleamed. A thin manuscript was placed precisely on one corner, a telephone and fax on the other.

Eden sat in the specially made executive chair that facilitated Gelham's access from his wheelchair, then dialed the Manhattan area code and telephone number from memory. She identified herself as Lisa Hollister. Britta's secretary put her on hold, warning the wait could be several minutes.

Keeping the receiver to her ear, Eden turned to Chris. "How did it go with Margo and her husband? Will she be all right?"

"Ed had a 9:00 a.m. surgery scheduled. He apparently left as soon as they got back to the house." Chris scrubbed his eyes with his fists. "I can't blame him for believing I put his family at risk."

Eden couldn't, either. Her cheek cramped. "But does he understand that they're at an even greater risk if he calls the authorities? He doesn't know Broussard. Most ordinary people would have a very hard time believing men like Broussard exist outside of the movies."

Chris agreed. "He knows, though, Eden. Anyway, he knew after Catherine was blown away." He stared out the window a moment, then took a deep breath. "He would still get off on seeing me toasted, but he's smart. He realizes the stakes are too high. I don't know." He shrugged. "Maybe he thinks when all this is over, I'll get what's coming to me anyway."

"What about the Mustang?"

"Margo is taking care of it. She promised to call the doctor and tell her where the car is. Margo thought she could convince the doctor just to leave the car for a while, knowing it's being looked after—and not in some potentially disastrous high-speed chase with a madman at the wheel."

Eden gave a smile and started to make some smart remark when Judith's literary agent came on the line. "Lisa, my dear. How are you? How is Judith? Nothing is wrong, I hope?"

"Hello, Britta," Eden responded. "I just wanted to check with you. I had to leave Jackson Hole unexpectedly. Judith promised to fax you a letter—to let you know how she is. I was hoping you could tell me."

"Eden, I'm sorry, but I haven't received anything from Judith. Does she even know how to fax? How extraordinary!"

Eden's heart sank. Fear for the dear old woman flooded her. She held the receiver with both hands, as if she could hear better, hear something else. "Britta, are you sure? Could you just check with your secretary?"

"There's no need of that as I'm quite certain. Lisa, dear, you're giving me a bit of a fright. I thought you were living permanently with Judith. What's going on?"

Eden began to shake. "Britta, it's very complicated. Let me call you back."

"Please do. I'm very concerned—"

"So am I—but I will find out and call you back. Goodbye." Eden shakily replaced the receiver. "Chris, I have a very bad feeling about this."

He gritted his teeth, then snatched up the receiver and dialed an operator. "This is a police emergency, Operator. Please connect me to the Park County Sheriff's Department in Wyoming." He punched the speakerphone button and waited, saying nothing, knowing Eden wouldn't tolerate empty reassurances, wanting badly to find some way to assuage the guilt out of her glittering gray eyes. "What's the sheriff's name, Eden?"

"Ross something." She combed anxiously through her hair. "No. Donald Ross."

Chris ID'd himself as a United States deputy marshal and his call as an emergency, then asked for Ross. He repeated his introduction without naming himself. The sheriff acknowledged that much, but Eden could hear antagonism ringing in Ross's voice.

Chris cut straight to the point. "Sir, we're in custody of the relocated witness who was living with Judith Cornwallis. Have you seen or spoken to her in the past few days?"

"No, sonny, I haven't, and let me tell you why. You federal yo-yos left an unholy mess. One of my men is dead, and Miz Cornwallis's cabin went up like a tinderbox. You fellas come back here anytime soon and I'll personally kick your butts to hell and back. Am I making myself crystal clear to you, *sir?*"

Chris made some conciliatory noises Eden couldn't even understand as words. Shock-ridden, she stared at the speakerphone, listening to the sarcastic and angry disembodied voice of the Park County sheriff, a man who'd been a friend to Judith for many years. She felt as if some internal flame, some essential light she depended upon to carry her through, had guttered out. But the sheriff wasn't quite done even when she thought she'd heard the worst of it.

"I've just had word your own damn pilot got himself whacked."

"Dan Haggerty?" Chris choked out, the color draining from his face.

"That's the one. So you save your sorries, sonny. Sorry don't get it. Don't come close. You tell your witness I said she'd be better off waving a red flag at a goddamned bull moose than hanging with you boys."

Chapter Fourteen

Eden rose and turned and fled. The guilt inside her turned to a solid, freezing chunk of ice in her chest. Her blood ran as cold as a winter slurry. She ran, gasping for air, and ran still farther, out the door, behind J. J. Gelham's house as far as her legs would carry her. She came to a pond surrounded by oak trees, dotted with lily pads. She dashed headlong into the pond, crying, splashing the still, stagnant water, hoping wildly that the pond would swallow her alive.

But the water rose no higher than her hips, and by the time she knew it would take sinking to the bottom to drown her pain, Chris had grabbed hold of her.

Standing thigh-deep in the lily pond, she clung to him, choking on her sobs, on the guilt, on Chris's own angry words in the Jackson airport. *Listen to me. Listen well. Get this, Eden Kelley. Try to remember. Innocent people die when you're around.* "It's true," she cried. "It's true."

Chris didn't know exactly what her cries meant, but he could guess. The rage inside him matched her pain. He knew it like an old enemy, like the familiar throb inside his head. He held her and stroked her hair and let her rage burn itself out. His own legs and feet grew numb with water that wasn't so cold but cold enough to sap whatever resilience was left in her. He lifted her from the pond and carried her to the house. Grim-faced, J. J. Gelham led the way to a hot shower, then laid out clothes of his own and discreetly wheeled himself elsewhere.

Crying softly and as lifeless as a rag doll, Eden let him strip off her sodden clothes, and then he shed his own and helped her into the shower. She felt so small and delicate, her flesh like a newborn's. He soaped himself, soaped her, praying with all his withered faith that the shower would wash away the horror and somehow restore Eden's spirit.

Torn up inside by her bottomless sorrow, he framed her face in his hands and kissed her and they clung to each other for a long time. After a while, he got out and left her standing alone beneath the needle spray of hot water.

At some point, Eden didn't know when, perhaps when her fingers brushed the stitches beneath her collarbone, a cold fury began to displace the guilt and sorrow, and she knew she could never run and hide again, no matter what. For Broussard to attempt to pick her off every time she surfaced for air was one thing, even if, in the end, he succeeded in riddling her body with bullets. But for him to cold-bloodedly murder all the innocent bystanders in her life was quite another.

Gelham had suggested Broussard *was* still vulnerable because of his obsession with her. She knew in her heart that must be true. There could be no other explanation. Broussard dealt internationally in illicit arms. He could have found complete safety and supported his insatiable appetite for fine living in high style in any number of exotic foreign locales. If he'd left the country, he need never have worried about her or prosecution for trafficking in illegal arms ever again.

If it was arrogance on his part to stay, it *must* be his overweening obsession with her that made him send his assassins to punish the people who'd kept her alive.

For murdering Judith and Dan Haggerty, she would make him pay or die trying.

She shampooed and rinsed out her hair, then stepped out of the steam-filled shower and toweled herself dry.

Gelham had left on his bed a pair of his own designer jeans and a beautiful navy-and-gray mohair sweater. The jeans, somehow, fit her perfectly. When she emerged from the master bedroom, Chris and Gelham were putting together ham sandwiches.

Standing at a cutting board on the kitchen counter, Chris stopped slicing the meat. In his wheelchair, spreading mayonnaise and mustard on slices of bread, Gelham gave a low, appreciative whistle. "I had no idea my jeans could look so good."

A tear spilled over her lashes. Anything either one of them said might have earned what must be her last possible tear, but a compliment raised fresh guilt. She wiped away the tear and nodded.

Chris cleared his throat. "Are you okay?"

She lifted her chin. "Of course."

"Eden..." Gelham began. "May I call you that? Eden?" When she nodded, he went on. "Eden, you're going to have to lighten up. None of this is your fault."

"I may not have pulled the trigger or set the fire, Mr. Gelham, but the people who tried to help me are dead. And if it's the last thing I do, I will see Broussard in that little piece of hell you described."

THEY SAT DOWN to the sandwiches and glasses of a merlot wine and waited until dark to drive away from Gelham's place in the tiny hunter green Karmann Ghia.

Chris took the secondary highway running parallel to I-90 headed toward Boston. Though Eden knew he was uneasy, she put off telling him what Gelham had suggested until they were well under way.

Not surprisingly, he disagreed. Violently disagreed. He whipped the steering wheel around, spinning the little Ghia off the highway onto a damned convenient side road, jammed the pedal to the metal and tore through a couple miles of dense, black-as-coal forest.

He spilled out of the Ghia and came around to her door, hauled her by the wrist out of the low-slung car until she stood toe-to-toe with him. Even then he didn't let go. "What the hell are you thinking?" he demanded. "What makes you so damned stubborn?"

Her chin shot up defiantly. "Self-preservation," she snapped. "And don't waste your time thinking you can intimidate me out of what I'm choosing of my own free will to do."

"Broussard will make hash of your free will, Eden," he barked. Anger roiled inside him, clawing at him. The last thing he wanted to do was cram down Eden Kelley's throat the fact that there was nothing she could do to save herself. "He will chew you up and spit you out in little pieces and you'll be lucky if you even know what hit you."

"That's ridiculous," she uttered fiercely. "He's a coward who has never once come after me himself." She jerked her wrist, trying to free herself but she could never overcome his strength, and he didn't release her. "Let me go, Chris."

He released her and swung away, jabbing his hands into his pockets, yelling at her now. "Do you think Broussard survives dealing illegal weapons to terrorists because he's a coward?"

"Of course not," she shouted back, catching his arm, trying in vain to make him face her. "That's not the point and you know it! When it comes to me, to dealing with *me*, he's vulnerable."

"Oh, yeah," he sneered, pacing in the tangled grass beneath a thick canopy of trees. "Winston Broussard is a regular soft touch when it comes to you. How naive do you want to be about this, Eden? Tell me that," he demanded, wagging a finger under her nose. "You want to get in and have me drive you right up to his front door tonight? Really take him by surprise?"

"What I want is to use whatever slim advantage I have!" Her hands balled into fists. She wanted to lash out at him, to haul off and hit him. Hot tears pricked at her lids because he stubbornly refused to understand. "Get this through your thick, macho, *lawman* skull, Chris Tierney. There's a reason why he never touched me—"

"Because he wanted something untainted in his miserable, misbegotten existence?" Chris gibed.

"That's exactly right," she returned, fighting tears, fighting the pounding in her head. "Because he *is* vulnerable to me. Because deep inside, all Winston Broussard craves is a little redemption."

"Oh, that's rich, Eden," he mocked.

She shook her head. "It's the only thing that makes any sense. Even your friend, Gelham, could see that. I want this to end, Chris, and if that means exploiting Broussard's twisted need to have me around, then I'll do it." She took a deep breath, trying to calm herself. "I don't want to live like this anymore, and I'll do whatever I have to do, with or without you, to make it all go away."

"Broussard has to be dead and buried for this bloodbath to stop, Eden, and you know it."

"And you're still willing to play executioner?" she demanded right in his face.

"As willing as you are to play the virgin sacrifice," he taunted cruelly. "Baby, it's too late for that, and don't think Broussard won't smell it on you."

"You bastard!" she hissed. "Don't you dare cheapen what we did, what we had, like that. Is that what making love to me was all about, Chris? Inventing an excuse to go off and murder Broussard? Can you do that?"

He cocked his jaw and stood staring bleakly at the ground. Where his heart should have been, there was only the burning coal of pain instead. He'd been avoiding the question—avoided even asking himself the question—like the plague. He had no answer, and she knew it. He believed with all his heart that Broussard could not be stopped in any way short of his death. But she knew there were his two nephews he cared for too much to get himself killed or sent to the slammer for life—and that he was in love with her. He knew her question came down to whether he would flush all that down the toilet, because that's what would happen if he took Broussard out.

Chris had known all along what kind of sacrifice would be required. A trade-off. If he succeeded, he took the risk of losing his own life or freedom, but Broussard would be dead. Until last night, Chris could never have envisioned any reason not to kill Broussard and be done with it.

Now, in Eden Kelley, he had the only reason he would ever need. With a single twist, like the turn of a kaleidoscope, everything had changed. Now he knew what love was, what was possible. He swallowed. Now if he sacrificed his life or his freedom, he would lose all that. And lose her.

The greater risk was still that Broussard would kill her. Everything Chris stood for in life focused down to that one overriding fact. One of them would die. Eden or Broussard.

Chris chose Broussard. So at last he told her. "I don't need an excuse, Eden. I will do what I have to do."

"Then get in the car and drive away without me, Chris," she said woodenly.

"Oh, that's a good idea. Like you'd survive out there alone for two minutes."

She crossed her arms over her breasts trying desperately to ward off the terrible pain. "Take me to the nearest police station, then. I'll go in and ask for protective custody. Tafoya will come for me in a flash, I'm sure, and then you'll be free to go commit murder."

Her blunt words hit him like a club. His neck and shoulders knotted at the prospect of leaving her alone. "You'll be dead before the forty-eight hours are up."

She swallowed hard, shoving what amounted to a desperate bluff to the very edge. "That's stretching credulity just a little, isn't it? Broussard is deadly, I know that. No one knows that better than I do," she cried fiercely. "But he can't know everything. There's no way he can know where we are. And David Tafoya managed to keep me safe for months before the trial."

Staring hard at her, he advanced toward her, the whites of his eyes glittering in the pitch dark. "Do you believe I won't, Eden?" he asked, his voice gravel low and knife-edged.

His tone was fraught with many more levels of meaning than she wanted to deal with. She wouldn't let him intimidate her. "I didn't mean he's better than you—"

"Good. That's a start."

"Please don't be sarcastic with me!" she cried. "You know I didn't mean it that way. Tafoya had the advantages of a safe house and a dozen armed guards. But I'm not going to stay in protective custody and I'm not going to cower in fear from Broussard or go into hiding again for another minute of my life! I'm in love with you, damn it—"

"Forget me. Just drop—"

"And I will not watch you throw your life away on the likes of him."

"Eden, you can't—"

"Yes, I can! Don't you get it by now? I will not stand by and watch one more person I care about be murdered on Broussard's command. You can either help me and stay with me and love me, or you can get the hell out of my way and leave me. So choose, Chris, and do it now."

He clamped his mouth shut, his chin sticking out in that impossible, implacable position. He grabbed her by the arm and pushed her back into the passenger seat of the Ghia, then got in and exploded backward down the rutted rural lane, backing onto the blacktop without caring who or what else might have been coming down the road.

He drove hard. It was a stupid risk. He knew that, but if speeding got him pulled over, he'd be arrested and Eden could have her way. They'd throw away the key on him and turn her loose. She could have the arresting officer call Tafoya and she would be free to make her own choices and do what Gelham suggested—what she thought she wanted to do.

He almost wished for that outcome, because getting himself tossed in jail would be a hundred times, a thousand times easier than making the decision to give up his plan to kill Broussard and let Eden try to get him her way.

Which was the right way.

The straight-arrow way, the only way he could ever explain to Tiffer what the hell he'd been doing to get his face plastered all over the morning news as an armed and dangerous man holding captive a woman he'd taken as hostage.

There was no radio in the little car so the silence after Eden's ultimatum hung heavily between them, and heavy on his soul. He'd been driven for so long by passions he could not placate that he didn't know how to let go. He hadn't known how to let go of Catherine, so she'd gone out and done the one thing sure to force his hand.

How desperate she must have been. Catherine didn't have the time of day for Tiffer or Jake. She wouldn't have allowed a child of her own to make a dent in her life-style, either, whether the baby was his or whether it wasn't.

In the end, Catherine knew exactly which of Chris's buttons to push to get what she wanted, which was out of any commitment to him or their marriage. She just hadn't lived long enough to experience his reaction or savor her victory.

Chris had nowhere to take his own betrayed, howling rage but to the streets, but when even that didn't appease the demons inside him, he started out to get Broussard. To punish the man who'd robbed him of the chance to have it all out with Catherine.

She hadn't been worth fighting for. Margo had tried to tell him that so many times it was a joke gone stale. And then, right beside him, beside her decorated United States marshal husband, Catherine had been shot to death.

What Broussard and his thugs had done to Chris's life, he'd done to Eden's over and over again, piling on her the guilt for the lives lost that Broussard didn't regret for a heartbeat. Dan Haggerty, Judith Cornwallis, and those were only the ones he could name.

But Chris's insides were eaten up with the other side of all of this. He could make a logical case for accepting

Eden's terms, but he knew in his heart he couldn't allow
her to do what she wanted.

Broussard would kill her. He might spend a lazy after-
noon taunting her first, making her see the error of her
ways, but in the end he would kill her. Either way, Christian Tierney and Eden Kelley had no future.

If he'd never met her, he would still sooner or later have
taken Broussard out and done the world a big favor. He
would willingly have paid the price civilization demanded, if it came to that. He would never have known
what he'd missed.

He wanted to howl at the Fates, to shake his fist at God.
What kind of depraved universe foisted on him a woman
who turned him on and then inside out when he looked at
her and when he listened to her—because she loved him for
all the right, straight-arrow reasons?

He had saved her life, made love to her, come to know
her for a woman who demanded respect and craved commitment and had given herself to him with no thought of
gain or making him pay for loving her.

It was going to kill him to have had all that within his
grasp and then have to turn around and walk away in order to spare her life. But he would do it. He had only
thought he knew what pain and sacrifice meant when
Catherine had died in his arms, pregnant with some other
man's baby.

Chris came up suddenly on a much slower car, a brown
sedan, so he slowed, then encroached into the oncoming
lane and passed the car. The driver was on a cellular
phone, not paying attention to the road. All at once feeling intuitively uneasy, Chris brought his own speed down
to within the limit. He couldn't afford to attract unneces-
sary attention or be stopped and get himself tossed in jail.

He couldn't allow Eden her straight arrow way, either. He would have to find a place to hide her away and then go after Broussard alone.

He checked his speed again, then glanced over at Eden. He knew she wouldn't look at him, knew she was waiting on his answer. He wanted his response to be different. He wished he could say *I'll help you. I'll stay. I'll love you.*

His chest tightened. The unspoken words sounded like vows to him, vows he wanted to make to her. The longing was so thick inside him that he almost pulled off the road again to say those things aloud to her, but he couldn't. He could only make her believe he had changed his mind.

He drew a deep breath. Lies in the line of duty came easily, smoothly, off his tongue. This one, the implication he was about to make, stuck in his craw. He cleared his throat. "Promise you'll trust me, Eden."

She turned to look at him. Hope filled her voice. "Does that mean—"

"I'm serious about this," he interrupted, knowing he couldn't give her a simple yes because that was too big a lie. Her willingness to believe him hammered craters in his heart. "You have to promise me you won't go off and do something half-cocked."

"Okay." The light that had flickered and guttered out in her eyes only a few hours before returned. She gave a brazen smile. "Fully cocked or nothing at all."

His heart was hemorrhaging but he laughed out loud. Should have known she could make him laugh, too. "Where do you want to start?"

She took his right hand off the stick shift and held it in her lap, massaging his fingers and palm. "Ultimately, I want to go straight to Broussard wearing a wire like Gelham suggested. I'm sure David Tafoya will jump at the chance to help us nail him for murder.'' She stared out the side window a moment, then went on with her thought. ''Assuming, of course, that Broussard doesn't gun me down on the spot.''

Chapter Fifteen

She gave a nervous laugh. "I think I can push him into taunting me with everything he's done," Eden went on. "All the hired guns, all the reasons I don't deserve to live, all the reasons why he's saving my immortal soul by his actions."

Chris grimaced. His hands tightened on the steering wheel. None of this was going to happen, but he had to come off sounding worried. "How can you possibly believe he won't kill you on sight?"

She swallowed. "I know Gelham and I are right, Chris. Broussard is obsessed with me. He won't be satisfied until I'm dead, but he'll want to rub my nose in my failures and shortcomings as a woman and a human being first. Most of all as a woman." She hesitated, realizing all at once that Chris had forever changed her. In their lovemaking, she'd seen more clearly than ever her strengths as a woman. Her power. She would never again see herself as Broussard wished. "By the time he's done with humiliating me," she concluded, "he'll have incriminated himself, and Tafoya can move in and make the arrest."

"You're willing to stake your life that Broussard won't blow you away on sight?"

"I'm not wild about it, no." She swallowed hard on a knot of very real fear in her throat. "I just know there is no other way. If there's any justice—" she paused and shrugged "—then this will work."

Chris slumped in his seat. "Some days I'd settle for mercy." He glanced over and touched a kiss to her nose with his finger. "So. Go on. Where do we start?"

"I thought about trying to call Sheila. This can only work if Broussard believes I'm alone and desperate."

He didn't know if that meant Eden now believed that her best friend would betray her. "Is it even possible to talk to her without Broussard knowing about it?"

"No." Eden shook her head. "I would bet Sheila's calls are all screened or recorded. But that would be the point— to let Broussard think I'm alone and just desperate enough to come crawling back—and scared enough to ask Sheila for help." Eden chewed worriedly on her inner lip. "I want to talk to Monique first."

Chris frowned. "Why?"

"I know blood is thicker than water, if that's what you're worried about. Monique is Broussard's cousin, but she has a mind and a heart of her own. She has never allowed him to dictate to her."

"That doesn't mean she'll cross him, Eden."

"No. You're right. It doesn't. But she never came to the trial to stand by him, Chris, and there were fifty or more of his family and friends and business associates in the courtroom every day. Monique never came."

Concentrating, Chris flexed his hand in her lap. She began rubbing the base of his thumb. "Tell me why you want to see her."

"Two reasons. One is that I think she may know who it was that Broussard ordered to kill me after I left the courtroom that day."

Chris took his eyes off the road and stared at her. "You're kidding me."

"No. I'm not."

He shook his head in disbelief. "Why would Monique know such a thing?"

"I don't mean Broussard *told* her, just that if I describe the killer to her, she'll know who he was. They all know each other, Chris, all of Broussard's minions. They all come from the same place. They all speak the same Cajun-French dialect...." Eden shrugged. "If Monique doesn't know, I bet she knows someone who does."

"Eden, that shooter wasn't carrying any ID. He had no driver's license, no parking stubs, no receipts, no permit to carry a weapon and no fingerprints on file in any jurisdiction. He had no ties to anyone even remotely involved—in fact, half the investigating officers believed the guy was on some wild-eyed vendetta against me—that he meant to get Catherine."

"Didn't they eventually conclude that I was the target?"

"Yes. But there was no way to make a case based only on your having seen the shooter in Broussard's office so many months earlier."

"Well, all any of that means is that Broussard sent home to New Orleans or Baton Rouge for fresh blood," Eden said. "That's the way he operates. He trusted no one who doesn't owe him—big time. And the ones who owe him are family members and friends of family that he's plucked out of some pretty god-awful, impoverished lives."

"Almost sounds noble," Chris sniped. "If you ignore the fact that he plucks his own family from one ugly habitat and turns them into mindless-robot killers in another."

"He commands a lot of loyalty, Chris. I never heard of anyone complaining about life after getting transplanted to Boston."

He downshifted and sped around a van, then settled back into the eastbound lane. "Okay. Explain this. Why didn't David Tafoya know Broussard's family tree up one side and down the other by the time you were done spilling your guts to him? Why wouldn't he have followed up on your instincts about the shooter?"

Eden opened her mouth to respond, then closed it, trying to remember. "The subject of Broussard's family connections never came up in that context. In the first place, my direct testimony had far more to do with his international customers than with the drones in his own organization. Also, I met dozens of cousins and uncles and their wives, but I rarely saw any of them more than once or twice."

"So you didn't really know them?"

"No. Not at all. I would have been doing well to remember their names, and I sure didn't know how they were connected to Broussard or what dirty work they did for him. Everything I'm telling you now, about how he operated, about how he only worked with people who owed him, those were all Monique's observations, not mine."

"How did you recognize the shooter, then?"

"Only by his eyes. The night I left Broussard, this guy was in his office. I remember thinking Broussard didn't even want me to see the other man, but I saw his eyes. It was the same man, Chris. I know it was. Monique will know, too."

Chris heaved a big sigh. "I still don't understand, Eden. If you believed Monique could identify the shooter, then I don't know why Tafoya didn't go after whatever information she could give him." They'd reached the I-95, which circled the western edge of the metropolitan area. Chris drove on through Waltham, staying off the Circumferential interstate. "There is no statute of limitations on murder, so it's never too late to start building a case against Broussard. That's the plan?"

Eden nodded. "Yes. Plus, I would like to know more than he thinks I do when I confront Broussard." She heard Chris draw an uneasy breath. His jaw tightened. Even in the dark, Eden could feel his resistance to the idea. It reminded her of coming up against that solid brick wall. "I know. It's very scary."

"Scary." He was mocking her.

"Yeah, Tierney. Scary. Like bad dreams and monsters hiding out in your closet," she snapped. "You *know* scary."

"Yeah, Kelley. I know scary."

"Good!" She clasped his warm hand in both of hers. "Chris, I don't mean to be flippant about this, but I don't want to think about *how* scary. Does that make any sense?"

He nodded. "It's the way I feel every time I go after some fugitive who has nothing to lose by putting a bullet between my eyes."

Eden looked away. She didn't ever want to think about the risks he took, the job he did apart from her. She wouldn't think about it now, either. "The other reason I wanted to go to Monique is that she may know what's going on with Sheila. Whether she's really... in love with Broussard, or what."

Chris slipped his hand from hers to downshift at a red traffic light. "Don't you think it's too much to expect Monique to say anything about Sheila one way or another?"

Eden tilted her head, letting it rest against the window. "Maybe. But if nothing else, Monique will understand that I have to go to Broussard to end this nightmare." Eden chewed at a broken nail. "She was always a great one for pulling yourself up by your own bootstraps. And if the worst happens and she won't talk to me, then Broussard simply knows we've been there and that she threw us out. No harm done."

He stretched his legs and reached over to rest his hand on her knee. "Don't be naive about this, Eden. You have to remember that everyone has their price. Even Monique Lamareaux."

FORTY MINUTES LATER, driving through the upscale brownstone neighborhood where Monique lived, he vetted three streets to the north and south. The vintage Karmann Ghia didn't look terribly out of place, but they left it two blocks down the street.

Monique's brownstone had lights on only at the second level, in the study that looked out over the street. To Eden that meant she was either not at home, or alone. Suddenly confronted with the enormity of taking on Winston Broussard, Eden drew a shuddery breath. Chris rang the doorbell.

The lights came on in the entry and sitting room, then a set of dead bolts were opened after several seconds. Monique Lamareaux opened the door. Raven-haired, fashion-model thin and dressed to kill even alone at home in the evening, a look of dismay filled her darkly attractive eyes. "Mother of God, Eden, what are you doing here? And who is this man?"

"Christian Tierney, United States Marshal Service. Ma'am, do you mind if we come in and get off the street?"

"You mustn't! No!" she responded peremptorily. "*Chère*, you must go away. Web will kill you!"

"Monique, please. We have nowhere else to go and I must talk to you."

Broussard's cousin made her decision quickly but not happily. Reaching out, her wine-colored nails like talons, she pulled Eden hurriedly inside. Chris followed, then closed and bolted the door and quickly scanned the drawing room and hall. "Is anyone here but you, Ms. Lamareaux?"

"No. Of course not." Despite her reluctance to admit them to her home, she hugged Eden tightly, then held her away by her shoulders. "I have missed you terribly, but you should never have come back here. After everything that had happened, what can you be thinking of, Eden?"

Chris watched the older woman closely, studying her movements, her voice, her hands, as she clutched Eden tightly to her thin body, then drew her into the sitting room where they sat together on the sofa. With bay windows at the front and on the side, the two women made a sweet set of targets in this room, like a pair of ducks in a carnival shooting booth. He pulled the shades.

Only the slightest trace of the woman's Cajun roots lingered in her cultured enunciation. Enough to be charming—and more pronounced under stress. She was much older than Chris had imagined. He had believed her to be a contemporary of Broussard's. Her slightly brittle posture and her age-spotted hands gave her away. Monique Lamareaux was at least fifteen years older, maybe twenty, which made her old enough to be Eden's mother.

What stunned Chris was Monique's instinctive, almost maternal fear for Eden, and her naked warning. *Web will kill you.*

"Monique," Eden was saying, "do you know what he does? Do you know people die all over the world—"

"I know, *chère*. I know," she answered dully. "After the trial, how could I not know? But he cannot be defeated and it is foolish of you to think otherwise even for a moment."

Eden's stomach lurched. She had never known Monique to behave or talk this way. She had always maintained a healthy respect for her cousin, but she had never been intimidated by him. Of all the Louisiana transplants, all Broussard's family and friends, retainers really, only Monique had never asked "How high?" when Broussard said "Jump!" "What has he done to you?"

Monique leaned stiffly back against the sofa, her arms wrapped around her waist. "One gets tired, Eden. One begins to grow weary of the subtle, constant threat of retribution. I have no argument with him. What he does is no concern of mine. Considering what he did to *Eden's!,* I am lucky that he allows me to mind my own business."

"It's worse than that." Eden exchanged glances with Chris and dropped the shoulder of J. J. Gelham's navy-and-gray mohair sweater. Monique could not avoid seeing the black stitches and puckered flesh.

"Mon Dieu," Monique murmured, averting her dark eyes. Her tone was more resigned than angry. Eden's heart sank. The spirit had gone out of the once energetic and vivacious woman, and the tragedy was that Eden understood why. It had taken no single act of cruelty or domination on Broussard's part to do this to Monique, only the accumulated weight of a thousand threats disguised as solicitous concern.

"Monique, you must fight back!" Eden begged. "You are not yourself anymore."

"I have nothing to fight back with. I exist by his leave and his good graces. He has fewer with each passing year."

Eden moved closer. "Then help me. He is only a man, only flesh and blood!" But Monique was already shaking her head. "You have already endured much more than this," Eden persisted. "If it weren't for you, he would still be trying to hack a living out of the bayou! He cannot have forgotten his debt to you."

"What debt?" Chris asked, as much to reinforce in Monique Lamareaux's mind that Broussard owed her as to learn of it himself.

Monique only tossed her head and stared at the Louis XVI clock on her mantel.

"Monique was a model," Eden explained, picking up on Chris's strategy. "The first in their family to make it big outside the Louisiana parishes. She is the one who gave Broussard his chance, the one who brought him to Boston. He knows his debt to Monique can never be fully repaid."

"You are wrong." Monique's hand fluttered anxiously before her eyes, settling at last at her temple. "He considers his debt more than repaid. What you don't understand, Eden, is that he blames my attitude toward him for blemishing your perception of him. That I influenced your betrayal."

"But that is ridiculous! And so typical of him to believe that I have no mind of my own. Monique, I'm so sorry that he blames you. It's true that you gave me a job and a home. That you made me feel capable and clever and gave me courage when I had none—"

"Stop, *chère!*" Monique cried, covering her ears. "Please say no more. I do not want to hear these things or be responsible for your betraying him."

"You're not, Ms. Lamareaux," Chris assured her quietly, but Monique only waved off his opinion as irrelevant.

"What Web believes is the only thing of consequence."

"Why is Sheila with him?" Eden blurted, desperate for other answers.

"Because he wishes it," Monique answered blankly, as if that were a given. But she looked up quickly, belatedly understanding Eden's question. "Sheila enjoys the lifestyle he provides her."

Eden felt hollow inside, sick to her stomach.

"Who wouldn't, *chère?*" Monique went on bitterly. "Even you were enamored of his largess. His—" she swallowed "—his power and good looks and charm."

Chris got up from the silk brocade wing chair and began to pace. Eden swallowed. This was to have been their cue, that if he felt the interview with Monique was not going well or could not succeed, Eden would bring it to a conclusion and get out. She had promised to listen to him, to trust his instincts, but however bitter the pill, she couldn't go without asking what she had come to find out.

"Monique, please tell me this. Do you know who it was that Broussard sent to kill me?"

"No!" she denied. But all trace of color drained from her face.

Eden reached out to her. "Monique, you were like a mother to me! Please try. Please listen. I saw him once before that day. In Web's office above *Eden's!* He had eyes the color of amber, like fire—and he spoke the patois—"

The distraught woman shook her head in tiny, jerking movements. "Do not ask, *chère.* I cannot say." Hopelessness made her eyes dull, listless.

She knew the answer to Eden's question; there could be no doubt of that. But because Broussard held Monique

Lamareaux accountable in her attitude for Eden's betrayal, he might as well have been standing over Monique holding the puppet strings, his smile contemptuous and his charm deadly.

The image transfixed Eden. The lines descending from each side of Monique's bloodless lips had deepened; her jaw now resembled that of an antique marionette.

Chapter Sixteen

Paul Maroncek kissed his wife goodbye, then sank into her mocha-colored Nissan to make the drive back to their home in the Boston suburb of Belmont. Janna was staying in Worcester with her sister for a few days. He hit the turnpike after fifteen minutes and followed it east to the tollbooths, tossed in his change and sped on.

Intending to get off on I-95 and head up to the Waltham exit, he'd switched on the CD player and listened to a Neil Diamond disc for twenty minutes or so when the cellular phone trilled.

He wished to God he'd left the thing home. Now he'd have to listen to someone else's harangue regarding Christian X. Tierney.

The whole of Massachusetts was keeping score now, all four districts, not only Boston, as if Tierney was starring in some kind of sexy, modern-day version of *Bonnie and Clyde*.

He punched the Off button on the CD player and barked into the phone. "Maroncek."

A cloying female voice came on the line. "Chief Deputy Paul Maroncek?"

His stomach knotted. "Yes."

"Please hold for the attorney general."

Maroncek sighed. This would not be just anyone's harangue.

The A.G. wasted no time on pleasantries. "I was promised an update, Paul. I want Christian Tierney found. I want that witness alive and back in custody and I want it *all* yesterday."

Frigging eight-thirty at night on a Tuesday, he thought disgustedly. Tierney had been gone five days now, and on every one of those days, Maroncek had been held personally accountable for his deputy's reckless disregard of the attorney general's express wishes.

It wasn't that Christian X. Tierney's bloated reputation didn't need a reality check, Maroncek thought. Too many people in too many high places had begun to think he walked on water with the captures he'd turned in over the last year and a half.

The specter of Tierney getting crosswise of the attorney general herself had suited the hell out of Maroncek. Only now, well in advance of Tierney getting his due, knocked down a peg or two or several, or, alternatively, off his pedestal altogether, Maroncek found himself getting raked over the coals.

"We all understand your directives," he replied evenly. "I've got every available man on the case, and Tafoya—"

"You're not suggesting, are you, Chief Deputy, that the combined forces of the Boston FBI and Massachusetts districts of the United States Marshal Service aren't up to the job of bringing in one of their own, are you?"

"Certainly not." Maroncek grimaced, smarting from the sarcastic remark, although why the hell he cared, he didn't know anymore. He'd talked himself blue in the face for the past five days. Even Tafoya admitted Tierney had saved Eden Kelley's life, but all the steps Tierney had taken after that were ones Maroncek could not justify—except to reiterate over and over again that at least with Christian Tierney, the witness was still alive.

"Tierney has got to be brought in," the A.G. pressed on. "The media is turning this fiasco into an ongoing circus. I want it resolved, Paul, and if that means you get *your* ass out there beating the bushes, then by God, you do it. Clear?"

"Perfectly," he snapped, moving over a lane to take the eastbound Brandeis exit.

"Good. Have a productive evening, Paul." She spoke softly, as was her habit, leaving the unspoken words "or else" hanging threateningly over his head like the proverbial big stick.

So angry he lost track of exactly where he was and what he was doing, he broke the connection and jerked the cellular phone battery adapter from the cigarette-lighter port about the time a small car came up fast behind him, slowed, then passed him. Automatically, Maroncek registered the vintage model, the license plate, the dark color.

The car reminded him of J. J. Gelham, whom Maroncek hadn't spoken with in several months. A year?

No, more. Needing a distraction from his anger at the attorney general, he fell to reminiscing. Gelham was a man's man, not in appearance, but in ways that counted. He had a rapport with the judges like no other attorney Maroncek had ever seen. A way of framing things for the liberal bench in such a manner that he got whatever he went after—warrants, wiretaps. Name it, J. J. Gelham got it.

All that talent going to waste, Maroncek thought, was a damned shame. He could use Gelham's advice about now. Gelham would have some brilliant strategy for keeping the attorney general at bay.

On the other hand, he and Tierney had been as thick as thieves. Drinking buddies in addition to schemers extraordinaire. Gelham would be busy transforming the media frenzy into a heroic, crime-busting platform from which Tierney's next step would be the White House.

One caustic thought after another flew through Maroncek's head. He pulled into his dark driveway in a very foul mood. Just as well Gelham was out of the picture, tinkering with his antique Karmann Ghias.

Just short of opening the door of his wife's Nissan to get out and go inside, Maroncek froze. He sat there absolutely dumbfounded, replaying the sight of that dark vintage Ghia passing him on a secondary highway that traversed most of the state, linked up with other secondaries that came out of Saugerties, and coincidentally, passed within a couple of miles of J. J. Gelham's place in Westfield.

Maroncek cursed and banged his fist off the steering wheel. He'd been within spitting distance of Tierney and the Kelley woman and never known it. He comforted himself with the knowledge that he alone knew how to find his run-amok deputy.

He picked up the cellular and made a few calls, setting into motion an unofficial, off-the-record all points for the Karmann Ghia, concentrating in the central Boston area and all points of access north to Marblehead. Unless he was way off base, which was rarely the case, Maroncek thought, Tierney would now go after Winston Broussard with both barrels blazing.

Maroncek could already taste the sweet satisfaction of having been the one to bring Tierney in. A part of him hoped Tierney beat out the Feebs and got to Broussard first.

MIRED AGAIN IN FEELINGS of loss and guilt that could never be assuaged, Eden stroked Monique's fragile cheek. "You will be free of his clutches and his threats, Monique. I swear it."

"Do not swear to such a thing, child. It brings the worst kind of luck." She got up from the sofa and sighed. Eden rose, as well. "I am going to bed now. Eden, *ma chère,* if you care anything for me, you will please be gone before I awake in the morning."

"Monique." Eden held out her arms, but the older woman stood stiffly, rooted to the floor in her black leather pumps, her arms wrapped tightly about her.

"I beg you," Monique whispered. "I have kept your room as it was when you left so many months ago. Collect what you want and then run away, as far and as fast as you can." She turned on her heel and fled up the stairs.

Eden stood watching after Monique, tears brimming at her lashes. Chris went to her and took her in his arms. She rested her head against his shoulder.

"I'm sorry, Eden. I know you thought she could help you, but it looks as if she's just not up to dealing with Broussard anymore."

Eden wiped her tears away and stood apart from Chris. "I can't believe he blames her for what I did."

"He had to blame someone. He sure as hell didn't believe you were capable of taking him on. It's his own failing, Eden. Not Monique's. Not yours."

"Not Sheila's, either." Eden straightened her shoulders. "But that will be his downfall. He won't quite get it that I'll never say die." She switched off the lamps. Weariness gnawed at her bravado. She wasn't so sure of anything anymore, not with Monique crumbling as she had. "Come with me upstairs. I left a few things. Some clothes, shoes."

She walked back across the entryway and turned off the light, then led the way through the kitchen toward the back staircase. Chris followed her in the dark up four flights of stairs to the topmost floor of the brownstone.

Eden opened the door to her old room and stepped inside. The door creaked in a familiar way as did the floorboards. The only light was cast by street lamps. "Do you think it's safe to turn on a light?"

Chris let his eyes adjust to the dark another few seconds, then moved past Eden and the old-fashioned dressing screen to the solitary window overlooking the street. Standing to the side of the window, he watched for a few moments. "I don't see anything to worry about."

Eden angled her head. She could only see Chris in profile. "I assume your instincts are usually right."

"Usually," he answered dryly, pulling the shade anyway. "Aren't those candles? There on the bedside table?"

Eden shook her head. "Of course. And a box of matches." The faint, lingering scent of perfumed candles should have reminded her. Maybe they were too much a part of her memories of this haven to trigger her conscious thoughts about what to do now.

She went and sat on the four-poster double bed. The coverlet was a thick, hand-tatted lace over an ivory linen spread. Her fingers went to the patterned lace, but with Chris standing at the window, dominating her old room, she was unwilling to get caught up in old memories the coverlet aroused. She snatched her fingers back. "I'll just light these." The wooden match flared. She lit two candles, then glanced around. Chris was watching her way too closely. "What?"

"Nothing, Eden." She didn't believe him. Her expression must have conveyed her skepticism. He crammed his hands into his pockets, then gave a crooked smile. He shrugged. "I was just thinking it's been a long time since I was in a girl's room. A girlfriend's bedroom."

She blinked and stared down at her hands, then tossed her hair back and met his gaze. "Is that what I am, Tierney?"

He blinked slowly back at her. "Yeah, Kelley. That's what you are."

Her throat tightened. A frayed cabbage rose paper decked the walls. A primitive kind of long-legged stuffed cotton bunny rabbit lay on the spread. Frilly curtains matched the dust ruffle. "I *was* a girl here. For a while. But no boys ever came in here."

"Good."

"You knew that, Chris."

Fending off a grin, he shrugged. "I knew no one stole home, Eden. That doesn't mean some little creep with sweaty hands and high hopes never went to bat here, or got to first base."

She gave him a quelling look, then let her gaze follow the line of the molding at the ceiling. "This was the first place I remember feeling safe."

"Even counting St. Anne's?"

Sitting back on the bed, she nodded. "There were a lot of girls there who had more experience than a grown-up hooker. I would listen to them talk and think about going off to join a nunnery."

Chris cleared his throat. "I'm glad you didn't."

The heat in his eyes and the gravelly desire in his voice made her flush and shiver at once. "Me, too."

Desire flared in her to match his. She got up off the bed and crossed the small room to a high, narrow dresser. She pulled out a mauve satin bustier, turned toward Chris and held it up against Gelham's sweater at her midriff. She felt brazen and daring and scared.

"I could have spent my life mending hospital bed sheets. Instead . . . I made this. Do you like it?"

"I'm not sure." His voice was gritty. He shifted his stance.

Eden gulped, startled, aware for the first time in her life what it meant when a man shifted like that. She flushed hotter and caught her lower lip between her teeth.

He closed his eyes momentarily and shifted again. "Maybe you should put it on for me so I can . . . decide."

She nodded, blushing, and turned away, but she did not retreat behind the screen. She put the bustier on top of the dresser and pulled off Gelham's sweater, baring her back to Chris, then slid her arms through the satin shoulder straps.

Her heart raced. Her breasts tingled, felt full, and her nipples had already drawn tight. She turned back, half-way through closing the garment up with its old-fashioned hooks and eyes and ties.

She watched his eyes following the upward path of her fingers. She smoothed the fabric when she was done, drawing her hands down the slick mauve satin to her waist. "There."

He knew she expected an answer now, but he felt as if he'd swallowed his tongue. The candlelight flickered and glowed on the satin molded so perfectly to her breasts. He had never felt more vulnerable.

Never.

He wanted her too much. He ached low and outside his torso. He knew in his head that the top floor of Monique Lamareaux's brownstone was not the place for this, but this was where he was, *how* he was. He could no more walk away from Eden Kelley or wanting her or needing to show her how he felt about her than he could let her sacrifice her life so Broussard would stop killing people.

He unbuckled his belt and unzipped his jeans and began to unbutton his plaid flannel shirt.

Eden didn't need any other answer. When he stroked the sides of her bustier and groaned and slipped the satin straps from her shoulder so he could kiss her there, she forfeited forever the notion of taking herself off to a nunnery. But a part of her grieved every kiss, every touch, every thrust of his supremely masculine body.

Deep inside her soul where it had always been apparent to her that she could never *belong,* she believed Broussard would win.

And that this would be the last hour she would ever spend in Christian Tierney's embrace.

AT TWO-FORTY in the morning of his sixth day with Eden Kelley, Chris got up from the bed where she had spent the last of her girlhood. He put on his socks and then his jeans and flannel shirt and moved silently down the four flights of stairs, carrying his boots and her mauve satin garment. He went to Monique Lamareaux's study and sat in the high-backed executive chair, staring in the dark at the phone on her desk.

His body was well sated, his heart little more than a mechanical object witlessly pumping away. He knew what he must do, knew how to do it and knew this was the moment, while Eden lay sleeping, trusting him.

There was the rub. He'd led her to believe she could trust him. He had lied at worst, misled her at best. The best he could do now was to ensure her safety and put her in the hands of the only other man she trusted—David Tafoya.

Chris held her satin bustier to his face and inhaled deeply. The scent of her lingered on the fabric. The slick texture sent tactile sensations through his fingers. His whiskers caught against the fine grain. His throat swelled.

His chest tightened and heaved and he came as close to tears as he had come since he was younger than Tiffer.

He picked up the receiver and dialed the Boston FBI. Following recorded instructions, he punched zero for the operator. When a woman answered, he identified himself as an informant seeking Special Agent David Tafoya and asked to be put through to Tafoya's home.

The Feeb picked up on the third ring. Chris choked. Tafoya barked a second hello. Chris shook his head at his indecisive waffling and made himself do what had to be done. "This is Tierney."

"Tierney who?" Tafoya demanded.

Chris could imagine the Feeb wetting himself. "Tierney, Christian Xavier, deputy marshal, United States Marshal Service, Boston." He rattled off every kind of identifying government number from his birth date to his date of hire to his clearance IDs and sandwiched Monique Lamareaux's address somewhere in the middle.

"Is this some kind of test?" Tafoya asked.

"Two conditions," Chris snapped, "or I'm out of here with the witness for good."

Tafoya placated him. "You're doing the right thing, Tierney. I'll put in a good word for you with the A.G. What conditions?"

Chris didn't think even St. Peter putting in a good word would salvage his badge. After he finished with Broussard, his job would be irrelevant. "One," he answered, "you come for her now—"

"I can do that—"

"And two, you keep her away from Broussard, no matter what."

"What the hell is that supposed to mean, Tierney?" Tafoya demanded. "I'm the one who was looking out for

Eden Kelley a long time before you ever heard of her. Why would I let her anywhere near Broussard?''

"Because she'll ask. She wants to go in wearing a wire. I want your word that won't happen."

"Done," Tafoya agreed. "Tierney, let me say this one more time. You've done a hell of job and put yourself on the line—"

Chris interrupted with a lone succinct curse. He didn't want to hear it, didn't want the Feeb extolling his actions. It didn't matter that Chris had saved her life. What was uppermost in his mind and heart was that he was about to betray Eden's trust. He knew, as far as she would be concerned, he might as well put a bullet through her heart himself.

"Just keep her alive, Tafoya."

"You know I will."

"Yeah." Chris's hand closed tight on the satin. "See to it." He hung up the receiver and sat a moment longer, then got up and slipped like a shadow out the front entry. Broussard's life was now measured in hours.

THE SUN HADN'T YET come up when Eden awoke in her old room, alone in the antique four-poster. Foreboding swamped her. Switching on the bedside lamp, she climbed off the bed and dressed quickly in Gelham's jeans and a sweater of her own. She checked the bathroom and then the other two rooms on the fifth floor of Monique's brownstone, then descended the stairs to the kitchen where there was a small light on and the scent of freshly brewed coffee.

"Chris?" She came around the landing and saw not Tierney, but the familiar short, solid shape of David Tafoya.

"David." Eden stopped short, still on the bottom stair. It took no great ration of reasoning ability to understand, but the implications took her agonizing long seconds to assimilate.

Christian Tierney had left her to go end Broussard's life.

Between one beat and the next, her heart caved in on itself. She should have known Chris would do this. He had changed his mind too easily to be true.

"Sorry to disappoint you, Eden," David said, pouring a cup of coffee from the automatic drip decanter. He gave a half smile. "But I thank God you're alive." Dark-haired, solidly muscled, wearing khakis and a gun in a shoulder holster over his light, short-sleeved shirt, he handed her the cup. "And looking well," he added.

"Thank you." She accepted the cup of steaming coffee, trying to disguise the bitter disappointment. "Where's Chris Tierney?"

"'You're looking well, too' comes next, Eden," he chided gently. Or, 'Boy, it's good to see you again.' Something like that."

She shivered. Her teeth clenched. She trusted David Tafoya and she knew very well that it had been her own plan to seek his help, but she found herself utterly unable to offer up inane clichés.

As he watched her reaction, Tafoya's blunt-featured face softened. "He's gone, Eden. I don't know where."

"He called you?"

"Several hours ago."

Shaking, feeling betrayed, Eden held her cup with both hands. "I was going to do that."

"Call me?"

She nodded. "I just thought—" she swallowed hard "—I just thought Chris would stick around."

Tafoya put down his cup and leaned against the kitchen counter. "It's best this way." He folded his thick arms over his chest. "Tierney was looking out for your best interests. We all are, you know."

His patronizing, we'll-take-care-of-you tone upset her deeply. "I intend to look out for my own best interests, David. Broussard has got to be stopped. I can't go on like this."

"Of course not." He drained his cup. "We'll get you back into protective custody, see to it that you're safely relocated once and for all so you can put all of this behind—"

"No." Pain roared through her like a distant train, heard, felt, not seen. There wasn't even any room for anger, only for keeping her focus. "I want to do this again, David. I want to go after Broussard."

"For what, Eden?"

"Murder." She shook her hair back. "Conspiracy to murder, whatever you call it. Catherine Tierney's murder and Judith Cornwallis's and Dan Haggerty's. I need your help."

Tafoya shook his head. "Tierney said you would ask. I'm afraid I promised him it wouldn't happen."

"You had no right to make a promise like that, David!"

"Eden—"

"Don't you see I have to get to Broussard before he and Chris kill each other?"

"My God!" Tafoya stared at her, incredulous, as if he were seeing her clearly for the first time. His features took on an ugly twist. "You've gone and convinced yourself you're in love with Tierney, haven't you?"

Chapter Seventeen

"That's what this is all about, isn't it?"

Eden's insides quaked. Hot coffee slopped on her hands. "David . . ."

His face darkened. "How sickeningly trite! What went on here, exactly?"

His inflection sent prickles down her spine. Stunned, she fought against shrinking from him. "That's none of your business, David."

"Oh, I beg to differ! Carnal relations with a witness isn't in the handbook, Eden. It's abusive and despicable." He snatched the cup of coffee from her hands, not caring that the hot liquid splashed on his own hands, and thrust it crashing onto the counter. He grabbed her by the wrist. "Show me, Eden," he commanded, hauling her back to the stairs. "Let's just see what's been going on."

He dragged her with him. Fighting him, she tripped on a riser and fell, banging her knees, but he only kept dragging her along up one flight and the next and the next.

"David, stop it!" she cried. If he thought she'd been sexually abused at Chris's hands, why was he treating her like this? "What are you doing? Let me go!"

But he didn't stop, didn't let her go until he had hurled

her into the room at the top of the stairs and stood staring at the tangle of bed sheets, blocking her way out.

"Tell me Tierney forced you," he commanded coldly. "Make it good, Eden. I will try very hard to believe you."

"David, it didn't happen that way." His frenzy chilled her to the marrow. *Dear God, what had she done?* Goose bumps broke out on her flesh. She no longer recognized David Tafoya at all. He wasn't the same FBI agent who had been so intent, so vehemently determined to get Broussard, so dedicated to protecting her. "Why are you doing this? Why are you so angry? Why does it *matter?*"

He ignored her questions. "You let Tierney take advantage of you," he sneered. "You just don't ever get a clue, do you?"

"David, what are you talking about?"

"Or am I giving you too much credit?" he went on as if she hadn't asked anything at all. "Did you beg him, Eden? Did you begin to see him as your savior? Did you think you owed him? Did you, Eden?"

"No—"

"It's a common enough phenomenon among female kidnap victims and hostages," he lectured, pacing the floor of her small room. "A woman will submit every time to her captor's despicable sexual advances in her gratitude for his having kept her alive."

Fear spread through her chest and congealed into a lump in her throat. She could *feel* Tafoya's eyes on her, as if he'd suddenly gone schizo, half of him violently condemning Chris, the other half insanely jealous, wanting her for himself. Her skin crawled. Her heart pounded as fear gnawed at her. "It wasn't like that, David. Please. Can't we go back to being allies, to working together to put Broussard behind bars forever?"

"I'm afraid I don't see that happening." He smiled. "You see, Winston Broussard paid me—exceptionally well, I must say—to see that the witnesses against him never testified."

Eden shivered violently. "No...you—"

"Oh, yes. You've been living on borrowed time, Eden. For way too long."

"David, no," she cried, anguish spilling through her. The blood rushed from her head. Her denials were meager hope, too meager. "You spent years going after him, years—"

"Exactly. Too many. I lost my wife and kid over it. Do you suppose my quality of life hasn't improved a thousand times by the simple choice of letting it be? Broussard was never going to be convicted. At a certain point," he explained, as if it were all really very simple, "all that zeal burns itself out and you're left holding the bag of ashes, wondering what the hell happened to your dreams."

Eden sank to her bed. "Why didn't you just kill me when I insisted on going through with my testimony?"

He gave a faint smile. "You were removed from the safe house in Maine after that. Even I didn't know where you were—but in any case, the decision was Broussard's. Suspicion might have fallen on me. He thought it much more valuable to have a...friend on the inside. He never believed he would be convicted even of jaywalking on your testimony alone. He paid dearly, didn't he, for the mistaken belief that he could bring you to heel?"

All hope withered away, Eden shook her head. "Not dearly enough."

He smiled nastily, then pinned her with his dark, righteous gaze. "Now, you insipid, foolish little slut, you have gone and squandered the only coin that has ever bought you any more time. And I'll be lucky if he doesn't hold me accountable because you are no longer his unspoiled little virgin." Tafoya scowled. "What was it he called you? Eden, his little garden of secret delights? Well..." He pulled the gun from his shoulder holster and aimed it straight at her heart. "All our dirty little secrets are out now, aren't they?"

Sickened and terrified, Eden bolted. Before she even made it as far as the door of her room, Special Agent David Tafoya lifted his arm and cracked her on the head with the butt of his gun.

CHRIS STUCK AROUND in the deep shadows of an outdoor stairwell across the street long enough to make sure that Tafoya arrived to take Eden back into protective custody.

He watched the Feeb drive up in a late-model BMW, watched him adjust his shoulder holster, pocket the keys and check out the street for any signs of trouble. The Feeb mounted the steps two at a time, approached the building without a trace of hesitation and then performed an illegal entry into Monique Lamareaux's brownstone.

Tafoya was good. Maybe too good. It took him well under sixty seconds to get in. Doubts clung to Chris like old sweat. His mouth tasted bad, his instincts railed against leaving her in anyone else's hands—but if Tafoya could keep her safe for a few hours more, just a few measly hours, she would be safe from Broussard for all time.

Keeping to the shadows, Chris walked the two blocks down the street to the Karmann Ghia, got in and drove off before he could think of better reasons to go back than that the Feeb was too good.

He drove to a seedy little motel off the highway on the northeast side of Lynn, Massachusetts, parked the Karmann Ghia in back, paid cash and went to his assigned room. He stripped out of his clothes and stood under the inadequate, too-low shower head for as long as the hot water lasted. He hoped it would be long enough, or the soap sufficiently strong, to purge Eden's scent from his flesh.

Reminded of her in any way, he couldn't focus on turning himself into the cold-blooded murderer he needed to become. Even to gain access to Broussard's property would require every professional wile, every finely tuned instinct, every fiber of his being.

He had never believed he could pull off this hit on Broussard on his own territory. He was too well guarded, his private estate patrolled day and night by dogs and human killers. Chris's plan had always been to bait Broussard elsewhere with Eden Kelley, to lure him away from his overwhelmingly secured property, but those plans had long since crumbled. Chris would have to deal with all of that protection and stay alive long enough to do the job.

When the hot water ran out after just twenty minutes, he stood under the drizzling cold. Afterward, he ate the rest of the crumpled package of Oreo cookies and went through the small arsenal of weapons he carried in his pack, making sure he could lay his hands on what he needed when he needed it.

The sky was still dark when he set out jogging to Winston Broussard's property, which backed up to the ocean bay, and barely light by the time Chris reached a vantage point above the road in the woods opposite the guardhouse where he could see down into the estate. He figured dawn for his best chance at catching the guards and dogs unaware.

He climbed a tree, pulled out his binoculars and scoped out what little could be seen through the enormous wrought-iron gate. The drive extended from the gates at the guardhouse for a quarter mile down a tree-lined lane.

At the southwestern corner, the pavement divided. To the left, the lane continued on into a circle drive at the front of the beautifully maintained 1930s-era house. He guessed that to the right, the road continued on around the house to a service entry and parking garage.

He began figuring out his strategy and mapping out in his mind the route he would take in avoiding the surveillance cameras, recognizing how dangerously hobbled he was because he wouldn't pick off the men who protected Winston Broussard.

Crouched in the tree, still running through his options, Chris listened to the low thrum of an approaching automobile. When he saw the BMW round the bend in the road and pull up to the wrought-iron gates, his heart all but stopped.

FIVE MILES BACK UP the road, a local cop spotted the hunter green Karmann Ghia, double-checked the plates and radioed his station. Maroncek heard about the sighting less than ten minutes later. He drew a shaky breath on the good-news, bad-news information. He now had the legal wherewithal to go after Tierney and, at the same time, invade Winston Broussard's fortresslike estate. With any luck at all, Broussard would resist and consequently go down in a barrage of government bullets.

But Maroncek figured Christian Tierney would be lucky to survive at all. And the witness . . . who knew?

EDEN CAME TO WHEN David Tafoya stopped the BMW and blasted the horn outside the gates of Winston Broussard's Marblehead estate. Tossed unceremoniously into the front passenger seat, her hands cuffed behind her, she could barely move and her head throbbed horribly.

Still, the black wrought-iron bars looming above Tafoya's windshield gave her a powerful sense of her existence having been preordained, as if everything in her life had prepared her to deal with this moment.

Being abandoned and shuffled about, reinventing herself time and again, hoping to be valued, because there was precious little love to go around for a ward of the state.

Judith's shattered mirror more powerfully described Eden's life than words could ever recount. And then there was Chris, who'd taught her that even with her nose pressed to the glass—forever on the outside looking in— she didn't have a monopoly on suffering.

He had given her something else to draw on, as well, an inner sense of her self, of what it was to belong and what it was not. She had never belonged to Broussard, or with him. He had no power to hurt her. He could not win.

Staring up at those bars, which were meant to impress and to intimidate all comers, she felt neither.

Tafoya bellowed angrily out his window when the guards failed to open the gates quickly enough. She heard the creaking, metallic noise, the lock releasing, the gates swinging open, and then Tafoya drove through and the gates clanged shut behind the car.

He hadn't noticed that she had regained consciousness. When he stopped the car on the driveway in front of the entrance and came around to drag her out, she straightened.

"I'll get out myself . . . David. Thank you."

He recoiled at her pleasant tone. "Ah, bravado," he said mockingly. "There's a clever girl." His lip curled. "You always were too clever by half."

She twisted about and put her feet on the driveway. "Not so clever as you," she responded sweetly. "Or else I would have known you for what you are, wouldn't I?"

"Cute." He grabbed her upper arm and hauled her to her feet. "Let's see how long your smart mouth lasts, shall we?"

He manhandled her to the massive front door. The butler must have been waiting because the door swung open before Tafoya could bang the knocker.

Eden had been to this estate several times. She recognized the scrawny old black man, Jameson, whose accent was so Cajun-French thick that she had never clearly understood him. He was a brilliant and loyal servant, rarely heard from, so his accent didn't matter.

His eyes, instinctively shuttered because he took Tafoya for a cop—*good cop, bad cop, makes no difference,* he once told her, explaining his trouble *back home back south*—flew wide when he recognized her. "Miz Kelley?"

She smiled. "Hello, Jamie. How are you?"

Tafoya swore. "Put a lid on the old home-week routine, Eden." To Jameson, he said, "Where's Broussard?"

The old man's eyes slid away again. Eden answered. "At the poolside, almost certainly. Isn't that right, Jamie?"

"*Mais oui.* Follow me."

He led the way through the house Eden remembered well. Fresh, hothouse orchids sat scattered in assorted cut-crystal vases. She felt a sliver of panic. Out the back double French doors, Broussard sat in a black satin robe casually sipping his coffee while he read through the morning paper. In the distance, sunlight glinted off the rippling waters of the bay. A sailboat bobbed at rest, its masts bare.

Tafoya's suddenly sweaty hands shoved Eden out the door onto the pristine white deck surrounding the swimming pool. "The prodigal at last," he said.

She saw two or three armed guards patrolling the perimeter, accompanied by dogs. Broussard's own bodyguard stood discreetly in the shadows beneath an upper balcony.

When Broussard deigned to look up at Tafoya's greeting, he ignored the man and let his sultry, lascivious eyes rake over her.

"Eden. *Ma douce amie.* To what do I owe the honor of your return?"

For all her bravado, she couldn't prevent the primitive dread he conjured up in her. She fought with everything in her to thwart the fear taking hold inside her. He fed on fear, thrived on it. Revulsion, she would dare show. Fear, she could not.

"I mean no honor, Broussard." She tossed her head. Pain shot though her shoulders, and her wrists chafed in the cuffs. "But you must know that."

"*Mais oui.* I do. A pity," he agreed, turning next to Tafoya. "You have finally earned your keep, but at what cost to me, I mus' wonder. Our little captive, it appears, has grown quite bold."

Tafoya shrugged. "For all the good it will do her."

Broussard folded his newspaper and sat back. "Where is your savior, Eden? The equally desperate and daring Christian X. Tierney?"

She managed a blank expression, but already Broussard had divined the weakness in her armor. "I don't know."

"Ah, Tafoya. You disappoint me again," he said, looking at Eden while he spoke. "Can this be true?"

"Tierney will be caught," Tafoya assured Broussard. "It's only a matter of hours before he's apprehended. His keepers will throw away the key on him."

"Eden!" All three of them turned toward the door. Sheila Jacques stood poised at the threshold. She wore a black satin robe matching Broussard's—a robe Eden knew was far and away more elegant and pricey than anything Sheila had ever owned in her life.

Her hair had been cut in a new and stunning style, and colored to tone down its fiery hues. When she stepped out onto the deck, she moved with more reserve and precision than Eden had ever seen.

Sheila was transformed, gorgeous, coldly aloof. None of her warmth showed, no spontaneity remained. Nothing about her resembled the girl with whom Eden had shared a room at St. Anne's. Eden turned to Broussard. The look of mocking satisfaction he shot at her filled Eden with despair.

"Sheils," she murmured to break the tension, "you're stunning."

"Thank you," the other woman responded, moving as if on a leash next to Broussard. He patted her backside. Eden flinched. "Winston," Sheila said softly, "perhaps Eden could have those grotesque handcuffs removed and sit down?"

"But of course!" he answered. His hand slid possessively down Sheila's thigh.

Eden would have been mortified had he touched her like that in the presence of anyone else. But that's what he intended, she thought. To defile and humiliate her best friend in her presence. To show her exactly who was calling the shots.

To bait her.

Now, when it was far to late, Eden was willing to admit that she needed Christian Tierney's help.

"What can have become of my hospitality?" Broussard was saying. "Tafoya," he ordered, "kindly remove the shackles."

The dirty FBI agent moved to comply. He jerked her hands unnecessarily high and unlocked the cuffs. Stabbing pain shot through her shoulders and arms as her circulation returned. Rubbing her chafed wrists, Eden shot Sheila a grateful look, but her friend wasn't looking. Deliberately not looking.

"Are you happy, Sheils?" she blurted.

"Shut up, Eden," Tafoya snapped, shoving her into a patio chair at the same table with Winston Broussard. "You're playing with fire."

Broussard's brow rose. "Indeed—" Eden staved off a shudder "—your question is a legitimate one. After all," he went on, "this was once all within your grasp." He gestured broadly over the panorama of all that he owned. "Answer your dear old friend, *ma belle,* Sheila Marie. Are you happy?"

Sheila met Eden's gaze. "I am happy, Eden."

Her response sounded parrotlike to Eden, but Broussard patted Sheila again, as if rewarding a dog for rolling over.

"Now, perhaps fair Eden will indulge a question of my own," he suggested equably, but his expression altered subtly. "What do *you* think, Eden, of your dear friend Sheila whoring herself at my whim?"

Sheila's expression never changed, but Eden quaked inside with fury at his stunning cruelty. "Your whim disgusts me," she snapped. "Your Madonna/whore mentality sickens me."

Broussard began to laugh in her face but Tafoya snickered. "Except there are no Madonnas left here, are there? Get closer, Broussard. She reeks of Christian Tierney."

Eden's breath stuck in her throat, but before she could think why Tafoya would risk Broussard's wrath, his arm lashed out and he backhanded her hard, sending her crashing down on the deck.

Her blood spilled and smeared on the immaculate white paint. Stars blinked before her eyes. It felt as if his blow had shattered her cheekbone. Tafoya righted the chair and jerked her up by her arm, then tossed her like a rag doll back into her seat. Her lip was split and bleeding. Sheila had turned stark white.

Eden battled back her tears. She had to be smarter than this, smarter than to give up the battle by letting him knock her senseless. With all her heart, she wished Chris were here now, but that was unlikely to happen. He could never breach this stronghold of Broussard's, and she had no one to help her anymore. Not Tafoya, not Sheila.

She swallowed painfully and met Broussard's brutal eyes. "What now?"

"Now?" He blinked.

But before he could answer, an explosion reverberated through the air, splintering glass and wood, and the estate alarms began to wail.

Broussard twisted his head around at the sound and swore violently in his native tongue. "Tierney!" Broussard stood and roared at the armed guards running everywhere. His own bodyguard took off. "Take him alive! I want him alive!" Then he spat on the floor at Eden's feet. "Now, *chère,* it seems we will wait upon my guards to apprehend your lover. And then," he snarled, "we will see how you will whore yourself to spare his life."

Horror nearly paralyzed Eden, but Sheila turned on Broussard, crazed with fury. "You sick bastard," she screamed, galvanized from her apathy into a rage. "Eden will never, *never* give in to you!"

She flew at him, clawing at him, fighting like a rabid shrew gone mad. Another blast exploded, nearer this time, and flaming debris showered down on the deck.

Growling fiercely, Eden launched herself at Tafoya to prevent his attacking Sheila from behind. She knocked the gun from his hand, but her momentum carried Eden into Broussard's range.

He shrugged Sheila off him with a mighty burst of anger, grabbed Eden's arm and twisted it high and hard behind her back. "You will die now, whore," he threatened, "because I will squeeze the life from your tainted and spent body myself."

But from behind him, Chris appeared, scaling the deck fascia to hurl himself over the low, white, wrought-iron fence. He must have used the explosions for a distraction so that he could approach from the rear.

"Let her go and call off your guards, Broussard, or you're a dead man."

Jerked tight to Broussard, Eden saw Chris from the corner of her eye standing only eight feet away and to the side of the arms dealer. Bloodied and bruised, his clothes and flesh ripped open by the attack dogs, relentlessly, recklessly determined, Chris trained his automatic on the back of Winston Broussard's head. In the distance, dozens of police sirens blared, and on an upstairs balcony, Broussard's bodyguard crept through a door, raised his gun and aimed at Chris.

"Above you!" she screamed, but a shot from behind and inside the house caught Broussard's bodyguard in the back and sent him hurtling off the balcony.

Tafoya bolted. Sheila stood paralyzed with fear. Chris dropped as if he'd been shot. Eden cried out, screaming in horror, believing he had been. Reacting to Eden's cry, Sheila threw herself at Broussard again, but he hurled Eden to the deck, enraged, crazed, ignoring even the threat to his own life in his dark, deranged obsession with choking the life from her.

His eyes flaming, his strength was wildly inhuman. Distantly, Eden felt her lungs burning and the cartilage in her throat ready to snap. In his own primitive rage, Chris grabbed hold of Broussard from above and threw him into the wrought-iron railing. Still he lunged back at Eden.

Humiliated and enraged at the man who had destroyed her best friend's life and then picked at the sores of her own self-esteem until she bled, Sheila Jacques picked up Tafoya's gun and shot Winston Broussard squarely in the chest.

She dropped the gun and flew to Eden's side. Christian Tierney held them both in the midst of the devastation while Maroncek burst through doors with twenty or so deputy marshals, and on the balcony, old Jameson blew the smoke from his sawed-off shotgun.

Epilogue

ON THE JET DESTINED FOR Los Angeles and beyond to Hawaii, a passenger jet this time, and not one appropriated from the government, Eden Kelley Tierney snuggled close to her husband.

The ragged peaks of the Tetons rose to bid them goodbye, but they would welcome them back in three weeks' time, when the house going up in the narrow valley where Judith Cornwallis's old cabin had stood was completed.

Eden and Chris were clearing out of Dodge City anyway, Boston in this case, so the old Brit expatriate poet had insisted. Spent quite enough time shambling around in the foothills on her own, she said, after taking her twelve gauge up and blowing the propane tank to kingdom come, igniting the blaze to send up her cabin and convince the wise guys she was already dead.

The ruse had saved her life. Her old silver-backed mirror had been restored, and Eden was officially adopted to assuage Judith's maternal ancestors. The Bancrofts threw one hell of a bon voyage party.

Sheriff Ross had spent a few hours metaphorically kicking Tierney's butt to hell and back, and then hired him. Jackson Hole made one perfect upscale resort location for the reincarnation of Eden's lingerie boutique. The high school accepted the application of Sheila Marie Jacques.

And the wedding had come off without a hitch in the spectacular mountain meadow where elk bugled and moose ambled and trumpeter swans performed their song.

Christian Tierney was at peace telling himself the truth these days, which was that he was wildly in love with a woman who told him the truth . . . which was that she was wildly in love with a reckless and dangerously potent man.

Kirsten Cornwallis Tierney was born on the Fourth of July, followed, one per year, by Evan and Dylan and baby Meghan Marie.

BRIDE'S BAY RESORT

UNLOCK THE DOOR TO GREAT ROMANCE AT BRIDE'S BAY RESORT

Join Harlequin's new across-the-lines series, set in an exclusive hotel on an island off the coast of South Carolina.

Seven of your favorite authors will bring you exciting stories about fascinating heroes and heroines discovering love at Bride's Bay Resort.

Look for these fabulous stories coming to a store near you beginning in January 1996.

Harlequin American Romance #613 in January
Matchmaking Baby by Cathy Gillen Thacker

Harlequin Presents #1794 in February
Indiscretions by Robyn Donald

Harlequin Intrigue #362 in March
Love and Lies by Dawn Stewardson

Harlequin Romance #3404 in April
Make Believe Engagement by Day Leclaire

Harlequin Temptation #588 in May
Stranger in the Night by Roseanne Williams

Harlequin Superromance #695 in June
Married to a Stranger by Connie Bennett

Harlequin Historicals #324 in July
Dulcie's Gift by Ruth Langan

Visit Bride's Bay Resort each month wherever Harlequin books are sold.

HARLEQUIN ®

BBAYG

What do women really want to know?

Only the world's largest publisher of romance
fiction could possibly attempt an answer.

HARLEQUIN ULTIMATE GUIDES™

How to Talk to a Naked Man,

Make the Most of Your Love Life, and Live Happily Ever After

The editors of Harlequin and Silhouette are
definitely experts on love, men and relationships.
And now they're ready to share that expertise with
women everywhere.

Jam-packed with vital, indispensable, lighthearted
tips to improve every area of your romantic life—even
how to get one! So don't just sit around and wonder
why, how or where—run to your nearest bookstore
for your copy now!

Available this February, at your favorite retail outlet.

HARLEQUIN®

I N T R I G U E®

Into a world where danger lurks around
every corner, and there's a fine line between trust
and betrayal, comes a tall, dark and handsome man.

Intuition draws you to him…but instinct keeps you
away. Is he really one of those…

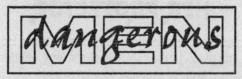

You made the dozen "Dangerous Men" from 1995 so
popular that there's a sextet of these sexy but
secretive men coming to you in 1996!

In March, look for:

#361 LUCKY DEVIL
by Patricia Rosemoor

**Take a walk on the wild side…with our
"DANGEROUS MEN"!**

HARLEQUIN®

I N T R I G U E®

A woman alone—
What can she do…?
Who can she trust…?
Where can she run…?

Straight into the arms of

HER PROTECTOR

When danger lurks around every corner, there truly is
only one place you're safe…in the strong, sheltering
arms of the man who loves you.

Look for all the books in the
HER PROTECTOR miniseries:

#354 *Midnight Cowboy*
by Adrianne Lee (January)

#359 *Keeper of the Bride*
by Tess Gerritsen (February)

#364 *Belladonna*
by Jenna Ryan (March)

Feel safe in the arms of **HER PROTECTOR**!

PROTECT2

HARLEQUIN®

I N T R I G U E ®

Angels should have wings and flowing robes—not tight black jeans and leather jackets. They should be chubby cherubs or wizened old specters—not virile and muscular and sinfully sexy.

But then again, the AVENGING ANGELS aren't your average angels!

Enter the Denver Branch of Avenging Angels and meet some of the sexiest angels this side of heaven.

Sam—THE RENEGADE by Margaret St. George
(#358, February)

Dashiell—THE IMPOSTOR by Cassie Miles
(#363, March)

and the littlest angel-to-be
Ariel—THE CHARMER by Leona Karr
(#366, April)

Kiel—THE SOULMATE by Carly Bishop
(#370, May)

They may have a problem with earthly time—but these angels have no problem with earthly pleasures!

Yo amo novelas con corazón!

Starting this March, Harlequin opens up to a whole new world of readers with two new romance lines in SPANISH!

Harlequin Deseo
- passionate, sensual and exciting stories

Harlequin Bianca
- romances that are fun, fresh and very contemporary

With four titles a month, each line will offer the same wonderfully romantic stories that you've come to love—now available in Spanish.

Look for them at selected retail outlets.

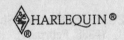

HARLEQUIN

A M E R I C A N ◆ R O M A N C E®

In Name Only

...because there are many reasons for saying "I do."

American Romance cordially invites you to a wedding of convenience. This is one reluctant bride and groom with their own unique reasons for marrying...IN NAME ONLY.

By popular demand American Romance continues this story of favorite marriage-of-convenience books. Don't miss

#624 THE NEWLYWED GAME
by Bonnie K. Winn
March 1996

Find out why some couples marry first...and learn to love later. Watch for IN NAME ONLY!

INO

INTRODUCING...  WINNER'S CIRCLE

A collection of award-winning books by award-winning
authors! From Harlequin and Silhouette.

Heaven In Texas
by Curtiss Ann Matlock

National Reader's Choice Award Winner—
Long Contemporary Romance

Let Curtiss Ann Matlock take you to a place called
Heaven In Texas, where sexy cowboys in well-worn jeans
are the answer to every woman's prayer!

"Curtiss Ann Matlock blends reality with romance
to perfection!"
—*Romantic Times*

Available this March wherever Silhouette books are sold.

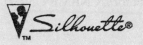 *Silhouette*®